The Renaissance Imagination
*Important Literary and Theatrical Texts
from the Late Middle Ages
through the Seventeenth Century*

Stephen Orgel
Editor

Volumes in the Series

1. *Arte of Rhetorique* by Thomas Wilson
   edited by Thomas J. Derrick
2. *An Enterlude Called Lusty Iuuentus* by R. Wever
   An old-spelling critical edition
   edited by Helen Scarborough Thomas
3. *The True Tragicomedy Formerly Acted at Court.* A Play by Francis Osborne Transcribed from the Manuscript in the British Library by John Pitcher and Lois Potter
   edited, with an introduction, by Lois Potter
4. The Comedies of John Crowne
   A critical edition
   edited, with Prolegomena, by B. J. McMullin
5. The *Pearl* Poems: An Omnibus Edition.
   Vol. 1: *Pearl* and *Cleanness*
   edited by William Vantuono
6. The *Pearl* Poems: An Omnibus Edition. Vol. 2: *Patience* and *Sir Gawain and the Green Knight*
   edited by William Vantuono
7. *The Swisser* by Arthur Wilson
   edited by Linda V. Itzoe
8. *Greene's Tu Quoque Or, The Cittie Gallant* by J. Cooke
   A critical edition
   edited by Alan J. Berman
9. A Critical Edition of *I Sir John Oldcastle*
   edited, with an introduction, by Jonathan Rittenhouse
10. The Tudor Interludes: *Nice Wanton* and *Impatient Poverty*
    edited by Leonard Tennenhouse
11. Pageants and Entertainments of Anthony Munday
    A critical edition
    edited by David M. Bergeron
12. *The Fancies, Chast and Noble* by J. Ford
    A critical edition
    edited by Dominick J. Hart
13. Buckingham: Public and Private Man. The Prose, Poems and Commonplace Book of George Villiers, Second Duke of Buckingham (1628–1687)
    edited by Christine Phipps
14. *The Pastyme of People* and *A New Boke of Purgatory* by J. Rastell, with a facsimile of *The Pastyme*
    A critical edition
    edited by Albert J. Geritz

15. *The Passions of the Mind in General*
 by Thomas Wright
 A critical edition
 edited by William Webster Newbold
16. *Thomas Heywood's Pageants*
 A critical edition
 edited by David M. Bergeron
17. *The Obstinate Lady* by Aston Cokayne
 edited by Catherine M. Shaw
18. A Critical Old Spelling of the Works of Edward Sharpham
 edited by Christopher G. Petter
19. *Sicily and Naples, Or, the Fatall Union.*
 A Tragœdy by S. Harding
 edited by Joan Warthling Roberts
20. The *Aeneid* of Thomas Phaer and Thomas Twyne
 A critical edition introducing Renaissance metrical typography
 edited by Steven Lally
21. A Critical Edition of Abraham Cowley's *Cutter of Coleman Street*
 edited by Darlene Johnson Gravett
22. A Critical Edition of Abraham Cowley's *Davideis*
 edited by Gayle Shadduck
23. An Old-Spelling Critical Edition of William Davenant's *The Platonic Lovers*
 edited by Wendell W. Broom, Jr.
24. A Critical Edition of John Fletcher's *The Humorous Lieutenant*
 edited by Philip Oxley
25. A Critical Edition of John Fletcher's Comedy *Monsieur Thomas or Father's Own Son*
 edited by Nanette Cleri Clinch
26. The Prose of Fulke Greville, Lord Brooke
 edited by Mark Caldwell
27. A Critical Edition of *The Play of the Wether* by John Heywood
 edited by Vicki Knudsen Robinson
28. A Critical Edition of *The Isle of Ladies*
 edited by Vincent Daly
29. A Contextual Study and Modern-Spelling Edition of *Mucedorus*
 edited by Arvin H. Jupin
30. A Critical Edition of Ferdinando Parkhurst's *Ignoramus, The Academical-Lawyer*
 edited by E. F. J. Tucker
31. A Critical Edition of Alexander Ross's 1647 *Mystagogus Poeticus, or The Muses Interpreter*
 edited by John R. Glenn
32. A Critical Edition of Thomas Salter's *The Mirrhor of Modestie*
 edited by Janis Butler Holm
33. An Old-Spelling Critical Edition of James Shirley's *The Example*
 edited by William F. Jones
34. Stuart Academic Drama: Three University Plays
 edited by David L. Russell
35. A Critical Edition of George Whetstone's 1582 *An Heptameron of Civill Discourses*
 edited by Diana Shklanka
36. An Edition of Robert Wilson's *Three Ladies of London* and *Three Lords and Three Ladies of London*
 edited by H. S. D. Mithal
37. The School of Cyrus: William Barker's 1567 Translation of Xenophon's *Cyropaedeia* (*The Education of Cyrus*)
 edited by James Tatum

THE VIII. BOOKES OF XENOPHON,

CONTAININGE THE Institutiō, schole, and education of Cyrus, the noble Kynge of Persye: also his ciuill and princelye estate, his expedition into Babylon, Syria and Aegypt, and his exhortation before his death, to his children.

Translated out of Greeke into Englishe by M. William Bercker.

Imprinted Anno Domini
M.D.LXVII.

The School of Cyrus
William Barker's 1567 Translation of Xenophon's CYROPAEDEIA (THE EDUCATION OF CYRUS)

edited by
James Tatum

The Renaissance Imagination
Volume 37

GARLAND PUBLISHING, INC.
NEW YORK & LONDON
1987

© 1987 James Tatum
All rights reserved

Library of Congress Cataloging-in-Publication Data
Xenophon.
[Cyropaedia. English]
The School of Cyrus : William Barker's 1567 translation Xenophon's Cyropaedeia (The education of Cyrus) / edited by James Tatum.
p.   cm.—(The Renaissance imagination ; v. 37)
Translation of: Cyropaedia.
ISBN 0-8240-8417-9
1. Cyrus, King of Persia, d. 529 B.C.—Fiction. 2. Iran—History—To 640—Fiction. I. Barker, William, 16th cent. II. Tatum, James. III. Title. IV. Series.
PA4495.C5   1987   883'.01—dc 19   87-30442

Printed on acid-free, 250-year-life paper
Manufactured in the United States of America

THE EIGHT BOOKS
OF XENOPHON,
containing the
Institution, school, and education
of Cyrus, the noble king of Persia: also his
civil and princely estate, his expedition into Babylon, Syria and Egypt,
and his exhortation be-
fore his death, to his
children.

Translated out of Greek into
English by Mr. William
Bercker
{London, 1567}

Edited for the Garland Series.
Stephen Orgel, General Editor.
by
James Tatum

Contents

Editor's Preface	i-iv
Barker's Preface to the Earl of Pembroke	1
His Preface to the Early of Surrey	6
The Proem of Xenophon	9
The First Book	11
The Second Book	43
The Third Book	64
The Fourth Book	87
The Fifth Book	112
The Sixth Book	142
The Seventh Book	163
The Eighth Book	182

Editor's Preface

In *The Illusion of Power*, the Editor of this series observes how central the notion of the ruler as exemplary figure was to those who thought about kingship in the Renaissance.

> An Aristotelian might maintain that to be a good king it is necessary to have all the virtues, and a Machiavellian object that it is necessary only to seem to have them; but in either case it is the *image* of the monarch that is crucial, the appearance of virtue, whether it accords with an inner reality or not.

The production of this image, as well as the conception of political power as a theatrical event, are themselves notions that run back through Machiavelli and other tutors of princes, to the Classical world. For the first of all mirrors for princes in western literature is Xenophon's *Cyropaedeia* or *Education of Cyrus*.

The present volume is a transcription of the first translation into English of the *Cyropaedeia*, by William Barker, first published in 1567. Editions would proliferate until the beginning of the next century, when Barker's version was superseded in 1632 by the incomparably more accurate translation of Philemon Holland. Yet accuracy has never been the chief attraction of the first English translators of the Classics. Barker's English is as vivid and fluent as his orthography. In many places he is eloquent and his version worthy of comparison with North's Plutarch (1579) or Addlington's Apuleius (1566). For better or worse he provided English readers with the only *Cyropaedeia* they had, from 1567 until the appearance of Holland's version of 1632. That translation was dedicated to Charles I and symbolizes for us as well as anything could the end of the *Cyropaedeia*'s usefulness as a mirror for princes.

How well known Xenophon had been in the preceding century is a question that remains to be answered. Spenser's remark in his *Letter of the Authors to Sir Walter Raleigh* of 23 January 1589 is often cited.

> For this cause is Xenophon preferred before Plato, for that the one is the exquisite depth of his judgment, formed a Commune welth such as it should be, but the other in the person of Cyrus and the Persians fashioned a government such as might best be: So much more profitable and gratious is doctrine by ensample, then by rule.

Familiar also is Roger Ascham's approval in his *School Master* (1570), as well as Sir Philip Sidney's praise in *The Defence of Poesy*. For Sidney, the *Cyropaedia* was "an absolute heroicall Poem."

There is good reason to suspect that Cyrus and his ideal education may have been woven more deeply into the fabric of English literature than even these familiar comments suggest. Xenophon was available to English scholars long before Barker appeared on the scene. To name but two possibilities, there was the elegant Ciceronian Latin translation of Poggio Bracciolini (1447), or the less graceful but more accurate version of his rival Francesco Filelfo (1476). Whatever his source, Elyot opens his preface to *The Boke Named the Governour* (1531) with a variation on the opening reflection of the *Cyropaedia* (*ennoia poth hemîn egeneto* . . ., "the thought once occurred to us . . ."):

> I late consideringe (moste excellente prince and myne onely redoughted soveraigne lorde) my dutie that I owe to my naturall countray with my faythe also of alliegeaunce and othe, more over theaccoampt that I have to rendre (that once little talent delivered to me to employ as I suppose) to the increase of vertue, I am (as god judge me) violently stered to devulgate or sette forthe some part of my studie, trustynge thereby tacquite me of my dueties to you, your hyghnesse, and this my country.

Comparison with the opening of the *Cyropaedia* in Barker's version shows how Elyot has particularized the general reflection of Xenophon and made it pertinent to the needs of a loyal Christian scholar writing in the service of his king.

Even more suggestive is what seems to be a sardonic echo of Xenophon in the wish of a certain Shakespearean monarch to exchange his kingdom for a horse. Cyrus poses the idea of such an exchange in a conversation on horses and kingdoms in Book 8 of the *Cyropaedeia*.

Whatever the implications of his translation may have had for English literature, William Barker himself was most assuredly caught up in the political world of his century. His surname is variously spelled "Bercker," "Bercher," as well as our standard "Barker." He was a fellow of Magdalen College, Oxford who also served as secretary to Thomas Howard, Fourth Duke of Norfolk. This service brought him his only notoriety. He was examined in The Tower of London twenty-one times and gave very damaging testimony to his former master. In Neville Williams' judgment, no one's testimony did more to bring Norfolk to the block than the testimony of William Barker. His confession of September 5, 1571 has been preserved:

> I confesse I did very evill to medle with any suche cause, although I did yt for good zele to my Master, which hath formed to the contrary, whereof I am sory, and hartely repent me, humbly beseching hir Majestie to pardon myn offence, and I protest never to enter into the lyke foly againe, but shall live quieately and obediently, as I have ever desired to do; whose Highness Almghty God long preserve. Amen.

Barker was pardoned in 1574. Norfolk dismissed him as an "Italianated Englishman." Several of his other publications are well as his own comments in the prefaces to the present translation reveal a scholar devoted to Italy: a translation from the Italian, *The Fearful Fansies of the Forentine Couper* (1559) and the *Epitaphia et inscriptiones lugubres a Gulielmo Berchero cum in Italia animi causa peregrinaretur collecta*, 1556 (*Mournful Epitaphs and Inscriptions Collected by William Barker When He Was Traveling About Italy to Improve His Mind*).

The Schole of Cyrus was dedicated to William Herbert, First Earl of Pembroke. It is not likely that Barker's translation played any role whatever in Norfolk's scheme of things. On the contrary, the Duke of Norfolk exemplifies the kind of rebellious subject the *Cyropaedeia* teaches its princely readers to suppress.

The best available modern translation, with excellent notes and commentary, is the Budé edition of Marcel Bizos and Edouard Delebecque (Paris, 1971-1978). Walter Miller's Loeb edition of 1914 is the most recent translation available in English. There is very little in Classical scholarship in English that would be useful to the readers of this series; as of this date, I can recommend William E. Higgins, *Xenophon the Athenian* (Albany, 1977), pp. 44-59, and J. K. Anderson, *Xenophon* (New York, 1974), pp. 1-8.

* * *

This project began as a labor of love, in connection with my book on the Greek text of Xenophon's *Education of Cyrus*. The history of the reception of the *Cyropaedeia* is in many ways as fascinating as the *Cyropaedeia* itself. Nowhere did this influence seem to me to be of more potential importance than in English literature of the Renaissance. I leave it for scholars and students of the early modern era to make of Barker's *Cyropaedeia* what they will.

As with most such labors, the outcome has been not at all what was first expected. My principal debt is to Maura Nolan, presently an undergradute in the Dartmouth English Department. She actually made the first transcription from Barker's English. If she had not, the present volume would never have appeared at all. Unless I am seriously mistaken, she will never again confront a task so dull. So at least I hope.

Gail Patten produced the revised copy which is printed here. Virginia Close of the Baker Library was as resourceful as ever in helping me track down what little there is to be known about the first English translator of the *Cyropaedeia*. The cost of producing the transcription was underwritten by the Faculty Research Committee of Dartmouth College. To one and all, sincere thanks.

Department of Classics
Dartmouth College
September 22, 1987

James Tatum

A Preface to the Right Honorable William, Earl of Pembroke, Lord Harbert of Cardife, knight of the honorable order of the Garter, and President of the King's Highness Council in the marches of Wales, William Bercker wishes health and honor.

Those authors be chiefly to heard, which have not only by finess of wit and diligence of study attained to an excellency, but also have had the experience of manners of men, and diversity of places, and have with wisdom and eloquence joined those two together. For as general things and order of nature can not be perceived, but by them whose natural sharpness of wit is helped with earnest and continual pain, fullness of study so the private doings and dispositions of men only known by daily use and trial of them. And there be many skillful in the one, that be in the other kind very simple, and say much of generalities, but in particularities be utterly ignorant, and other again, who can talk well and wisely in singular points wherein they be experienced, but in the other kind they be in a manner without understanding. Or they who have been brought up in study, and know no more than they have attained unto by reading, be in general things, labored in by other, and found out by much debating of common reason skillfuller than the common sort, and therefore called better learned, and they who have whet the fine edge of their wit, and peered their doings and inclinations of other, with diligent making of the seen, and remembering the marked, be called witty and wise men, and have good praise of their sayings and doings in common life. And hereby happeneth that which is commonly said, the best learned men be not the wisest. Either for that they can not tell particular things, which be in daily and common use of life, or else for cause, although their reason be well furnished with reading and understanding what is best, yet their affections and moods be not hardened enough, nor strengthened with experience and trial of things, and therefore be in their doings many times unadvised and simple. And because each of these things require a whole man's life to grow to any perfectness therein, and it seldom chanceth and once in a man's age, that perfect study and perfect experience meet together in one man, and few painful wits be good, and fewer good wits be painful, therefore cometh it seldom to pass that there be many thoroughly wise men at one time and be more commonly talked of than seen and more looked for than found, and wished for rather than had. And this maketh that in all the course of learning and experience there be very few who satisfy goodly and well judging wits, and whom they would, that seek the price of fame, labor to follow in their writings, whole wits they marvel at in writing.

Some there be, who by diligence and nature have goodly understanding of praiseworthy things, and can find out well what is best to be done, and wittiest to be reasoned, but they lack the stream of eloquence, which floweth with delight to please the dainty ears and can roughly hew the matter to serve for good purpose, but yet lack the swift violence of sweet running talk, to carry away the indifferent mind to their intented purpose.

Other there be, whose wit melteth words sufficient to serve, and gusheth with abundance when they turn their cock, but it is muddy and troubled for lack of fined reason, and so serveth not the purpose well, although it be plentiful, but better unoccupied than spent in weighty causes. Thus Nature playeth well where she purposeth her show, and showeth what she liketh to open her diversity, and is fruitful to weeds if they lie untilled, and overgroweth her self with her own plenty, and by fruitfulness is unfruitful, except her fruitfulness be ordered, and wisom rules Nature, and pares away her excess wherewith she is overcharged, when she is unordered. The barren ground sometime with diligence is tilled, and bringeth forth such fruit, as such a ground can serve for, and what cunning can do where nature will not help, she showeth by her burden, and telleth us this lesson: That nature's want is helped where good husbandry is used, and if grounds well looked to, be of like value to the good grounds ill ordered and overgrown by sloth. Such hardness is it for good things well made to meet all in one man, and matchly to be copied, for nature and diligence to serve experience and study, all which things lightly fall not well together, except some godly grace from some diligent nature, which being well brought up and well disposed to, do furnish nature's beauty with the favor of good learning, and mark well in travail the common doings of men, and apply well together his learning and experience, and labor there unto join wisdom in talk by following of the wise and raising out his words of the nature of the matter, and driving to the end the order of his reason, and measuring by direction the affection of the hearer and draw him to the matter by cunning in conveyance, and not the matter unto him to serve his desire.

But Xenophon this Philosopher hath not only travailed in the general knowledge of true reason to have right understanding what is good and bad in life, and what is true and false in nature, but also travailed by experience to see the diversities of men's manners, and to acquaint himself with right order of civil government, and thereby hath attained to a great estimation of worthiness among the wise and learned, and judged a man most worthy, whose writings should be read with diligence, and travailed in for the fruits of wisdom. For he was Socrates' scholar, out of whose school can first the excellent philosophers, who were afterwards divided into certain sects, and filled all Greece with manifold knowledge, and being joined with the most notable men in schoolfellowship, got equal praise with the chieffest, and hath learnedly intricated the sum of well doings, in his book that he wrote of Socrates' worthy remembrances. For government and order of policy, he first travailed through not only Greece, but also remained with great estimation in the King of Persia's court, and understood not only the nature's of men, the usages of orders, the devices of council, the engines of war, but also the sports and pastimes most convenient for a leisureful life, and hath sorted with skill, that was engrossed by experience, and hath given rules of peace and war no learned man more, and furnisheth a gentleman with much goodly knowledge so much more to be commended than the other, that his rules be in practice for common life and not sought out of the depth of nature, whose perfectness as it is most commendable. So can it not best agree with the common use of life. But what is there that a wise man can with honesty desire, whereof not only the sparkles be scattered in him but also the great beams be largely set, that in such variety and plentifulness of good things, as it is not hard to choose the good, so is it very hard to choose the best. If knowledge of war be sought for, is there any that giveth truer and wiser rules, both for the captain to govern by and the soldier to be ruled after? Did not Scipio, as Tully citeth out of Polybius, think the books of Cyrus bringing up, so full of good instructions and warlike wisdom, that a good captain should never go without them? Was not Cyrus so well taught himself, that he learned not only obedience like a soldier, but government like a captain, and afterwards was fulfilled with all the noble virtues that may be wished with excellency in any ruler? And all those good lessons that either Cyrus learned, or Scipio praised, be contained in this treatise, and fit to be known at this time, not of that the kinds of war be not changed, but for cause those precepts which he gathered out of the everlasting and unchangable right of Nature's laws, do serve all men at all times, and come amiss to no country. The miseries and misfortunes of war, the shifts and escapes from the enemies, the forsight of dangers and avoiding of perils, be they anywhere more grievous or more manifold than in younger Cyrus going up against the King and in Xenophon's return again to Greece? If peace and quietness be looked for, can there be any better rules given for every man's private life , than the worthy remembrances of Socrates? which books contain a sum of manners and life, and what is to be followed as good, and avoided as well, and what honesty and philosophy doth look for, and what nature uncorrupted can naturally require, and which is the right and easy way to the true and reasonable happiness. If government and order of common wealth be sought, can we have a perfecter example of a good ruler, than the praise of Agesilaus is? Which hath prescribed all the worthy virtues that a man can praisably desire, to funish a ruler, which hath not hereon all the incommodities that longeth to governers, and plain demonstrations how in seeking for pleasures, they be furthest from pleasures, and last to attain that wherin they labor first. Be not these books like true glasses, that will show none other favor and beauty of conditions, than be the owners in deed? Nor will not by flattery make mean things great, and great vices small, but according to the true proportion of the qualities, show the visage of the fame? If hunting, riding, and other chosen pastimes be fit to learned of Gentlemen, and taught of skillful men, who did experience them more naturally, and write of them more cunningly than Xenophon hath done? The matters whereof be neither unpleasant to be known, nor unhandsome to be practiced. And yet the chief ground works of riding be so naturally said by him, that he is at this day counted the best horseman that keepeth his orders in riding best, and goeth nighest that true way, which he by wisdom hath of long time prescribed. All these things which severally be scattered and sparse in other, be almost all in one gathered together in this book of Cyrus bringing up and going forth under this title, is indeed a pathway to wisdom, and for matter most fit to be read and known of all Gentlemen, and for fineness of of style, most pleasant and perfect in his own tongue. And although herein I have a goodly occasion to commend the writer, that in the most eloquent and excellent tongue hath written most purely, yet because it carrieth the matter whole into another tongue, and keepeth his own fineness still in his own tongue, and our gross tongue is a rude and a barren tongue, when it is compared with so flourishing and plentiful a tongue. I will pass over this praise, with touching only the remembrance of it, and leave so large a matter until a better time, lest in commending his writing I might dispraise mine own, or else in an unneedful matter spend too many words. But shortly to conclude of all books which philosophers have written with judgement, and other hath translated with labor, no book there is which containeth better matter for life, order for war lines, policy for courtliness, wisdom for government, temperance for subjects, obedience for all states. I seem to praise this book too much; to the ignorant I may do, who can not judge, and therefore I pardon him, and yet least worthy pardon to rule over that he knoweth not, and be most busy where he hath lest skill, but to the wise I cannot, who weighing the matter and judging the examples, and examining the rules, shall find as much as plentiful wisdom wittily framed in this short treatise, and in other great volumes, having as expressly every part of wisdom as well set together, as a little tablet containeth the lively face by cunning of workmanship , which the great table for want of cunning sometime doth miss. But because I thought it praiseworthy, I thought it labor worthy also and began my travail of this good opinion, supposing that which of reason contented me, might by the same reason content others too. And besides the honest contenting which must needs be in well minded men, if any man learn anything that he is the better for, I trust he will yield me some thanks, by whose means he hath met with a good councellor, and learned plainly that he might long else have sought for, and therefore thank me for my pains herein at the least, if he further require me not to go on with the like. Therefore in devising to whom I might offer this honest travail of mine, well I trust bestowed, although of every noble man well, yet of no man better than of your good Lordship, whose virtues be better know unto me, than you yourself are, and therefore thought it fit to offer written virtues, where lively virtues dwell, to be better accepted where they see report of their ancient fame, and honor much esteemed. And if the thing is welcomed not, yet another might:

your children whom you love and bring them up in learning, and have chosen them of late a good schoolmaster, as I hear, whose diligence and discretion hath much always commended the good learning he hath, and other good qualities. The reading hereof to them may double profit them, both to learn the matter which is good and pleasant, and also to learn to turn Latin out of English, which way although it seem trifling to some, yet is it the readiest exercise that ever I could find, to make a child easily to attain to that profit, which else with labor they shall not (hit) at all. These things make me bold, although not much acquainted, to present to your Lordship the honor of my pains, most humbly desiring you to accept my boldness, moved yet with reason, and where the goodness of the matter, your Lordship's noble virtues, your children's bringing up, hath moved me here unto, you will for these causes accept well my good will, and I shall hereby think my self so bound to you, as other must to me, that hereby profiteth oughts, and desire the living LORD, whose rule goeth through all, to increase your Lordship's honor and nobleness always.

To the right honorable, my singular good lord, Philip, Earl of Surrey, son and heir to my lord and master the Duke of Norfolk's grace, William Bercker wishes furtherance in forwardance of learning with continuance of virtue and honor.

When Alexander the Great did pass by the place where Achilles was buried, he said these words: "O happy Achilles, that had such a trumpet as Homer, to sound thy glory to the world." Of this saying did grow a disputation: whether the valiant captain, that by courage and policy attained fame, or the skillful writer, that by learning and cunning makes report thereof, is more worthy of commendation. For as the doer of noble deeds gives matter to the writer of goodly books, so those deeds should soon die, if they did not live by writ. When Zopyrus, a noble man of Persia, had disfigured his body, and thereby won the city of Babylon, Darius, the king of that country, said: "I had rather have one such faithful subject as Zopyrus was, that ten such cities as Babylon is." Of which sentence rises this question: whether the mighty prince that commands what he will have done, or the worthy subject that executes the prince's pleasure, deserves greater praise. I will leave the matter in suspense, and suffer by silence the sentence to be given where it ought. And to your Lordship this I have to say: There is no gentleman alive has more occasion to be stirred by his ancestors' virtues, than you. For if I may remember unto you the noble acts that they have done, and singular services that they have showed, then must I say, that even from my Lords your great great grandfathers, to my Lord's grace your father, you have to receive examples of rare virtue, as well of warlike affairs done abroad, as of royal wisdom showed at home: whose steps to follow, you have two ways. The one is by learning, whereunto I rejoice to see you so well given. For by it, shall you receive such lessons in your youth, as the fame shall be instructions to your at more years. The other is experience, to the which I hope your will give yourself when time shall come. For as the one without the other hath a want, so both being joined together, makes a marvelous perfection. In the first you are yet to be trained with as good inducements as may be, and better can there none be than the reading of such authors as for the matter be most worthy, and for the manner be most skillful. Which being granted, I dare affirm, this Xenophon, whom I now present unto you, to be most fit for you. For he treateth of a prince that in his time exceeded all others, and in him he showeth a model of perfect and princely education. The handling of it is such, as for the excellency both in learning and experience can not be amended. For this Xenophon was scholar to Socrates, and proved so singular, as he was accompted concurrent with his schoolfellow Plato, who for his knowledge was surnamed Divine. This Xenophon was he, that after Cyrus the younger was slain in the expedition he made into Asia, brought home the Greeks that served in that voyage, amidst so many fierce enemies, over so many huge mountains, and through so many dangerous passages. And this was that Xenophon, whom Scipio the singular Roman, that overcame the valiant Hannibal of Carthage, had ever at his pillow, to receive instructions by night that he would practice by day. So as for both considerations, few or none have been found the like. Which although it be true, yet is there one thing that hath a while withdrawn me, from that I now am doing. And it is, that for your Lordship's further furtherance in learning, and for mine own poor estimation, I should rather have exhibited unto you something in Latin than in English, but as a forlorn scholar, not able to keep credit in learning, I do yet entertain myself studies not altogether devoid of learning, which I offer unto you. Indeed I must confess this translation to be done before I went into Italy, finding six books of the same enprinted when I did return, not by my desire, but only by the courtesy and good will of the printer, a furtherer of good learning. For these two later books I have often times been spoken to of diverse of my learned friends, whose requests at length I have satisfied. And because the only intent of the book is to show what a noble man by good education may prove unto, I have both by duty and skill made election of your Lordship, to be the last patron of it, as I made by very good Lord, the Earl of Penbroke, the first. To your Lordship the reading of such matter is convenient, to his Lordship, the judgement is to be referred. Your Lordship must talk of your book, his Lordship of his experience. For the which, joining him with you, as it were in commission, for the good will he hath born to my lord your grandfather, and for the friendship he beareth to my Lord your father, I dare say he will be both a father and a grandfather to you, if cause should require. I shall desire your Lordship, when you read, it to think the time will come, when you shall be called of your prince to take such journies as you shall see that Cyrus appointeth to such as you are, and to do such services as your most noble progenitors have done by the commandment of their princes, whose great glory shall ever so shine before your eyes, as you must needs forsee yourself to follow the same to the contentation of your prince, the benefit of your country, the joy of your parents, comfort of all your friends and servants: the which I among the rest do wish and trust to see. And so most humbly I take my leave of your Lordship. From my chamber at Howard house, the eighth day of this new year, 1567.

THE PROEM OF
Xenophon

I have thought oftentimes with myself how many of wealths hath been overthrown by them which would rather have any form of government than the commons. How often the rule of one or the power of few hath been of the commons overthrown. How many attempting tyranny, some forthwith have been deprived, some reigning any time, be in admiration, as men of rare wisdom and felicity: me thought also I had learned that among many matters of private families, some have had many servants, some very few, which few notwithstanding, they could never very well break and have at commandment. I perceive furthermore that neat herds be rulers of neat, and horsekeepers of horses, and that all other, which be called herdmen, be semblably reputed callers of the cattle that they keep. I though also I saw all herds, more willing to obey their keepers, than men their governors. For the herds going whether the keepers driveth, feeding on that pasture, which they appoint, departing from the fame when they compel, and suffering them to take at their pleasures all such profits, as of them ariseth: I never yet heard any herd to be rebellious or disobedient, or denying their keeper the fruit of their increase, but rather to be more untractable to all other, than to them which receiveth profit by them. But men do vie with none so much as them whom they percieve to go about to have dominion over them. When I had thus debated these things, I gave this sentence of them: That it is naturally given to man, to have more easily of all other creatures the sovereignty, than of only man. But when I remembered in my mind, that Cyrus being a Persian, had gotten so many sorts of men, so many sundry cities, and so many diverse nations obedient unto him. I was thereby enforced to forthink the same, because it is neither impossible, nor yet greatly hard, to have sovereignty over man, if a man did it skillfully or wittily. For we know that men willingly have been obedient to Cyrus, whereof some have been distant many days journey, some many months from him, some that never did see him, some that knew certainly they never should see him, yet would become his liege men. So much did he exceed all kings, as well inheritors to their fathers' kingdoms, as them to which by their industry, achieved the same. For the Scythian king, albeit the Scythes be in number great, can get dominion over none other nation, but is well apaid if he can govern his own country. And the Thracian, the Thraces, the Egyptian, the Egyptians. And of other nations we hear the like thing. And truly the countries of Europe, be yet as they say, free, and one of them dissevered from the other. But Cyrus beginning his reign after this sort, and invading the nations of Asia, being of separate regiment. With a small army of Persians, rule the Medes, the Hyrcanians, they frankly giving it him. He conquered the Syrians, the Africans, the Arabs, the Cappadocians, both Phryginas, the Lydes, the Carians, the Phoenicians, the Babylonians. He ruled the Bactrians, the Indes, the Cilicians. Likewise the (Datians), the Paphlagonnyes, and Magadidians with other very many nations, whose names a man could not well reherse. He governed also the Greeks that be in Asia, and making a voyage to the sea side, be subdued the Cyprians, and Egyptians. Thus he had dominion over these nations, which in language, agreed neither with him, or with themselves. Notwithstanding great portions of the earth could be gone throughout, by fear of his prowess, and he ruled all men, and none durst enterprise anything against him. Yet he could imprint so great desire in all men's hearts to be thankful to him, that they thought good evermore to be governed by his pleasure. He got the friendship of so many nations, as were a pain to number, whether so over a man will travail, from his palace either east, west, north, or south. We therefore have considered this man, as worthy estimation what kindred, what natural inclination, what form of bringing up he had, whereby he did which passed so far all other living men in princely dominion. As much then as I have either heard or known of him, so much I propose to declare.

The First Book

The Parentage of Cyrus

Cambyses, king of Persia, was father to Cyrus. This Cambyses was of the Perses family, who have their name of Perseus. Mandane was his mother, the daughter of Astyages, king of Medea. The saying is, and yet reported among the Barbarians, that Cyrus by nature was of most goodly shape, in heart most gently, of learning most studious, and of honor most desirous, is so much, that for glory or praise sake, he would endure any pain, and abide any peril. This is recorded of the nature, both of his mind and of his favor. He was brought up in the Persians' laws, these laws as it appeareth, hath in their beginning some respect of the commonwealth, for they go not that way to work that many other cities do. For the most part of cities suffereth every man as he lived, to bring up his children, and the ancients, to lead what life they will. Then they enjoin them neither to steal, to rob, to enter any house by violence, to strike any man unlawfully, to commit adultery, to be disobedient to their rulers and all such other things after like sort. If any do offend in these, a pain is appointeth for the same. But the Persians' laws proveth by foresight, that from the beginning none of their countrymen might be such in time to come, as should desire any evil or dishonesty, and this is their provision. They have a common place of free resort, as they name it, where the palace and all other royal things be placed, from which all buying and selling, all market men with their noise and rudeness, are rejected to another place, that the pureness of good nurture, should not be intermedled with the base multitude. This common place, compassing the palace, is divided into four parts. Whereof one is for children, another for young men, the third for them that be at the full state of men, the fourth for them, which for their years, be pardoned from wars. And by the law every of the theses is present at their place. Children by break of day, and likewise they that be at the full age or estate of men. The ancients when they may, except at days appointed, when as they must needs be there. But the young sort, lie also about the palace in warlike armor, except married men, which be not required, unless they be afore commanded to be present. Yet to be often away, it is not good. And of every of these parts, there be twelve governors: for the Persians be divided into twelve families. And they of the ancients be governors to the children, which be thought able to make them most honest. Over the young men, such of them of middle age, as seemeth to bring the young sort to best proof. Over them of perfect age, they which be thought most meet to cause them best to do such things, as be instituted and commanded of the chief ruler. There be also lieutenants or governor chose over the ancient sort, which do command that they also perform their duty. Now what is appointed to every age to do, we will declare, that it may be the more manifest, what diligence they take to make the citizens most honest men. Children that come to the schools, spend their time in learning. Justice, as men say, they go as diligently to this, as with us, to learn their letters. Their governors consume the most part of the day in giving judgement among them. For there be, as well among children as men, accusements one against the other, of theft, robbery, force slight or deceit, slander, and such other like. And whom they know to offend in any of these, they punish. They chastise also such as they find accusing without just cause they give judgement also of quarrelling or complaining, for the which men do hate one another most of all. They be also for in the judgement of unthankfulness. And whom they know able to requit thanks, and do it not, him they punish sharply, for they judge the unthankfull to be most negligent, both toward God, their parents, country, and friends. For of unthankfulness seemeth to follow unshamefastness, which as it appeareth, to all mischief, is the chief mistress. They teach their children soberness, and they be much furthered in learning to be sober, because they see the very ancients every day live so soberly. They teach them to obey their rulers. And in this also it much availeth them, because they behold the ancients very obedient to their rulers. They teach them to be moderate in diet, to the which also they be much moved, both because they see the ancients not to go to meat, before the rulers give them leave, and because the children be not fed before their mothers, but before their masters, and that when the governors do appoint. They bring from home, for their sustenance, bread, for their meat, cresses. And if any lust to drink, he hath an earthen pot to draw him water of the river. Over and beside all these, they learn to shoot and dart. And till the sixteenth or seventeenth year of their age, these things the children practice. After this time they come among the young men, which lead their life or be brought up in this wise. Ten years after their childhood, they lie about the palace, as it is said tofore, both for the custody of the city, and also of temperance, for this age, seemeth to have most need of good governance. They give attendance in the day, upon the princes, if they will have their service in any matter of the commonwealth. And when any need is, they all remain about the palace. When the king goeth on hunting, which he doeth often every month, he leaveth at home half the guard. They that attend upon him, must have a bow and arrows with a quiver, a short sword, or a woodknife in a sheath, a target and two darts, the one to pick at large, the other to use, if need be, at hand strokes.

Why they give diligence to common hunting, the king being their captain, as it were in war, which both hunteth himself, and provideth that others may hunt also, is because it seemeth a very true practice or exercies of warlike affairs: for he accustometh them to rise early to endure cold and heat. He exerciseth them in going afoot, and runing: and of necessity they must shoot and dart at the deer, wheresoever he cometh. And the mind in hunting must needs be quickened, when any cruel or fierce beast maketh against them. For when it approacheth, strike he must, and avoid the assault of it. Wherefore a man shall not lightly find in war, that doth not chance in this wild chase. Going on hunting, they have their dinner somewhat more, as reason is, than children, in all other things, like. In the time of their hunting, they may not dine. If there be any cause of long tarrying, either for the game, or that otherwise they will continue the hunting or chase, and sup with their dinner, and all the next day hunt till night. Then they accompt these two days, but one, because they spend but one days diet. Thus they do for their exercise, that is any like thing should happen in war, they might be able to do the same. And what game the young men killeth, that have they for their repast, if none, cresses. If any man think they have little pleasure in eating, because cresses are their only meat, and as little in drinking, because water is their drink, let him remember how pleasant it is, to eat course bread and gruel in hunger, and how sweet to drink water in thirst.

The other companies which remain at home, diligently exerciseth both, all other things learned in their childhood, and also to shoot and dart. And contending in these one with another, they spend their time. There be also of these feats, common games or gifts and rewards ordained or chosen for the same. And in which family be most cunning and forward, the teacher, not only that now is, but also that was in their childhood, is greatly praiseth and honored of the people. The rulers useth the youth remaining at home, if any need be of guard, of searching out transgressors, pursuing thieves or any other thing wherein quickness and strength is required. And thus the young men pass their time. After they have lived ten years, they be placed among them of perfect age, and from the time of their youth, they give attendance upon the high rulers, if any common cause needeth feats, either of knowledge or courage. If at any time they must go to war, they that by this taught occupy in warfare, nether bows nor darts, but such as they call armour for hand warfare; that is, a breastplate afore their breast, a target in the left hand, even such as the Persians have in painture. In the right hand, a sword or arming dagger. And of these men be made all magistrates, except the children's governors.

After they have spent these twenty-five years, they, being somewhat more than fifty years of age, be received among them, which both be in deed, and also called, ancients. These ancients go not to war out of their own country, but remaineth at home, discharging or dispatching all common and private cause, and judging matters of life and death. And they also do choose all other officers. If any of the young company, or of the others of perfect age, do in anything transgress the laws, the rulers of every family or any other, do accuse the same.

The ancients hearing the cause, give judgement, he that is condemned, liveth all his life in shame. Now that the whole Persian commonwealth may be made evident, we will a little repeat the same, being this briefly expressed, by the former declaration.

The Persians (as it is said) be in numbers, one hundred and twenty thousand, and none of all these is debarred by the law from honor and offices. It is lawful for all the Persians to send their children to the common schools of justice. But they only send, which are able to find them with ease, they that be not able, send not. They that have been taught in their childhood of the common schoolmasters, may, with the young sort, learn the young feats. They that have not been so taught, may not.

They that perform so much as the law requireth of the young men, may proceed among them that be at full age, and be partakers of honors and offices. But they that continue not out in the young men's trade, may not come among the perfect aged men. And they that remain their time without reproof among the men, be made ancients. So such be made ancients as have proceeded through all goodness. And this form of commonwealth they have which they?? using, be reputed best men. And yet a witness remaineth of their sober diet, and also of laboring out the same. For at this day, it is shame among the Persians, to spit, to snit the nose, or to be puffed up with wind. It is also a rebuke if any man be seen openly going to make water, or any other such thing. Which they could never do if they kept not both a moderate diet and also did so waste their moisture by much labor, that is is conveyed some other way. Thus much thought we good to speak of all the Persians. Now we will declare the noble acts of Cyrus, even from his childhood, for whose case we have begun this treatise.

The First Book

    Cyrus being trained in this discipline, till the twelfth year of his age and upward, did excell all his schoolfellows, both in quickness of learning, and also in handsome and courageous doing of every thing. At this time Astyages, king of Medea, sent for his daughter Mandane, and her son, whom he greatly desired to see, because he had heard that he was of no less beauty than honesty. She went to her father, taking with her her son Cyrus, to whom when they were come with speed, and Cyrus knew Astyages to be his grandfather, forthwith as a child full of natural nurture, he did salute him, as one that had been of old aquaintance, and embrace him as an ancient friend, and beholding his princely estate, by the painting of his eyes, the setting on or rubbing on of color, and by his made hair, which be lawful among the Medes, (and other attirements, as purple coats and garments, and chains about their necks, and bracelets on their arms) whereas the Persians at this day, being at home, use very coarse array and thin diet. Cyrus seeing this rich array of his grandfather, and looking upon him, said to his mother: "O Mother, how goodly is my grandfather!" His mother then asking of him, whether his father or grandfather seemed the goodlier, he answered thus: "Mother, of all the Persians my father is goodliest, but of all the Medes, that I have either seen by the way, or at men's doors, my grandfather is by far the goodliest. Astyages then welcoming him again, arrayed him with a robe of honor, and honorable apparelled him with chains and bracelets. And if he did ride to any place, he was set upon a horse, trapped with gold, even as Astyages was wont to ride himself.

    Cyrus being a child desirous of honesty and honor, was delighted with his robe, and glad that he learned the feat of riding, for in Persia, because it is hard to keep horses, and to use riding, by reason the country is full of hills, it is seldom that a man shall see a horse. Astyages being at supper with his daughter and nephew, and needing that the child should the less long to go home, served him with all kinds of dishes, sauces, and fine fare. And Cyrus, (as they report) said thus: "Grandfather, what a business have you to do in this supper, if you must move your hand to every dish, and taste of so many sundry meats?" Then said Astyages: "Doth not this supper (think ye) pass far your suppers in Persia?" To whom Cyrus thus answered: "No, Grandfather, for we go a more plain and straight way to suffice ourselves, than you do. For bread and flesh bringeth us to that, but you desiring that very thing, which we have, wandering up and down, as it were in a maze do scarcely at length, come to that, whereunto we attained long before." "But we, O son," said Astyages, "be not grieved when we do wander, and when you have tasted, you shall know how sweet they be." "But methinketh, Grandfather," said Cyrus, "that you be loathed with these meats." "Whereby conject you that?" said Astyages. "Because," said he, "when you touch bread, you do not wipe your hand, but when you touch any of these, forthwith you make clean your hands with a napkin, as though you were much grieved with the encumbrance of your excessive meats." "If you think so, son," said Astyages, "yet assay of the flesh that you may go home a lusty young man." And after he had said this, he caused all kind of flesh, both wild and tame, to be brought to the table. And Cyrus beholding so much meat, said: "Grandfather, do you give me all this meat, to do with it what I like?" "I give thee, son," said Astyages, "certainly." Cyrus taking the meat, did distribute it among his Grandfather's servants, saying thus to everyone: "Take thou this, because thou gladly teachest me to ride; take thou this, because thou gavest me a dart, for that I have yet. Take thou this, because though doest honorably serve my Grandfather; take thou this because thou doest reverence my mother." And thus he did, till he had given away all the meat that he had. "But you give nothing," said Astyages, "to Sacas my cupbearer, whom I esteem most. Thus Sacas was a goodly fellow, and had the offices to admit all them that had to do with Astyages, and kept back such as he thought to come out of season. And Cyrus quickly as a child, nothing afraid, asked: "Why do you (Grandfather) set so much by him?" And Astyages dallying with him, said: "Do you not see how neatly and comely he poureth wine? For these king's cupbearers, be most neat in giving wine and pure handling of the same. They bear the cup, and give it with the fingers, and so bring it, as thy may most easily deliver it him that shall drink." "Command, grandfather," said he, "Sacas to give me the cup, that I serving you of drink cleanly, may, if I can, get your favor." Astyages commanded the cup to be given him. Cyrus taking it, did so cleanse it, as he had seen Sacas done, and with a stable contenance, so prettily and seemly, bring and give it so his Grandfather, that he made both him, and his mother to laugh heartily. And Cyrus laughing for good company, ran to his

Grandfather, and embraced him, saying: "O Sacas, you be undone. I am like to thrust you out of your office: For I can give wine as well as you, and yet drink none myself. For kings' cupbearers, when they bear the cup, drawing of it into a piece, thy pour some into their left hand, which they drink, lest poison might be mixed, and they escape harmless." Then Astyages merely said, "Why do you (Cyrus) follow Sacas in all other things, and do not drink the wine, as he doth?" "Because," said he, "I feared that poison was mixed in the cup. For when you on your birthday, did feast your friends, I knew well that he gave you poison." "And how, son," said he, "did you know that?" "Because," said he, "I did see you distempered both in body and mind. For first, that you would not suffer us children to do, you did the same your fellows. You cried out all at once, one of you could not understand another. You sung, and that very foolishly. And whom you heard not sing, him would you swear, sung best, every one of you bragging of his strength, and rising to dance, in dancing you could not only keep no measure, but scarcely stand right up, so did every of you forget what he was, you, that you were king, and they that they were subjects. And then did I first learn, that it was a very confused talk which you did use, for you could never leave." And Astyages said, "son, when your father drinketh wine, is he not drunken?" "No", truly said he. "How doth he order the matter?" "He liveth with thirst, other pain he feeleth none. For I think, Grandfather, that this Sacas, doth never give him wine." Then his mother said: "What is the matter, son, that you be so heavy master to Sacas?" Cyrus said: "Because I have cause to fall out with him. For many times when I am desirous to come to my grandfather, he like an unkind fellow, keepeth me back. But I beseek you good grandfather, give me authority over him but three days." Astyages asked: "And how will you order him?" Cyrus said, standing in the entry where he is wont to stand, "I when he would come into dinner, will say, 'Back liar, my grandfather is busied with certain men'. And when he would very fain eat, I will say, 'he is with women'. Till I have put him off, as he hath delayed and kept me back from you." And such pleasantries Cyrus did minister at that supper. And from time to time, if he perceived any man having any suit to his grandfather or his uncle, it grieved him that any should prevent him in promoting their suits. And he was glad to do men pleasures to his power.

When Mandane had prepared to return to her husband, Astyages prayed her to leave Cyrus with him. Who answered that she in all things would gratify her father, but she thought it would be hard to leave the child there against his will. Then said Astyages to Cyrus: "Son, if you will tarry with me, you shall be master of my suitors, not Sacas. And when you will you shall come to me, and the oftener that you come, the more thank you shall have, my horses also shall be at your pleasure, and what you will beside. And when you shall depart, take with you, which of them you like. And because you love thin diet, you shall have it as you will. Moreover, I will give you in hand, the wild beasts in my gardens, and all that otherwise I can get for you. Which when you can ride perfectly, you shall chase, and by shooting and darting, overthrow them, and big men do. I will apppoint also chidren to be your playfellows, and all other things that you will, ask and have of me." After that Astyages had thus said unto Cyrus, his mother did ask of him, whether he would tarry or depart. Who without any study, answered shortly that he would tarry. She asking him again, for what cause? He answered: "Mother, because at home, I am counted and am in deed, best in shooting and darting of my companions. But here in riding, I know well I am inferior to my fellows. Which thing, Mother, as you know right well, doth not a little grieve me. Now if you leave me here, that I may get the feat of riding, when I am among the Persians, I trust, you think, I shall easily pass them that be good on foot. And resorting to the Medes, and being most-excellent in riding, I will endeavor myself to aid my Grandfather in war." Then said his mother: "But how son, shall you hereafter learn justice, seeing your teachers be in Persia?" Cyrus answered: "I am mother, very perfect in that." "How know you that," said his Mother. For my schoolmaster," said he, "did appoint me a judge over others, as one, that in justice was most cunning. And in judging one thing, I was beaten, for judging it not right, and this was the cause:

The Judgement of Cyrus

A great boy, having a little coat, did unclothe a little boy, having a great coat, and caused that the one did wear the other's garment. I being judge in this matter did give sentence that is was best for both parties, either to have his coat meet for him. At which sentence my master did beat me, saying, "When you are judge in a controversy of fitness and convenience, then must you judge after this sort. But when you must determine whose is the coat, then you must consider who hath right possession, whether he that taketh away a coat by violence, or he that hath caused it to be made for him, or else hath bought it. For that is just, which is lawful, that that is not lawful, is violent. Wherefore sentence must be given always of the judge according to the law." "Therefore, mother, I am perfect enough in justice, and if I lack anything, my Grandfather shall teach me. "But Son," said she, "the justice of your grandfather, and of the Persians do not agree. For he here in Medea, hath made himself lord of all; among the Persians to have equality is thought just. And your father first maketh the laws that he maketh for the city, but he also receiveth laws. He measureth things not by lust, but by law. How then can it be, but that you shall be undone with beating at your return, if you, for kingdom, have learned tyranny, whose nature is to have more than all other." "But my grandfather, Mother," said Cyrus, "is so wise, that he can teach men to have rather less than more. Do you not see, how he hath taught all the Medes to have less than himself? Therefore fear you not, mother, but he will so instruct both me, and others too, that when I shall depart, I shall not have more than he."

Cyrus after this sort, spake many things. In conclusion, his Mother departed. He remained and was brought up there, being soon acquainted with his companions, as with his familiar fellows. And he did straight away get the love of their fathers, in going to them and signifying how much he loved their children, insomuch, that if they had any suit to the king, they would bid their children desire Cyrus to do it for them. Cyrus, when the children did desire or require him, of his singular humanity and desire of reknown, had no greater pleasure than to speed their suit. And Astyages could deny no request that Cyrus made, but gratify him in the same. For when it chanceth that he was sick, Cyrus would never depart from him, never leave weeping, that every man might perceive how fearful he was of his Grandfather's death. For in the night, if Astyages called for anything, Cyrus would first hear him, and of all other most readily make haste to minister such things as he thought might please his grandfather. Whereby he was in most high favor with Astyages. But peradventure Cyrus was somewhat full of talk. For both by his education, wherein he was compelled of his schoolmaster to render cause of all that he did, when he was in judgement, and also because he was desirous of learning, he did ever ask many questions, of such as were present, how the world went with them. And whatsoever others did demand of him, he, for his quick wit, would give ready answer. By reason of all which things, a certain liberal talk was reputed in him. But as in young men, whose bodies be of great growth, there appeareth some young shape, that doth disclose their tender age; so of Cyrus' liberal talk, no boldness did appear, but a soft and gentle behavior. Whereby every man desired rather to hear him speak much, than to be in silence. But in continuance of time, growing in body and years to a young man's estate, he used fewer words and less noise. He was also so bashful that he would blush when he met with any ancient man. And his rudeness to praise in every company after a wanton fashion, he did no more use, but became very quiet.

Also with his equals he was most acceptable. For truly in such exercises as his companions did often use, he would never challenge his fellows in that he was superior. But wherein he well knew he was too weak, therein would he assay himself, affirming that he, one day, would do it better than they. And he began now to leap on horseback, to shoot and dart on horseback, before he could well sit his horse. When he was overcome, he would be most merry with himself, and not shrinking, though he were ovecome, to practice those feats, wherein he was inferior, but eftsoon enforcing himself, in assaying to do them better, in short time, he was as good in riding as his fellows, and in short space, by reason of his fervent desire of the feat, he did excell them all. In short time with chasing and shooting at the wild beasts in the park, he wasted and destroyed them all, in so much as Astyages could not provide him game. And Cyrus, perceiving that his

Grandfather being very desirous, could not provide them alive, often said unto him: "Grandfather, why do you trouble yourself so much in seeking for these wild beasts? If you will let me go on hunting with my uncle, I will think every wild beast that I see, to be kept up for me." And being very desirous to go on hunting he could not now desire in wantonly, as when he was a child, but was somewhat afraid to go about it; and wherein he before did reprehend Sacas, which would not suffer him to go to his grandfather, he was now become a Sacas to himself. For he would not ocme, except time served him, and desired Sacas to show him, when it were time convenient to go, and when not. Wherefore this Sacas, as well as all others, did wonderfully love him.

After that Astyages knew, he was so desirous to go on hunting abroad, he sent him forth with his uncle, appointing a certain guard of ancient horsemen to keep him out of dangerous places, and from the wild beasts that should be put up. Cyrus then asked earnestly of his waiters, which beasts were not for him to meddle with, and which he might boldly chase. They answered that bears, bores, lions and leopards have slain many approaching too nigh. But harts, goats, wild sheep and wild asses, be not so dangerous. And this they said more, that the danger of the place was as well to be regarded, as the very beasts. For many men, horse and all, have been hurled down headlong. Cyrus diligently marked these words. But when he saw a hind afoot he, forgetting all that he had heard, did pursue her, looking to nothing else but whether she fled. In so much that his horse leapt and fell on his knees, and had like to have cast him over his neck, nevertheless, he with much ado did sit him, and the horse recovered. Being come into the plain, he picked his dart, and overthrew the hind, a fair beast and a large, and he did not a little rejoice. But his rulers and tutors riding to him, did rebuke him, showing in what peril he was, affirming that they would tell his Grandfather. Cyrus stayed and alighted, being much grieved to hear such words. But when he heard any howling, he as past himself, leapt eftsoones on horseback, and seeing a boar chased, he rode against it, and threw so right that he hit it in the face, and made the boar to stay. Then his uncle, seeing his rashness, rebuked him, who notwithstanding his rebukes, desired him, that he might present his Grandfather with those, that he had taken. to whom his uncle answered: "If he should know, that you have chased he would not only be angry with you, but also with me for suffering you." "Let him beat me," said he, "if it be his pleasure, so I many present them to him. And you uncle, beat me to, as you will, so you do me this pleasure." And his uncle at length said: "Do as you list, for you are now as a king among us." So Cyrus presented the deer, and gave them to his Grandfather; and said, that he had hunted these for him. His darts he did not show, but left them bloody in such place, as he thought his Grandfather should see them. Astyages said unto him: "I accept (son) gladly, whatsoever you give me. But I have no such need of them that you should put yourself in jeopardy." "If you have no need," said Cyrus, "I pray you Grandfather, give me them to distrubute among my companions." "Take them," said Astyages, "and give them to whom you will, and anything else that you will desire."

Cyrus took them and gave them to the children, saying thus: "O Children, how did we trifle, when that we hunted deer in the parks. It is like, I think, as if a man would hunt beasts in prison. For first they were in straight place, then both little and unlusty, some of them halt, some lame. But the deer that be in mountains and forests, how fair, how fresh, and great they seem! The harts, as swift as birds, flying up to heaven, the boars assaulting, as the say, valiant men do. Whom, being so broad, a man can not lightly miss. Wherefore, I think, that these be fair being dead, than the others enclosed in house yet being alive. But will your fathers," said he, "give you leave to go on hunting?" "Readily," said they, "if Astyages command." "And who," said Cyrus, "shall be a mean for you to Astyages?" "Who," said they, "can better speed this purpose, than you?" But I," said Cyrus, "cannot tell in what case I am. For I can neither speak, nor look on my grandfather as I was wont to do. If I grow in this fashion, I am afraid, I shall prove an ass or a fool. What I was a little boy me thought I had tongue enough." "Nary," said the children, "you tell a shrewd tale for us, if you when we have need, can do nothing for us, that you may best do." Cyrus hearing this, was much grieved, and departing in silence, and enforcing himself to be bold, went forth, and waiting how he might without displeasure, speak to his Grandfather, and obtain his and the children's request, began thus: "Tell me grandfather, if any of your servants did run away, and you should take him again, how would you handle him?" "How else," said he, "but imprison him, and make him a slave." "If he did return of his own mind, what would you then do?" What," said he, "but after sharp correction, that he might no more so do, use him as I did before." "Then it is time," quod Cyrus, "for you to provide sharply to punish me. For I propose to run from you, and take my fellows with me on hunting." "It is honestly done," said Astyages, "that you give me warning. But I command you not to stir one foot out of these doors. Were it not a pretty pastime, if I, for a little venison, should lose my daughter's son?" Which thing Cyrus hearing, obeyed, and abode at home. and being heavy and sad, kept himself in silence. Astyages, perceiving him very sad, intending to please him again, had him forth to hunt, assembling many, both foot and horsemen, and the little boys too. And gathering the deer into the plains, he made a goodly hunting, and being himself present in royal manner, commanded, that no man should shoot, before Cyrus had his fill therein. But Cyrus did not suffer them to be forbidden, but said: "Grandfather, if you will have me hunt pleasantly, suffer all these that be with me, to chase and travail, and do the best that they can." Then Astyages gave then all leave, and himself stood still, beholding how they encountered with the deer and contended in chasing and darting at the same. Being much delighted in Cyrus, which for pleasure could not keep his tongue, but as a whelp of good hind, made a noise when he drew nigh the fame, and did encourage every man by name, rejoicing furthermore to see him laugh at one, to hear him praise another, repining? at no man, at length having great praise. Astyages departed, and had from thence forth such pleasure in this pastime, that at other times when he had leisure, he would go abroad with Cyrus, taking with him the other boys for Cyrus' sake. After this sort Cyrus continued a long season, to all men cause of goodness and pleasure, of hurt to no man. And when he was about the age of fifteen or sixteen years, the king's son of Assyria, which should marry, had great desire to hunt at that time, And hearing much deer to be in the marches of them and the Medes, which had been spared, by occasion of war, he coveted to hunt the same, and that he might hunt in safety, he took with him men of arms and light horses, which should drive the deer to him into the plains and champion ground. And being come to the places where his castles and garrisons were, he did there sup, that he might early hunt the day following. And when it was night, there came out of the city, that succeeded the former garrison, both of horsemen and footmen, wherefore he thought himself to have a great army. These two garrisons being joined, having himself many horsemen and footmen that came with him, he thought it therefore best, to make a drove? out of the Medes' ground, both that the pastime of his hunt should be the more notable, and also did think to have the more abundance to make sacrifice. So rising early, he set forth his host, and leaving ambushments of footmen in the borders, he, with the horsemen, which he hath both very good and many, did ride to the fortresses of the Medes and there remain, that the garrisons should not rescue them, that were chased. Then he sent band forth of the most forward men, to chase some one way, some another, commanding, and with whatsoever they met in their compass, they should drive the same to him. And so they did.

When it was reported to Astyages that enemies were in his land, he with such as he had about him, went to help the marches, and his son likewise with the horsemen that were present. And gave warning to all others to come in aid. When they saw many of the Assyrians in good order, and the horsemen not stirring, the Medes also stayed. Cyrus seeing other making them ready on every side, did so himself likewise. And that was the first time that he put on harness unlooked for, so desirous was he to be in arms with them, and truly they were very goodly and meet. Which his grandfather had do made for his body. Being thus harnessed, he took his horse and rode forth. Astyages seeing him, much marvelled at whose motion he came, and commanded him to abide with him. When Cyrus saw many horsemen, of the contrary part, he asked: "Be yonder horsemen, Grandfather, our enemies that stand on horseback so quietly?" "They be our enemies," said he. "And they too, that drive the praie??" "And they." "Now surely Grandfather," said he, "they look like cowards, and being horsed with iades? they drive away our goods. Is it not meet, that some of us make after them?" "What son," said he, "do you not see what a troop of horsemen stand in good array? If we chase them, they shall enclose us, or compass in, and our strength is not yet come." "Yet," said Cyrus, "if you tarry here, and repair your force, they being in fear, shall not move and they that desire the prey, shall let go the same, when they see the onset give them." When he had said this, he seemed to Astyages to speak somewhat, and marvelling at his prudence and forecast, commanded his son to take a band of horsemen and pursue them that pursue the prey. "And I (said he) shall let upon the other, if they move toward you. Wherefore they shall be enforced to have watchful eye at us." So Cyaxares taking the strongest horse and men, set forward against them, and when Cyrus perceived them marching forward, he marched forth among them and being the foremost, he led them a great pace. Cyarares followed and the others were not behind. The preydrivers, seeing them approach, left their booty and fled. Cyrus' company did encose and hurt them, that they overtook Cyrus being the foremost, and so many as had escaped prevented them, they chased and pursued, and did not cease, till they had taken some of them. And even as a dog of a good kind uncunnning, rashly runneth on the boar, so Cyrus rushed among them, only looking how he might strike him that was overtaken, regarding nothing else.

    Their enemies seeing their men in jeopardy, moved forth the troop of horsemen, thinking that the chase would cease, if they see them once to march forward, but Cyrus staying never the more, and for joy calling upon his uncle, followed the chase. And handling his enemies hard, made great slaughter among them. Cyaxares followed truly, perchance for fear and shame of his father. The others followed also, being thereby the more encouraged to pursue, yet in force and power inferior to their enemies. Astyages perceiving them rashly to pursue, and his enemies both in number great and in good array making toward them, being afraid, both for his son and nephew, lest they so scattered, falling in danger of their enemies well appointed, should be in peril, marched straight forth agaist his enemies, who, seeing the Medes making toward them, holding forth, some, their darts, some, their bows, kept their place, as though they would resist them being come within arrow shot, as oft as they were wont to do. For approaching somewhat nigh together, they skirmished, with shot at large, many times, till night. When they saw their men flee toward them so fast, and them with Cyrus following so fiercely, and Astyages with his horsemen, like shortly to be within arrowshot, they recoiled and fled, the other pursued with all their might, and took, hurt, and slew many valiantly, both horse and man, not ceasing, till they came to the Assyrian's footmen, there fearing lest some greater ambushment might be in cover, they stayed. And Astyages returning with his army was very joyful of his victory of horsemen, and of Cyrus could not speak too much, whom he knew to be chief cause of this feat, perceiving him to be hardy and fierce.

And whereas others returned home, only he could do nothing, but ride about, beholding them that were overthrown. And they that were appointed to bring him to Astyages, had much ado to get him away, he causing the same to go a good way afore him, because he saw by his Grandfather's countenance, that he was moved in beholding of him.

These things were thus done in Medea, and as all other men set forth Cyrus, in word, report, and song, so Astyages highly tofore regarding him, had him now in more estimation. Cambyses, Cyrus' father, hearing this report, was very joyful, and understanding that Cyrus played manly parts, sent for him, that he might be fully furnished with the discipline of the Persians. And Cyrus (as they report) said he would depart, both that his father should not be displeasesd, nor his country reprove him, wherefore Astyages thought is necessary to send him home, and giving him such horses as he desired to have, honorably dismissed him, all things, for that purpose, being prepared, because he both loved him, and had also great hope that he should prove such a man as might be able to do his friends good, and his enemies hurt. Cyrus at his departure, was accompanied of all states, children, his equals, men and ancients on horseback, and also Astyages himself, and as they say, there was no man, but that wept, at that departure. And Cyrus himself, as it is reported, departed with much weeping, giving many gifts among his equals, which Astyages had given him; in conclusion, putting off the Medish robe that he wore, gave it to one, declaring that he most entirely loved him. When they had taken and received these gifts, they did (as men say) show them to Astyages, who took and sent them again to Cyrus, which sent them quickly to the Medes, with these words. "O Grandfather, if you will have me repair to you without shame, suffer them to have my gifts, to whom I have given the same." Astyages hearing this, fulfilled Cyrus' request. And if I may recount somewhat of amorous talk, it is reported, that at his departure, taking leave one of the other, his kinsmen kissed his mouth, dismissing him according to the Persian's law, for the Persians at this day used so to do.

And one of the Medes, a man of much goodness and honesty, had long time marvelled of Cyrus' estate, beholding his kinsmen kissing him, he stood still, and when all other were departed, he went to Cyrus, saying, "Be you ignorant, Cyrus, that only I am your kinsman?" "What, are you my kinsman also?" "Yes surely," said the other. "Is that the cause," said Cyrus, "that you have so countenanced me? For I have marked you often so to do." "Truly," said the other, "being very desirous to come unto you, as God save me, I ever was too bashful." "But so you should not have been," said Cyrus, "being my cousin." And coming straight to him, he did kiss him. The Mede being kissed, asked, "Is this a law of Persia for friends to kiss one another?" "It is indeed," quoth Cyrus, "when they have not seen one another a certain space, or when one do depart from another." "Then is it now the time," said the Mede, "when you must kiss me again, for I must, as you see, depart from you." And Cyrus kissing him, eftsoons, left him and departed. They had not ridden very far, but the Mede returned again to him, his horse all in a sweat; whom Cyrus seeing, asked, "have you forgotten anything that you would have spoken?" "No truly," said he, "but I am come again after a long while." "Indeed, cousin," said Cyrus, "it is but a very short while." "What, short?" quoth the Mede. "Do you not know, Cyrus, that when I wink never so little time, it seemeth to me very long, if I do not behold you, being such a gentleman?" Cyrus then after his former weeping, first began to laugh, saying: "Depart and be of good cheer, for it will chance in short time, that you may behold me, if you will, and wink not."

Cyrus being returned into Persia, was one year more among the children, who at his coming, scoffed with him at his pleasant life that he learned in Medea; but after they saw him eat and drink as heartily as themselves, and in a festival day, when they had good cheer, perceiving that he would rather give away some of his part, than desire any of theirs, and also saw, that he in all other feats excelled them all, they had him in estimation again.

Being perfect in this trade of learning, he entered among the young men, in the which he appeared also to pass others, exercising all things requisite, endeavoring everything that was his duty, reverencing his seniors, and obedient to his governors. In continuance of time, Astyages, king of Medea, died, whose son, Cyaxares, and brother to Cyrus' mother, received the dominion of the Medes.

The King of Assyria subduing the Syrians, no small nation, having the Arabian king and the Hyrcanians subject unto him, now beseiging the Bactrians, thought if he might weaken the Medes' state, being the most strong nation of all his borderers, that he should easily achieve the dominion of all the country about him. Wherefore sending both to his subjects, and also to Cresus, king of Lydia, to the king of Cappadocia, and to both the Phrygians, to the Paphlagonians, to the Indes, the Carians, and Silicians, and accusing to all these, the Medes and Persians, declaring how these nations were great and strong, confederated and allied in marriage and perpetual league, insomuch, that except some man did by forecast abate their force, they were like by invasion to subdue all other nations, one after another. Some persuaded by his allegations, some inveigled by gifts and money, wherein he was most wealthy, joined with him in league. Cyaxares, Astyages his son, perceiving their trains and purveyance made against him, gathered straight of his own strength so much as he could, and also sent for aid to the Persians, as well the counsel, as to Cambyses, his brother in law, King of Persia. He sent also to his nephew Cyrus, praying him that if the counsel did send any aid, that he would labor to be captain of the same. At this time Cyrus had spent ten years with the young sort, and was in the company of men, whom when he approved the thing, the counsel, after consultation chose captain of the army into Medea. They also licensed him to choose two hundred of them that be equal in honor, and to every one of the two hundred, they have the election of four of the same peers, which number maketh one thousand, and to every one of this thousand they gave leave to choose of the commons ten darters, ten slingers, and ten archers, which amounteth to ten thousand archers, ten thousand throwers of darts, and ten thousand slingers, beside the thousand noble men. And this so great an army was committed to Cyrus, which being chosen, forthwith made his beginnning of God, and having prosperous sacrifice, did elect the two hundren, and when they also had chosen four more, Cyrus assembled them and thus he first spake unto them.

Cyrus' Oration

Friends, I chosen you, not now having the first experience of you, but beholding that from your childhood you have with much quickness and lustiness travailed in those things which the city reputed honest, and utterly abandoned those which it judgeth unhonest. Now for what cause I, not unwillingly am appointed to this business, and why I have assembled you, I will declare unto you.

I have considered that our ancestors, have in nothing been inferior to us, for they have travailed to accomplish all such things as be reputed the works of virtue, but what good, they, being of this sort, have exploited, either for the commonwealth of the Persians, or for themselves, that can I not yet perceive. Surely I think therefore, that virtue is not put in use among men, that good men should not be preferred to the will. They that refrain from present pleasure, do it not, because they would nevermore be in rejoicing, but that at length, by such temperance, they might the rather attain to many sundry delights and pleasures. And they, that study to excel in eloquence, do it not that they should never cease or stay from pleading of causes, but because they trust, that by persuading many men by their eloquence, they shall purchase themselves great avails. They that travail in feats of chivalry, do it not that they should never leave of fighting, but because they think that if they excel in martial proofs, they shall get both themselves and their country great riches, much felicity and high honor. And if some men, after such pains taken, before they can receive any fruit of the same, perceive themselves to be made impotent by age, they, as I think, be in case like to the husbandman, which would fain be cunning, so with well and planteth diligently yet when he hath need to take fruit of the same suffereth it ungathered, to fall to the ground. And if a champion, after intolerable pains and many guerdons of victory worthily won, would end his life, as one that never assayed feats of strength, he were not worthy, as I think, to be excused of his foolishness. But friends, let not us be in this case, but seeing we all do testify with ouselves, that from our childhood, we have travailed in good and noble feats, let us go against our enemies, whom, I certainly know, by that I have myself seen, be unexpert men of war in comparison to us, for such be too weak to match with us, which though they can shoot, dart, and ride perfectly, they quail when labor is required, but our enemies cannot away with labors, neither such as when they ought to watch, be overcome with the same, but our enemies cannot lack their sleep, neither though they be in these things able men, which be untaught how to use their aiders and how their enemies. But it is evident that our enemies be to learn in those disciplines, that be most expedient in war.

But as for you, you can away with night, as well as others with day; you repute pains, the guides to pleasant life. You take hunger in stead of meat, and you can away with water drinking, as well as lions. You have also laid up within your hearts, the most precious treasure of the commonwealth, for you be more in love with renown, than all other men, and they that be towers of renown, must needs gladly for it endure all pains and perils.

If I should thus speak of you, thinking otherwise, I should deceive myself. For if by you no such thing could come to pass, the less should it redound to me. But I trust, that by your experience and benevolence toward me, and by simplicity of our enemies, that this good hope shall not deceive me, but that we may boldy set upon them. And where we have abhorred to be reputed, unjustly to covet other men's, our enemies at this time, be authors of doing this injury, our friends call on us for aid. What is there, either more just, than to resist unjury, or more honorable, than to help our friends? And I think that you have not been negligent to make my beginning of God. For you being privy of many things with me, do know, that as well in weighty as small affairs, I use always to begin of God. To conclude: What should I say more? When you have chosen your men, and have them ready in all other things, being well appointed, set forth into Medea. I do return to my father, that when I have learned with all speed the state of our enemies, I may make the best provision for you that I can, that we may with God's help most honorable go forward with this enterprise.

They prepared themselves. Cyrus being come home, and his prayer made to Vesta and Jupiter his country's patrons, and the other gods, he set forth toward the army, his father bringing him on the way, and when they were come forth of the house, it thundered and lightninged on his lucky side. And when that was done, they using none other token, did set forward. As who would say, the high god did signify nothing else. As Cyrus set forward, his father began to speak unto him on this wise. "It is evident, O son, as well by sacrifices as celestial tokens, that the gods send thee forth with their help and favor, as thou thyself dost well know. For I have diligently taught that, these things that thou not through others interpretation mightest know the will of God, but that thy self seeing the sights and hearing the noises, mightest perceive it, and not go to soothsayers, which if they would, might deceive thee, showing thee otherwise, thee were signified of God. And that at no time thou shouldest be without an interpreter, or be in doubt what God meaneth by his signs, but knowing by divination, what God his will and pleasure is, thou mightest obey the same."

"Surely father," quoth Cyrus, "I will not cease to do every endeavor to the utmost of my power, according to your advertisement, that God may the rather be favorable and inclined to do us good. For I remember that I heard you once say, that of congruence be obtaineth more, as well of God as man, which doth not flatter, when he is in need, but when he is in his chief wealth, then doth most remember God. And the same consideration you said, ought to be had of friends." "Merely son," said he, "thou at this time, being so affected, doest come to God with more delight, by reason of the same regard. And thou doest trust to obtain the better thy want, because thou art certain in thy conscience, never to have been negligent in the same." "Without doubt, father," said he, "I am so affected toward God, as to my most assured." "What, son," said he, "doest thou remember what we once concluded? For men, which learn what God at any time give thee, and take diligent pains, do speed better than they that be idle. And they that provide afore, behaving themselves as they ought to do, liveth more in safety, than they that care for nothing. After this sort, we thought expedient, that men should make request to God, for all good things." "Truly father," said Cyrus, "I remember, I have heard this lesson of you, wherefore I am enforced to follow the same. And I know that you be of this mind, that it is not lawful for them that have not learned to ride, to ask of God victory on horseback; nor for them, that be uncunning in shooting, to desire better hand of them that be expert in the feat; nor for the ignorance of sailing, to wish the safeguard of ships that they take in hand to govern; nor that they, which soweth no corn, should desire they might have good corn to grow; neither the unware in war, to make prayer to win victory. For all such things be against God's ordinance. You said likewise, that they that ask of God ungodly things, were as well worthy to be said nay of God, as they to be denied, which make unlawful request of men."

"But have you, son, forgotten those things, which we did devise? That it is for a man a sufficient and honest part, of he can procure, to be indeed, in very good and honest case himself, and also in provision of necessary things, to be so diligent that he and his family may have sufficient. But to rule their men, and to sustain the labor thereof, it being so weighty that they might have abundantly all things necessary, and that they might all prove as they ought to do, this seened to us a thing of admiration." "Truly father," said he, "I remember that you did so say. And it seemed to me likewise a thing of much importance to rule well; and now it seemeth no less unto me, when I confide and muse with myself, what it is to rule. But when I behold other men, and do consider what they be that are in rule, and the condition of them that shall be our enemies, I think it a very great rebuke to me, to be afraid, they being of such sort, and not willingly to go with such companions, who, as I suppose, to begin with these our friends, be of this opinion, that you behold a ruler to exceed his subjects, in plentiful diet, in abundant treasure, in longer rest, and in all things to take less pains, than his subjects. But I think, quoth he, that it becometh a ruler to exceed his subjects, not in easiness of life, but in the care of provision and courage of travel." "But son," said he, "there be certain things, wherewith we strive not so much against men, as against the things themselves, which we cannot lightly overcome with ease. And you know," quoth he, "that if your army have not out of hand sufficient purveyance, your rule will soon decay." "Mary, father," quod he, "Cyaxares said he will provide for all, that shall go hence, how many soever they be." "And will you son," quoth he, "go forward, trusting to Cyaxares ability?" "I will," said Cyrus. "What?" quoth he, "know you how able he is?" "No surely," quoth Cyrus. "And do you give credit to things uncertain? Do you not know, that you shall have need of many things? And that you shall even now be enforced to spend much other ways." "I know," said Cyrus. "Then", said he, "if he lacketh money, or peradventure should dissemble of purpose, in what case then shall your army be?" "In no good case, as it appeareth. Therefore, father", quoth he, "if you see how I might make provision for money, show it now, while we be among our friends." "You ask, son, if any provision of money should be made by you; of whom is it more meet, that money should be provided for, that of him that hath power? You have, son, a company of footmen to go forth with you, as I know, you would not change for a far greater number. And as for horsemen, you shall among the Medes have the best aid with you. Then, what country, think you, that is nigh has not such power, will not both be glad to aid and succor you, but also fear some displeasure by you? Which things you, jointly with Cyaxares, must devise, that at no time you lack anything that ought to be had. And a revenue of money must be found out, to accustom you to it. But of all other, remember this, that in no wise you do not differ the provision of it, till that need enforceth you, but when you have most plenty, then ratherest provide against want. For you shall the sooner relieve your lack, of them you do ask, if you seem to have no need. And furthermore, you own soldiers shall have no cause to complain of you, but shall thereby cause others to have you in the more reverence. And if you desire with your power, to do pleasure or displeasure to any man, your men shall be the more ready to serve you, so long as they have all things necessary. And your words, as you well know, shall have the more pith to persuade, if you can evidently show, that you are both able to do pleasure and displeasure." "Me thinketh, father", said he "that you have spoken all other things very well, and that the soldiers will give me no thanks, for that they shall now receive, because they know for what case Cyaxares hath sent for their succor. But what any shall receive beside this tofore spoken, that they will think honesty to themselves, and render great thanks, as reason is, to the giver. He that hath a great company, with the which he may help his friends, by doing them good, and his enemies, if he have any, he may go about to get something from them, and them will be negligent in getting of it, think you it, to be a less shame, than if a man had both land and till men, wherewithto work, and yet would suffer his ground to be untilled without profit? Therefore, have this opinion of me, that I will never be negligent in studying for my soldiers' provision, neither being with my friends, nor with mine enemies." "Keep that mind still," quoth he. "But do you not remember, son, what other things we thought necessary to be cared for?" "I remember indeed," said he, "when I came unto you for a reward, to be given him, that said, he had taught me the feats of chivalry, which you giving me, did thus ask of me: 'Did this man, son, to whom you bore this reward, among his matters of war, make any mention of household governance? For no less need have the soldiers of things necessary to live in the camp, than servants in the house.' I, showing you the truth, that he made mention of no such matter, you did ask me again, if he said anything of health, and of strength, which should no less be cared for of a captain, than anything that belong to a captain's office. And when I had also did nay herunto, you asked more, if he taught me any way, how to make my men most expert and courageous in every feat of war? Which thing, I denying also, you required eftsoons, whether he had given me any precept, how to encourage and make hearty my soldiers, affirming that quick courage, did in all things, far exceed youthful hearts. When I had denied this too, you did demand, if he had taught me any way how to persuade an army. Which thing a man must most diligently assay. I utterly denying any such word to be spoken. Finally, you asked me, in what point he had taught me the knowledge of governing a host. I then answered, in setting an army in array. Whereat you smiling, showed me, by conferring one thing with another, that ordering an army should little profit, without knowledge of feats of war tofore mentioned, and without obedience, insomuch as you made it plain unto me. The ordering of array was but a little part of governing an army. I then, desiring you to instruct me in these things, you commanded me to resort to men of most experience in war, and with them to debate and learn how all these things might best be done. Since which time, I have been conversant with them, that have been reputed most politic in such affairs. As concerning victuals, at this time I believe there is sufficient purveyance, because Cyaxares must find us the same, for preservation of health, because I both have heard and seen that cities, which regard health, maintain physicians, and that captains for their soldiers' sake, lead physicians with them; even so I, being appointed to like office, will have diligent regard of it. And I hope, father, I have such men with me, as be very expert in physic."

Whereunto his father said: "These physicans, son, that you now speak of, be like unto butchers and clothiers of torn and ragged garments. For when men be sick, then they cure them, But you must have a more honorable and decent regard of health, than this, wherefore you must provide at the beginning, that your army fall not into sickness." "What way shall I go to work, father, to be able to accomplish this?" "If you shall foresee, that this place wherein you shall be long in camp, be of good and wholesome locality, wherein you shall not err, if you take heed. For men commonly report which places be healthsome, which unhealthsome; and men's bodies and colors, be evident witnesses of both. Furthermore, it is not enough to consider that the place be sufficient, but you must remember to have regard that yourself may be in ill health." "Then," Cyrus said, "I do first beware that I surfeit not, for that grieveth me much. Then with labor I consume that I receive. So methink I have the better health and stronger body." "Likewise, son," he said, "you must provide for all others." "May soldiers, father, have leisure to exercise their bodies?" "They may not only," said his father, "but be of necessity enforced to the same. For an army that shall do that it ought to do, must never rest, but be doing with some hurt to his enemies, or good to himself, for it is evil to nourish an idle man, and worse, son, to nourish an idle household, but to keep a whole army in idleness, it is a thing insupportable. Much it is that an army spendeth, and what it hath, it wasteth excessively. Wherefore it is not in any wise expedient, that an army should be idle." "Your saying, father, as I can guess, is this, that as of an idle husbandman cometh no profit, so of an idle captain cometh no good." "I allow," said he, "him for a hard-working captain, which, God not hindering, can provide, both that his army have things needful abundantly, and also prepare, that their bodies be strong and lusty." "Therefore, father, that they might have assay of every feat of war, methinketh if I did proclaim common games and appoint rewards for the same, I should best causee them to have a proof in everything, that when need shall require, I might have them prest and ready." "That is very well said, son," quoth he, "for in doing this be you well assured you shall perceive your bands of men, studying to keep their order, as it were in a dance." "Verily," said Cyrus, "concerning the encouragement of soldiers, I think nothing so good, as if a man could put them in hope of great avails."

"That is like, son," said he, "as if a man in hunting would always allow his hounds with the noise, which he useth, when they see the deer at the first, they will quickly harken to it. But if he deceive them often, the end will be, that they will not then believe him, when this deer is up indeed. Likewise, it is in hope, if a man many times put them in hope of gains and deceived them, it will come to pass, that when he showeth the certain hope indeed, they will not give credit to him. Therefore you must, son, refrain to speak that you do not certainly know. For though some men, sometimes perform like promise, yet, let that encouragement be reserved, till greatest dangers, that it may the rather continue in credit."

"Truly father," said Cyrus, "methink you speak very well, and this way delighteth me much, But to make my men obedient to me, methink, father, I am not to learn. For you even from my childhood, have taught me this, compelling me to obey you, afterward, you recommended me to schoolmasters, which did so likewise use me to the same. And being among young men, our governor was most diligent in this, and many of our laws seemeth to teach most these two things: To rule, and to be ruled. And therefore, pondering thoroughly all these things, I think, I see, that this were the best exhortation, to make obedient men, to praise and avaunce him that doeth obey, and the contrary to punish and condemn." "To make them," said he, "to obey by constraint, this is the readiest way, son, but to make them freely to obey, which is much better, there is a readier way than this, for whom men think wiser than themselves, for their avails, him, they gladly will obey. And as you may know, that this is true in many other things, so in sick men, which very gladly do call on thm, which do appoint and enjoin, what they ought to do. How carefully in the sea do the sailors obey the shipmasters, whom men think to know the way better than themselves, from them, they will not gladly be departed. But when they think that by obeying, they shall take hurt, neither will they be enforced, for pain, nor allured for reward. For no man willingly will take reward to do himself hurt."

"Then, father," quoth he, "your sentence is that there is no readier way to have obedience, than to appear wiser than his subjects." "It is so indeed," said he. "And how, father, may a man soonest bring to pass that opinion of him?" "There is, son," said he, "no readier way, than in those things to be wise indeed, in which you would appear to be wise. And marking this in every particular thing, you shall find, that I say true. For if you would seem a good husbandman, a good horseman, a good physician, a good minstrel, or any other like, and be not, consider what shifts you must make, to maintain this appearance. And if you persuade yourself, that many men do praise you, and think to get glory thereby, and have laid good foundations in every man, you do deceive them presently. But when you shall come to the trial, you shall betray youself, and forever be taken as a vain boaster." "But how can a man, father, presently be wise, in foreseeing profit to come?"

"It is evident, son, that so many things as can be known by learning you may by study attain to, as you did learn the ordering of an army. But such as men cannot learn, nor yet, be foreseen by man's wisdom, if you can understand them by divination, and God's oracles, you shall be thought to be wiser than other men. And when you know what is best to be done, if you will be careful to do it. For to be careful for things needful, is a point of a wiser man, than to be altogether careless. Furthermore, to be beloved of his subjects, which thing I think one of the chief, a like way is evident, as if a man would desire to be beloved of his friends. For I think surely, that he that doth well, must needs be notable, but this, son, is hard always to be able to show pleasures, to whom a man would. But to show himself to rejoice with them at their good chance, to lament with them at their hurts, and to be ready to relieve their lacks, to provide that they take no hurt, to foresee that they be not deceived, and also how they may most gladly accompany him.

And in doing feats, if it be in summer, that captain must manfestly suffer most heat. If in winter, most cold. And if labors must be endowed, most pains. All these things be most available, to get the love of subjects." "Do you say, father, that a captain must be in all things more painful than his subjects?" "Yes, son, so I say. But be not dismayed of that. For you know well, that the labors of like bodies, be not alike painful, in a ruler and in a private man. For honor in a ruler, maketh the labor lighter. And because he knoweth that whatsoever he doeth, it shall be notable." "But father, when an army hath sufficient, is in good lust, able to travail, exercised in feats of war, desirous to declare manhood, gladder to obey than to be stubborn, do you not think him wise, which at that instant, would encounter with his enemies?" "Yes, truly," said he, "if he may have the better hand. If not, as I think myself, to be in better state, and my men also better appointed, so much the more ware shall I be, even as those things, which I think to be of most price, them will I covet to be in most severity." "But how can a man soonest have the better hand of his enemies?" "It is no trifling matter, son, nor light thing, that you do ask of me. But know for certain, that he that shall bring this to pass, must be politic, close, subtle, taking his advantage, privily, catching, in every thing aforehand with his enemies." And Cyrus, smiling, said: "O Hercules, what manner a man, Father, do you describe me to be?" "Such one, son, as you may be a most just man, and keeper of the law." "Why then," said he, "when we were children and young men, did you teach us the contrary?" "So truly do we now," said he, "toward our friends and countrymen. But do you not know that you have learned many subtleties how you may do hurt to your enemies?" "No, truly, father." "For what purpose," said he then, "did you learn to shoot? For what purpose to catch wild boars with nets and pits? Whereore harts, with snares and traps? Why lions, bears and leopards? You did not match them of even hand, but always labored to encounter with them, you having the advantage?" "Yes truly, father," quod Cyrus, " concerning wild beasts. But if I were but suspect, to go about to deceive any man, I remember full well that I had many a stripe." "Indeed, son," said he, "we did not, as I think, trade you to pick a dart at a man, but we taught you to drive it to the hilt. And now, you may not hurt your friends in no wise. But if war did chance that you might be able to hit, to deceive, and get the advantage of men, we taught not you these feats in men, but in beasts, because you should not hurt your friends. Nevertheless in time of war, you should not be slack in such feats." "Then, father, if it be profitable to know the way both to do good, and hurt also to men, it had been meet, we had been treaded in the use of both, in men." "There is a saying, son, among our ancestors, that there was sometime a schoolmaster, that taught children justice, even as you now would have it. Not to lie, and to lie, not to deceive, and to deceive, not to slander, and to slander. Not to oppress, and to oppress. And did divide, which should be done to friends, which to enemies. And went so far, that he taught to be lawful, to deceive friends, for a good purpose, to steal friends' goods, for a good purpose. Children, being thus taught, must needs practice to do the same one against another, as yet the Greeks, men say, teach their children in the common school, to deceive and exercise them to be able to do it, one against another. Therefore, some being very toward to deceive cunningly, and to get advantage cunningly, and peradventure not untoward in coveting riches, did not spare their friends, but attempted to be enriched by them. By which occasion a law was made, which we use at this day, that children should one way be taught, as we do now teach our servants, to do truly, not to deceive, not to steal, not to be afore hand, which things if they transgress, we punish them. That thus being accustomed to this trade, they might be made the milder men. But being at that age which you now be, it was thought, they might safely be taught, what was lawful against enemies. For being trained in mutual shamefastness, it was not thought, that you would go so far, as to prove wild citizens. Even as we do not make any mention of natural pleasure to very young men, lest ease, joined to the vehement desire, might provoke the same, to unreasonable lust."

"Yet, father, if you can show any way, how I may get advantage of mine enemies, be not afraid to teach me, as one, somewhat dull in the other." "You must then endeavor," said he, "with all your strength, well appointed, to assail your enemies unprepared. You being armed, they unarmed. You watching, they stepping, they espied of you, you not of them, you being in sure place, receiving them in straits." "But how, father, can a man take his adversaries in such errors?" "Because, son, both you and your enemies shall of necessity suffer many such things. You must both needs send a foraging, both needs have herbigage, both needs in the morning stray out for necessaries, and with such way, as it happeth, you must be content, all which things, you must consider alone. And in what thing, you know your men to be most weak, in that must you be most ware. In what things you know your enemies to be most easy to be vanquished, in that you must fiercely set upon them." "Whither must we," quoth Cyrus, "get the advantage in these only, or in some others too?"

"You much more, son," quoth he, "in other. For commonly in these, all men use to keep sure watch and ward, knowing their own lack. If they that will deceive their enemies can make them have good comfort in themselves, and so unlooked for, assail them, and negligently pursuing them make them to dispair, and by retiring bring them into straits, then it is good to set upon them. And, son, you must be desirous to learn all these things, not that when you have learned you shall practice only these, but of your own policy, you must be inventing of sleights against your enemies, even as musicians do not only use the measures, which they have learned, but also study to invent every day new harmony.

And as in music, new and fresh stuff is had in most price, so much more in war, new policies be most set by, because they may soonest deceive your enemies. And, son, if you would turn those sleights upon men, which you devised in catching of little wild beasts, do you not think that you shall have advantage to set upon your enemies? For you, to take fowl, have risen in the night. And before the fowl could stir, your snares for that purpose were set for them. And the ground, that was moved, was like a thing not movable. And birds were caught to serve your turn and to deceive their own kind. You lay in court, that you saw them and they not you. All your purpose was, to prevent the same before they should flee away. And for the hare, which feedeth at night, and fleeth the day, you kept hounds that find him out by scent, and because when he is found, he swiftly fleeth, you had greyhounds taught to overtake him by footmanship, and lest he should escape them, you learned the course and place, whither the hare courted to flee. And there set privy nets, that he is his most fleeing might fall in them and trap himself. And that he should not here escape, you set watches for it, which being nigh, might straight come upon him. And these, which on the fore part, you taught to lie in wait, you made to be in covert. And you on the back half, with an hollow make in time, so astonished the hare with the noise that he was taken as it were, in a maze.

"Therefore, as I said tofore, if you will practice these feats against men, I know not, what you should need in feats of war. If it shall at any time so chance that you are enforced both to fight in plain ground and in open field, being both thoroughly appareled, then, son, your things, better appointed, afore, doeth much prevail. Which I say be these: If your men's bodies be well exercised, if their hearts be courageous, and well instructed in martial feats. This also you must well know, that so many as you think worthy to be obedient to you, they all will think you worthy to be a ruler to them. And you must never be negligent, but foresee overnight, what your men must do in the day, and in the day, that things as well at night. How the army may best be appointed to fight, how you may convey it in the day, how in the night, how in straits, how in the plains, how in hills, how in dales, how to camp, how to appoint the watch and ward, both in night and day, how to advance again your enemies, how to retreat from them, how to bring your army to a city being your foe, how to march to the walls or recoil from the same. How to pass forts, floods, how to order your horsemen, how darters and archers. Or when you lead your army against the wing, and your enemies set upon you. How you must array your men. If you set forth against the main battle, and your enemies appear in any other place, rather than at the front, how you may encounter with them. Also, how a man may best know what his enemies intend, or how they shall have little knowledge, what you intend."

"Why do I now reherse all these things to you? For what is there that I know, but you have full often heard. Specially if any other seemeth to have knowledge in any of these things, you have not condemned any of them, nor have been ignorant in the same. Wherefore you must, I think, when anything chanceth, use such of these remedies as you suppose may ever do you good. And learn these things of me, son, as chiefest, against sacrifices, and tokens, enterprise nothing. Neither alone, nor adventuring with your army, remembering that men by conjectures take matters in hand, not knowing, which shall redound to their wealth, but you may know by that that chanceth.

"For many men, being reputed most wise, have persuaded cities to make war against them, of whom they have been vanquished, when by persuasion, they have invaded. Many have increased, both cities and private men, by whom, being increased, they have come to extreme displeasure. Many, which might have used their friends, both doing and receiving pleasures, choosing rather to use them like servants than like friends, have been by them brought to nought. Some men, not being content with sufficient pleasure and happy life, but coveting to be lords of all, have thereby lost that they have afore had. Many possessing great treasure of gold, have by the same lost their lives. So men's wisdom does no more know how to choose the chief good, than he that goeth by lot, when he cast the same."

"But the gods, O son, which be immortal, knoweth all things, both past, present, and what shall of every thing come. And to men, that make request to them, if they favor, they do declare what they ought to do, and what they ought not. And though they do not show so much to every man, marvel not. For there is no necessity can compel them, to regard that they will not."

The End of the First Book

The School or Discipline of Cyrus

The Second Book

Devising thus together, they came to the end of Persia. Whereas an eagle appearing unto them with lucky token, became their guide on the way. They, making prayers to the gods, patrons and defenders of Persia, favorably and mercifully to dismiss them passed the marches of the same. Being past, they made eftsoones their prayer to the gods a vowers of Medea, as favorably and mercifully to receive them. This done, and after comely manner embracing on the other, they departed, the father returning into Persia, the son marching forward in Medea to his uncle Cyaxares. Whither when he was come, at their meeting, they embraced one the other, as was decent. Then Cyaxares demanded of Cyrus, what manner of army he had brought. He answered, "I have twenty thousand of them which heretofore have been in wages with you. And certain other of the nobility, which never yet came abroad, be now come with me." "How many be they?" quoth Cyaxares. "As for the number," said Cyrus, "it will not greatly delight you to hear, but this you must learn, that a few of these whom we call peers, or men of equal honor, do far pass a great many of other Persians. But have you any need of them? Do you not fear in vain? Do your enemies come?" "Yea, surely," quoth he, "and that very many." "How know you that?" "Because," quoth he, "many that come from these, do diversly report, but all to one purpose." "Must we then match with men?" "There is no remedy." "Why then," quoth Cyrus, "have you not told me what you know of their power? How great a company cometh? And likewise of your own force, that both being known, we may devise, how we shall best join with them." "Then hark," quoth Cyaxares, "Cresus, the king of Lydia, bringeth, they say, ten thousand horsemen, target men and archers more than forty thousand. Artacaman, the prince of great Phrygia, bringeth about eight thousand horsemen, spearmen, and targetmen, no less than forty thousand. Aribeus the king of Cappadocia, about six thousand horsemen, archers, and darters, no fewer that thirty thousand. Maragdus the king of Arabia, ten thousand horsemen, one hundred chariots, and slingers an huge multitude; but it is not yet certainly told, whether the Greeks that inhabit Asia, do follow or no. But the Phrygians that join upon Hellespont, do accompany Gabeus, having in the plain of Caustre, six thousand horsemen, and ten thousand target men. The Carians, the Cilicians, and Paphlagonians, being called, do not follow, as they say. The Assyrian himself, which is king of Babylon and all Assyria hath (as I think) no less than twenty thousand horsemen. Chariots (I am sure) not above two hundrend. and footmen (as I guess) an infinite sort. For so is he wont when he marcheth hither." "Then," said Cyrus, "you have declared our enemies to be in horsemen, three score thousand, in target men and archers above, two hundred thousand. Now what number have you of your own power?" "There be," quoth he, "of Medean horsemen, more than twenty thousand of target men and archers, may be made in our dominion, sixty thousand. Of the Armenians our neighbors shall come four thousand horsemen and twenty thousand footmen." "Then you say," quoth Cyrus, "that our horsemen be less than the third part of our enemies, and our footmen almost half so many as they." Then said Cyaxares, "do you account the Persians so few, which you say you have brought?" "Whither we have," quoth Cyrus, "any need of men or not, we shall consult hereafter. Now tell me the manner of your several fight." "The fight," quoth Cyaxares, " is of all, almost alike, for there be archers and darters, as well of them as us." "If they be," quod Cyrus, "thus appointed, must there not needs be skirmishing with arrow shots?" "Of necessity," said Cyaxares. "Then," quoth Cyrus, "the greater number must needs get the victory. for a few be sooner hurt and destroyed of many, than many of a few." "If the case standeth so," quoth Cyaxares, "what device were better, than to send to the Persians, declaring that the Medes' loss, must needs rebound to them, and requesting to have more aid of them." "You say well," quod Cyrus, "but you shall know, that if all the Persians should come hither, they were not able to countervail our enemies in number." "Do you," quoth Cyaxares, "espye any better way than this?" "I would," said Cyrus, "if I could, with all speed provide for all the Persians that shall come hither, such armor as they have, which, with us be called men of equal honor or peers. That is, a curert before the breast, a light target in the left hand, an arming blade or curtolays in the right hand. These, if you can provide us, you shall cause us to join with our enemies with most security, and them, rather desiring to flee, than abide the Persians, shall couple with them that tarry, and if any stay, we shall commit them to you and your horsemen, that they shall not be able, neither to retire, nor eftsoons to march." Thus

Cyrus said, and seemed to Cyaxares to say well, insomuch as he made no more mention of sending for more men. This armor rehersed tofore, was speedily prepared, and when it was well nigh ready, the noble men of Persia were come with the army of the same. When as Cyrus calling them together, spoke on this wise.

The Oration of Cyrus

"When as I (dear friends) perceived you to be so armed, and in hearts so appointed, as is meet to match with our enemies at hand, and the residue of the Persians that follow, to be so appareled, as serveth to fight at large. I was not a little afraid, lest you, being few, and abiding the brunt without succor, might haply fall in the danger of your enemies that be so many, and by occasion thereof be in no small jeopardy. But now seeing you be come with tall men's bodies, and no refuse, and they shall have even the same armor that you have, it must be your part to quicken and encourage their hearts. For it is the office of a captain, not only to be good himself, but also to care that his men be very good too."

Thus he said. They were all glad, because they thought they sould be well accompanied at the battle. And one of them spake after this sort.

"I shall peradventure seem to speak strangely, if I should exhort Cyrus to say somewhat of us, to them that shall be our warfellows, when they shall receive their armor. But I surely know, that they which be most able to do good or hurt, do most prevail in words, and soonest persuade the hearts of the hearers. And when such men giveth any gifts, though of less price than their familiars do, yet the receivers do much more esteem the same. Wherefore if the Persians were now exhorted of Cyrus, they would much more rejoice and regard it, than if they were to the like admonished of us. And when they shall be appointed to us of the nobility, they shall esteem the matter to be of more weight, beeing assigned of a King's son and grand Captain, than if they were if us moved to the same. Nevertheless our parts may not be behind, but with all means we must encourage and quicken the hearts of our men. For if they be good and valiant, it shall be profitable and commodious." When Cyrus, according to this device, had brought the armor into the middest of them and assembled all the Persian soldiers, he spake unto them after this sort.

"Friends Persian, you were born and bred in the same place that we were. You have bodies nothing inferior to ours, and your hearts ought to be no worse than ours. Being of this sort, yet in our country you have not equally been partakers with us. Not of us repelled, but enforced of necessity to seek for your living. But now that you may have even the like, I (with God's help) will provide, you may, if you will, have the same armor that we have, to endure the same peril that we shall, and to be advance equally with us, if any of you shall become valiant and hardy. Heretofore as well you as we, have been archers and darters, and though you do the feat worse than we, it is no marvel, for you have had no such opportunity to put the thing in use, as we. But in this armature, we shall not be any deal better than you. For every man shall have a meet curette for his breast, a target in his left hand, as we all are wont to bear, an arming sword or curtoloyse in his right hand, wherewith we must needs hit our enemies, and not fear to miss when we strike. Then, wherein do one of us pass another, but in valiant courage? Which you ought no less to declare than we? and for to desire victory, the which possesseth and saveth all wealth and felicity, why ought we more than you? Finally, to be conquerors, which giveth all that the conquery hath. Why is it more expedient for us than for you? to make an end, you have heard all. You see this armor, take every man that is meet for him, and give his name to a Captain of a crew, to be in like array with us, He that is content with the place of a stipendary soldier, let him remain and minister harness."

Thus he said. The Persians hearing this, thought themselves worthy all their life to live a wretched life, if they being called to like avails, would not be willing to take like pains. Wherefore they gave their names and took every man the harness. All that time that it was said, their enemies came, and did not, Cyrus travailled to exercies their bodies in feats of strength, teaching them to keep array, and quickening their courage against their enemies. And having ministers of Cyaxares, he commanded them to give to the soldiers all things that they should need. And by this mean, he left them nothing to do, but the only exercise of martial feats. supposing learning taught him, that men be made in every feat most excellent, when they leave all other things and set their minds upon one only. Dismissing also a part of their warlike exercise, and taking from them the use of bow and dart, he left this only to them, to fight with sword, target and breast plate. Whereby he fashioned their hearts to join with their enemies at hand strokes, or else to confess that they were unprofitable warfellows. But that were a grief for them to confess, knowing that they were found for none other purpose, but to fight for them that gave them wages.

Furthermore perceiving that men be most willing to exercise those things, wherein is contention and desire of victory, he proclaimed prizes or games of all things that were meet for the soldiers to put in use. And these that he did proclaim were these: That the private man should show himself obedient to the rulers, being ready to labor, and foreward to adventure with modesty, expert in things belonging to the army, brave in wearing his harness, and in all these to seek for honor. To the Quincurion or captain of five, to behave themself as becometh an honest private man, doing to his power, all things belonging to the office of that number. To the Decurion or captain of ten, the like in his number, even so the leader of twenty-four; to the band leader, to the Centurion or captain of a crew, and to every other ruler, after like sort, being careful to perform the captains commandments, they again might provide for them, doing their office accordingly. The requards of good Captains of a crew, which did best frame their men, was to be made a Tribune or captain of a thousand. The Band leaders, that best did teach their bands, did ascend to the place of a Centurion. The best Decurions or captains of ten, were appointed to rooms of bandleaders. The captain of five, to the captainship of ten. The private sort that most excelled, to the captainship of five. The chief regard of these captains was, to be honored of their men, the which being obtained, other advancements followed every man in comely wise.

Furthermore he proposed greater hope to them that were worthy praise, if any greater commodity should appear in time to come. He proclaimed rewards of victory to the whole crews, to the whole bands, likewise to the whole number of ten and five as they appeared most faithful to their captains, and ready to exercise these things tofore rehersed, and such rewards were appointed to them, as is meet for the multitude. These things were proclaimed and put in practice in the host. Furthermore he provided pavilions for them, according to the number of captains of crews, and so big, as was able to receive a crew. And in every crew was one hundred men, and so they had their tents according to their crews. In camping thus together, he thought this commodity would ensure for the battle and should be, because he perceived that they being kept together, should have no pretense of cowardice, that one was better or worse taught than another, concerning the coupling with their enemies, it seemed also to profit, in that they should know one another being camped together, and in knowing one another, they should be more ashamed one of another. For when they know not one another, they seem to be the more given to sloth, as men living in darkness.

Wherefore he thought that this camping together, should much profit to the perfect instruction of his men. The centurions and their crews so living, as every crew might march by himself, the bandleaders, the captain of ten, the captain of five, after the same manner. And this order of every band seemed very profitable, as well not to be disarrayed, as if it should so chance, to be soon in order again, even as wood and stones, which must be framed, though they lie cast hand over head, be easily set together, if they have notes, whereby it may be perceived, for which place every one serveth. It seemed also profitable to them the less willing to forsake one another, because he saw that beast feeding together had great desire to them that chanced to stray away.

Cyrus had regard of this also, that none should go to dinner or supper, except they had labored and sweated tofore; for either he lead them on hunting and so caused them to sweat, or else devised such pastimes as might move them to the same. And if it chanced anything to be done, he would begin the feat, that they should not return without sweat. For he supposed this to be profitable, as well to the better lust to meat and health of body, as to the enduring of pain, and to be the more gentle one to the other. For horses accustomed to like labors, stand the more quietly together. And soldiers be made the more couragious against their enemies if they be assured to be well exercised. Cyrus prepared for himself a tent, that might be sufficient for the receit of them, whom he called to feast. He called commonly such captains of crews, as seemed meet to him, and sometime bandleaders, sometime captains of tens, and five; sometime soldiers, sometime the whole number of five and ten, sometimes a band and a crew. He called and advanced such as he saw doing, that he would have all to do. He service was ever equal, and all one for himself and his guests. And the ministers about the army he made partakers of everything. For he judged those mininsters of the camp to be no less worthy advancement than heralds and orators. Wherefore he would have them expert and cunning in things belonging to the army, and also hardy, quick, ready, and stable. And he appointed that they shold have even as much as they that were reputed best, and so to use themselves, as thy should refuse no labor, but think it their duty to do whatsoever the general did command them.

Cyrus also had regard, that when they made merry, such talk should be ministered as was pleasant and might stir them to manhood. And on a time he chanceth to talk on this wise. "Friends," quoth he, "doeth other men seem inferiors to us, because they be not trained after our sort? Or is there no difference at all betwixt them and us, neither in behavior, nor in things appertaining to the trade of war?"

Hystaspas answered and said: "What they be in warlike matters, I can not tell, but in behavior and company, there be some (by my say) rude enough. For of late Cyaxares sent to every band and company sacred meat, and we had three dishes of flesh every man or more. The cook began the first meal at me. And when he came the second time, I had him begin again at the hindermost. Wherefore one of the soldiers that sat in the middest, cried out and said: 'By god this gear goeth not indifferently, if not man shall begin at us that be in the middest.' Whichwhen I heard, I was grieved, that he should think he had too little, and called him unto me. He very modestly obeyed me. When the meat came at us, and the lowest had taken their part, there was, I think, but little left. Whereat he was again grieved, as he did plainly express. And said to himself: 'What ill luck had I to come hither, when I was called?' And I said: 'Take no care for the matter, for he shall straight begin at us, and you shall be first and take the most.' And with that he brought in the third and last course. And this fellow took next unto me. When the third man had taken, and seemed to take more than he, he laid aside that he had taken, intending to take another. The cook, thinking he had no list to meat, bore it away before he could take another piece. Then he was grieved at his evil chance, because that he had taken was eaten up. Wherefore being in a rage and fury for so evil fortune, he overthrew the sauce that was left him. Which, when the bandleader that sat next unto me, saw, clapped his hands and laughed heartily. And I made as I had had the cough, for I could not refrain from laughter. Such one of your soldiers can I show you, Cyrus," quoth he. At the which tale they laughed, as they might well.

Another of the captains, said, "This man, Cyrus, as it seemeth, was not well contented, but I, when you had taught us, and sent us forth to our crews, commanding every man to teach his company, as you had taught us, did my duty as other men did. So I came to teach one band. I placed the band leader first, next him a lusty young fellow, and than other as I thought good; then standing afore, and looking to the band, when I saw my time, I bade the band march. And this fellow your lusty young man, coming before the bandleader, marched foremost. And when I saw him, I said: 'Good fellow, what doest thou?' 'I march,' quoth he, 'as you command.' Then I said: 'I bid not thee alone, but I bid you all to march.' And he hearing this, turned to his fellows, and said, 'Do you not hear, that he biddeth us all march?' And the all going before the band leader, came about me. And when the bandleader had brought them again to their places, they grudged, and said, 'Which must we obey? Now the one commandeth us to march, the other will not let us.' I took the matter in good part, and placed them eftsoons in order, saying that none of the hindermost should move, till the former did set forth, and that they all should have regard at this, to follow the former. When it chanced that one went into Persia, he came unto me, and bade me give him letters, which I had written home, and I bade the bandleader, which knew where the letters lay, to run and fetch the same. He ran forth. This young fellow followed the bandleader with his breast plate and arming blade. All the remnant of the band, seeing him run, followed and fetched my letters. Thus hath my band, quoth he, perfectly learned all that you have taught them."

The others that were there, laughed at the warlike bringing of these letters, but Cyrus said, "O Jupiter and other gods, what fellows have we to our friends? They be so tractable, that some of them will be won with a little meat. Some be so obedient that before they know what is commanded them, they obey the same. I can not tell what kind of soldiers a man ought rather wish to have, than such." Cyrus laughing with them, thus praised the soldiers.

It chanced that at this feast there was one of the captains named Aglaitadas, a man in manners like to testy and forward men, who said in this wise: "Do you think, Cyrus," quoth he, "that these fellows say true?" "Why should they," quoth Cyrus, "desire to lie?" "Why," quoth he, "but becase they would move laughter, and therfore speak after this sort, to avaunt themselves." "Speak honestly," quoth Cyrus, " and call them not avaunters; for the name of an avaunter seemeth to be made, as I think, of them that pretend to be richer than they be, valianter than they be, and not able to perform that they take in hand; and that be evidently known to do this for lucre and advantage sake. But they that move laughter in company, neither for their own advantage nor the hearers hurt, neither for any other kind of displeasure they ought of right rather to be called pleasant and fine, than avaunters." Thus Cyrus answered in their defense that moved laughter.

Then the bandleader that told the merry tale of his band, said, "Aglaitadas, if we should make you to weep, you might right well blame us. As some men in their verses and orations recite lamentable matter, to provoke weeping. And now when we, as you know, would have you merry, doing no man hurt, you have us for the same in much disdain." "Yea, by God," quoth Aglaitadas, "and that justly. For he that maketh his friends to weep, doeth, as I think, a great deal better, than he that maketh the same to laugh. And you shall find, if you weigh the matter well, that I speak rightly. For by weeping, fathers make their children sober, and the schoolmasters their scholars well learned, and the laws enforced citizens, by making them to weep to keep justice. But wherein can you say that they which move laughter do profit, either the body or mind, to be the more apt to govern families or commonwealth?"

Then said Hystaspas, "Aglaitadas, if you will follow my counsel, among you enemies, be bold to be liberal in this, as in a very precious thing, and do your best to make them weep. But with us your friends, I pray you be more liberal of laughter, because it is a thing of little price. For you have neither spent it youself, neither willingly among your friends or aquaintance uttered the same, so that you can make none excuse, but that you have a great deal of laughter in you."

And Aglaitadas said, "Do you think, Hystaspas, to move laughter of me?" And the band leader said, "Mary, then he were a fool, for I think a man shall sooner beat fire out of thee, than get laughter." At this all the other laughed, considering the manners of Aglaitadas, and he himself also smiled.

Cyrus being him somewhat merry, said, "You do not well to corrupt this our sober man, in moving him to laugh, he being such and adversary against all laughter." When this was spoken, Chrysantas said thus, "Cyrus and all you here present, I think that there be come with us some of more price, some of less. But if any good luck shall happpen unto us, they will all think themselves worthy to have like avail. And I judge nothing to be among men, so unequal, as that the good and bad should be reputed alike."

To this Cyrus said, "Friends, we could not do better, than propound this matter to be debated of the army, whether, if God giveth us any good of our travail, it be the feats of every man being considered according to the same the rewards to be employed." "What need you," quth Chrysantas, "propound this to be reasoned, and not rather proclaim that so you will do? Have you not already proclaimed common games and rewards for the same?" "Yes certainly," quod Cyrus, "but they be not like. For what as they shall get in their soldier fare, that (I think) they will take to be common to them. As for the governance of the army, they peradventure thought to be in me before they came forth. Therefore though I appoint the order of the same, I suppose they think I do them no wrong." "And do you think, "quod Chrysantas, "that the multitude will decree, every man not to have equally, but the best to be preferred in honors and advancements?" "I think so," quoth Cyrus, "partly by your exhortation, and partly because it will be a shame to speak against it, that he which travaileth most, and profiteth the common, should not be worthy most reward." "And I think," quoth he, "that the very worst and refuse, will suppose the best to be preferred." And Cyrus was the more willing that this decree should be made, for the noblemen's sakes. For he thought they would do the better, if they knew their travails should be considered and their worthiness regarded. Wherefore he thought the time meet, to have this decree made, because the noblemen, repined at the equal regard of the commons. Every man at this feast, thought it meet to be debated, and that every manly man should accord unto it.

One of the captains smiled and said, "I know one of the common sort which will agree, that equal reward shall not be had." Another asked who it was. "It is," quoth he, "my tentfellow, which in all things requireth to have more." "What," quoth another, "in labors too?" "Nay by my faith," quoth he, "there I lied. For in labors and such other, he is alway very gentle to let him that will have more than himself." "But I," quoth Cyrus, "do determine such fellows, as he now speaketh of, to be banished our army, if we intend to have a valiant and obedient army. For I think it the part of soldiers one to induce another. And the good, will do their duty, to induce to goodness, the evil, to lewdness. And for the most part, the lewd have more agreeing to them than the good. For lewdness coming with present pleasures, serve the same, as joint persuaders, to allure the multitudes; but virtue, leading to hardness, is not able to draw unto it out of hand, especially where do incite to ease an displeasure. There be also some, which only be evil in sluggardy and leisuring, whom I repute, as drones, hurting the common weal, only be wasting. But they that in labors be lewd, and stout and vehement to have with the most, they be also leaders to lewdness. For many times they may boast and show that their lewdness prevaileth. Wherefore in any wise, see that they be banished from us. And do not regard to fulfill your number with your own countrymen, but as in horses, you speak them that be least, not of your country, even so in men, of all other, take them, which seemeth most meet for the strength and honor of your fellows. This also witnesseth with me for the best, that neither a cart can be swift, which hath slow horses, nor a house well governed where be lewd servants. And less loss it were to have no servants, than be troubled with evil servants. You know well, friends, that this profit shall not only come, by weeding out the lewd, that all lewdness shall cease, but also they that remain, and were infected with others' lewdness, shall eftsoones be purges of the same. And the good seeing the evil rebuked, shall with the more courage embrace virtue." Thus he said, which pleased all his friends, and did accordingly.

Then Cyrus began to jest again, for perceiving that one of the captains had brought a guest to make merry, which was a man hairy and deformed, he called the captain by his name, and said thus: "Sambaulas, do you after the Greek fashion, which is commendable, lead about that young man, which sitteth next you?" "Yes surely," quoth Sambaulas, "for I have a pleasure to be in his company, and behold his countenance." When the other at the table heard this, they looked upon him, and when they saw his face so evil favored, they all laughed, and one said: "Good lord, Sambaulas, by what mean hath this man won your favor?" "Mary I will tell you," quoth he, "when so ever I call him, wither by night or by day, be never maketh any excuse for his case, nor obeyeth me slowly, but every runneth when I bid him do anything; and I never see him labor, but he sweateth. And doth declare not in word, but in deed, how all the other like companies should behave themselves." And one said, "If he be such one, why do you not kiss him as your kinsman?" To this the foul fellow answered, "By God, because he listeth not to take pain; for if he would kiss me it were enough for all his other exercises." Such matters both of mirth and importance, were ministered at this feast. In the end, making thrice oblation, and praying God to send them good chance, they broke up the feast and went to bed. The day following, Cyrus assembled all the soldiers, and said thus:

"Friends, the battle is at hand, for our enemies cometh. The rewards of victory if we overcome, certainly our enemies be ours, and all our enemies' goods. But if we be overcome (for this must we ever both speak and practice) all the goods of them that be overcome, to be evermore present rewards to the conquerors. This you must think. When men that indifferently be doers in this war, shall assure themselves to have no commodity, except they play the valiant men, then they will without delay do many valiant feats, for they will bear anything undone that ought to be done, but when every man shall think, that another may travail and fight, and he take his case, through such (be you sure) all kind of displeasure shall redound to all.. And God worketh after this sort, for to such as will not appoint themselves to do good, he hath made others their rulers.

"Therefore now let some man arise and say his mind of this matter, whether he thinketh that virtue shall the rather be put in use among us, if he that shall most travail and adventure, shall have also most advancement, or if we perceive that it maketh no matter, to be a coward, because all shall have equal reward." Then Chrysantas arose, one of the nobles, no big man, nor strong to see to, but of singular wisdom, and spake thus unto them.

The Oration of Chrysantas

"I think, Cyrus, you do not propound this case, because you think it meet that the evil should have equally with the good, but to prove, whether any man will show himself to be of this opinion, that doing no good nor laudable feat, would have equal part with them, that shall achieve honor by their virtue. I am neither swift in feat, nor strong in hands. And I am sure, if I be judged, by that I shall by my body do, I shall neither be the first, nor second, no not the thousandth as I guess. And peradventure not the ten thousand, yet this I know for certain, if they that be valiant shall receive for their travails any commodity, my part shall be so much as right requireth. But if the evil do nothing, and the good be out of courage, I fear me, lest I shall be partaker of more than I would of anything rather than of good." Thus Chrysantas said.

After him Pheraulas, one of the Persian commons, and to Cyrus at home familiar and pleasant in body, not unbeautiful, and in mind not unlike a gentleman, arose and said thus:

The Oration of Pheraulas

"I suppose Cyrus and all you Persians here present, that we all equally be moved to the trade of virtue. For I see that we all do nourish our bodies with light diet, and all be entertained in like companies, like commodities being laid before us all. For to obey the rulers, is indifferently appointed. And he that seemeth to do the same without grudge, I see that he doth get honor at Cyrus' hand. And to be valiant against our enemies, is not propounded to some, and the goodliest thing, and to some not, but indifferently to all. Now battle is declared to be at hand, in the which I see, that courageous men be made cunning by nature, even as other creatures hath each one learned a certain fight of none other schoolmaster, than of nature, as the cow to strike with the horn, the horse with the hoof, the dog with the mouth, and the boar with the tooth. And they know to avoid all things, of the which they ought most to beware. And these they learn without any schoolmaster at all.

"I being a child, knew straight how to defend myself aganst him, of whom I thought I should be beaten, and if I had nothing, I would hold forth my hands, and as much as I could, let him that beat me. And this I did, not taught, but was beaten for the selfsame, if I did defend myself. And being a very child, I would get a sword, when I could see it, learning this neither, how to take it of none other, but of nature, as I say. And this I did forbidden, not taught, as other things, which being restrained of father and mother, I did being enforced of nature. And truly I would privily strike with the sword, all that I could. For it was not only natural unto me, as to go and run, but methought I had a certain sweetness in doing the thing, that nature moved. Seeing therefore, that all one fight is left unto us, in the which rather courage than cunning is required, why should not we with pleasure, contend with noblemen? For the rewards of virtue be equally propounded.

"And if we be compared together, we be not like in adventures. For they live an honorable life, which is pleasant; and we a painful life, without honor, which is displeasant. But friends, this doth most encourage me to fight, that Cyrus is the judge, which doth not judge partially, but as God knoweth, and I dare swear, whom he seeth valiant, them he loveth no less than himself. To them I see he hath more pleasure to give, than himself to keep. I know these gentlemen be high stomached, because they have been brought up to endure hunger, thirst and cold, ill perceiving that we be taught the same, of a better schoolmaster than they. For there is no schoolmaster so good, as necessity, which hath taught us to be very perfect in the same. They learn to labor, when the bear their harness, which all men have devised to make most light and easy to bear. But we have been compelled to go and run with great burdens, insomuch as the bearing of harness seemeth to me at this time, more like feathers than burdens.

"Therefore, Cyrus, so take me as one that will do my best, and whatsoever I be, think it meet that according to their worthiness, so men should be advanced. And friends of the commons, I exhort you, that you will encourage yourselves to contend in this fight with these well brought up gentlemen. For now men be taken to a fight of the commons."

"Thus Pheraulas said. And many others arose and accorded with them both. Wherefore it was decreed, that every man should be rewarded after his worthiness, and that Cyrus should be judge of the same. Thus his matters went forward. Cyrus in a time, called an whole crew of men with their captain to supper. He saw him place the one half of his crew against the other meet to fight, both having breastplates and targets in their left hands, in their right hands he have the one half good round wasters, the other he bade take up clods and throw what they saw time. When they stood in order of battle, he gave a token to fight. Then they threw their clods and hit some on the breastplace, some on the target, and some on the shins and legs. But when they came together, they that had the wasters struck some on the legs, some on the hands, some on the thighs. And as they stooped to take up more clods, they hit them on the backs and necks. At length they were put to flight, and the waster bearers chased them, and struck them with much sport and laughter.

Cyrus being delighted at the witty device of the captain, and the due obedience of the other, because they were exercised and also recreated. Being at this delighted, he called them all to supper. And when he saw in his tents some having their legs, some their hands bound up, he asked, what they ailed. They answered that they were hit with clods. Then he asked them again, whether it was when they met together, or when they were asunder. They answered, when they were asunder. For when they met together, the waster bearers said it was a pleasant pastime, but they that were striken with the wasters cried, that it was not pastime to them when they met together, and showed the stripes of the wasters, some in their hands, some in their necks, some in their faces. And thus one laughed at another, as they might right well.

The day following, the plain was full of all the host, counterfeiting these. And ever when they had no weightier thing to do, they used this pastime. He saw at another time a captain leading his crew from a river on the right hand one by one, and when he saw his time, commanded the hindermost band to lead the third and fourth into the front, when the bandleaders were in the front, he commanded to lead every band two by two, then the captains of ten lead into the front. When again he saw it time, he commanded to lead a band by four a rank, then the captains of five were the leaders, and every band went four by four when he was at the tenth gate, commanding them to go two by two, he led in the first band, and commanded the second to follow at the tail of it. So likewise the third and fourth, he led them all in. And so sat at supper as they entered.

Cyrus being delighted with their mildness, device and practice, called this crew to supper with their captain agan. There was another captain at supper which said: "Cyrus, you call not my crew to your tent, which when it cometh to supper, do even the like. And when supper is done, the tail leader of the last band, leadeth the band, having the last, first to fight. Then after them the tail leader of the other band, and the third and fourth after like sort, whereby they know how to go back, when they shall retreat from the battle. If we be appointed to walk a course, and it be in the morning, I lead, and the first band is first, the second, third and fourth followeth, as they ought, so long as I command. When it is night, the tail leader and the last goeth first, and nevertheless obeyeth me coming last, that so they might be accustomed both to follow and to lead, being alike obedient."

Cyrus said, "Do you this always?" "So often," quoth he, "as we go to supper." "Then I bid you to come," quoth he, "both because you trade your men going and coming, night and day, and also exercise your bodies by walking, and profit your minds by learning. And because you do all things double, it is right we make you double cheer." "For gods' sake," quoth the captain, "not in one day, except you also give us double bellies." And thus they made an end of the feast. The next day Cyrus called that crew to his tent, as he had said overnight, which other perceiving, from that time forth, all followed these.

As Cyrus was mustering his men in that exercise, and setting them in order, there came a messenger from Cyaxares, saying that an embassage was come from the Indes, "Wherefore Cyaxares would that you should come with all speed. I have brought you a goodly robe from him, that you should come most comely and civil, because the Indes shall behold you when you come."

When Cyrus heard this, he commanded the captain that was first in array, to stand at the front, leading his crew one by one, placing himself in the right hand. And commanded him to give the like charge to the next, and so throughout. They obeyed him, and warned the other, so that shortly the charge was given. And in a while there was in the front about two hundred (for there were so many captains) and in breadth, one hundred. When they were placed, he had them follow as he marched, and went on a good place. But after he knew the way which went to the palace, to be more straight than all could go in the front, he commanded the first thousand to follow in place, and the second at the tail of it. When it was so done throughout, he marched forth without stop. The other thousands followed every one at the tail of the former. He sent two ministers at the entry of the path, that if any man were to seek, they should tell what ought to be done. When they came to the gates of Cyaxares, he commanded the first captain to lead his men by twelve a rank. And the leaders of every twelve to stand in the front about the place, and commanded like charge to be given to the next, and so throughout all, and they did accordingly. He came to Cyaxares in a Persian robe, not of the worst sort. When he saw him, he was glad of his speedy repair, but offended with the baseness of his garment, and said: "Why have you done thus, Cyrus, so to appear to the Indes? I would you should have been seen in most goodly wise. For this had been an honor to me, to have had my sister's son set forth most royally."

To this Cyrus said, "Whether should it have been more to your honor, if I being clad with purple and dashed with bracelets and chains, and ruffling in my robe, should have acomplished your will, or as I now have with so great a power and so speedily performed the same to your high honor, garnishing myself with sweat and diligence, and honoring you, by teaching others how to obedient to you?"

Thus Cyrus said. And Cyaxares thinking that he had said well, commanded the Indes to be brought in. Being come in they said, the Indian king had sent them and commanded to inquire the cause of the war, between the Medes and Assyrians. And your answer heard, to go to the Assyrian king, to make the like demand of him, and in fine, thus to say unto you both: "The king of India sayeth, he will stick to him that hath the wrong."

To this Cyaxares answered, "Then this is mine answer. I have not done any wrong at all to the Assyrians. Now go to him and learn what he sayeth." Cyrus being there, said, "May I, Cyaxares, speak any thing?" And Cyaxares bade him speak his mind.

"You then," quoth he, "shall thus say to the king, that we, except it seemeth otherwise to Cyaxares, make this answer. If the Assyrian shall say he hath wrong by us, we choose the king of Indes judge thereof." When they heard this answer, they departed. When the Indes were gone,

Cyrus began thus to talk with Cyaxares: "Sir, I came from home with no great store of money, beside mine own, and how much so ever it was, there is but a little left, for I have spent it upon my solders, hwereat you may marvel how I have spent it, seeing you find us. But you shall well undertand, that it is employed upon none other thing, but upon the advancement and encouraging of my soldiers by some benefit. For I think, it is better for him that will have at all bands good helpers in any matter, to incite the same, by well speaking and well doing, rather than by cruelty and compulsion. Likewise he that will make courageous travailers in warlike matters, must (I think) allure the same with good words and works. For they must be friends, not foes, which shall be unfeigned fellows in war, neither envying their captain in wealth, nor betraying him in woe. Which thing I considering, perceive I have need of money. And that you should care for all, whom I perceive liberally to give so much, I think it not convenient. Wherefore it is meet, that you and I indifferently should device, that money do not fail us. For if you have plenty, I know I shall have part at my need, specially if I take it for such purpose, as may profit you by the expense thereof. I remember I heard you say of late, that the Armenian despiseth you at this present, becasue he heareth, that enemies be coming against you, neither sending you an army, nor paying you your tribute, which he oweth." "He doth even so, Cyrus," quoth he. "Wherefore I am in doubt whether it were better for me to make him war, and compel him to pay me, or more for my profit to let him alone at this present, lest I should increase mine enemies by him." Then Cyrus asked, "Be his houses in sure places or easy to come to?" Cyaxares said, "They be in no very sure places, for I have marked that . But there be hills, whether if he can come, he is straight in safety from being taken, himself, and all the he bringeth with him, except a man would lie at long seige, as my father sometime hath done."

Then Cyrus said, "If you will send me, and appoint me so many horsemen as shall seem sufficient, I trust with God's help to make him send you an army, and also pay your tribute, And I trust further, that he shall be more assured to you than he now is." And Cyaxares said, "But I think they had rather come to you, than to us. For I hear say, there be some, which were poor companions in hunting when we were children, which peradventrue had rather come again to you, but if we can make some sure, our will shall be fulfilled." "Then," quoth Cyrus, "is it not good to keep this device close?" "The sooner," quoth Cyaxares, "should some come into our hands, and if a man would go against them, he should take them unaware." "Then hark," quoth Cyrus, "what I say. I have many times with all the Persians which were with me, hunted abut the borders of your ground, and the Armenians, and have taken boars of my friends there, and gone forth. Wherefore if I did the like now, I should not be suspected. But if my company be more now, than it was wont to be in hunting, it shall be suspected. But we may make a shift for this, that shall seem somewhat true. That is, if some man would report among them, that I intend to make a great hunting, and have made an open request to you for horsemen." "You say well," quoth Cyaxares, "and that I will give you, but a few, because I will got to my forts, which be next Assyria." "For so I will in deed," quoth he, "to make them so sure as I can. And when you be gone with the power you have, and hunt, I shall send you within two days sufficient horses and footmen, which I have gathered, whom you shall take, and then invade. And I, having another power, shall do my duty, not to be far from you, that when time requireth, I may show myself."

So out of hand, Cyaxares gathered horsemen and footmen for his forts, and sent wagons with with vitayles the way that wnet to the same. Cyrus made sacrifice for his journeys, and desired Cyaxares to have his younger horsemen, and he granted him but few, very many being willing to go. Cyaxares being gone his journey to his forts with power of foot and horsemen, Cyrus had lucky sacrifice to go against the Armenians, and so marched forth as appointed to hunt. Going forth in the first field an hare was started, and an eagle flying on the lucky side, and espying the hare running, made his flight and struck him, took him up and bore him away. And going to the next hilltop, seasoned on his pray as he would. Cyrus seeing this sign, rejoiced, and thanked Jupiter king, and said to them that were present, "Friends, this shall be a pleasant hunting, I trust in God."

When he was come to the borders, straight he hunted as he was wont. And the multitude of footmen and horsemen, coursed to and fro to put the deer up. The best of the foot and horsemen were divided to stand at receipt of the deer put up, who chased and killed many boars, hearts, goats, and wild asses. For in those place there be many asses at this day. When he had done hunting, and drew near the marches of Armenia, he supped, and the next day early hunted again, going nigh the hills, which he coveted to have. When he had done, he supped. And hearing that Cyaxares' host was at hand, he sent unto them, bidding them keep two Persian miles of, foreseeing the commodity of closeness. When they had supped, he bade their captain to repair to him.

When he himself had supped, he called his captains unto him, and said: "Friends, the Armenian hertofore, hath been confederate and tributary to Cyaxares; but now hearing of the coming of our enemies, he despiseth us, and neither sendeth army, nor payeth his tribute. Now therefore we must hunt him, if we can. And thus I think good to do. You, Chrysantas, shall go into his land to far as you may, and take with you half the Persians. You must walk over the hills, and take the same, whither they say he fleeth, when he is in fear. I shall give you guides. And they say the hills be thick, so that I hope you shall not be seen. You shall also send before your army quick fellows, like to these, both in number and array. And they if they chance upon any of the Armenians, shall take them and keep them from telling tales; and whom they cannot take, they shall drive them so far off, as they shall not espye the whole army; but shall make provision as it were against them.

"Thus shall you do. I, by the break of day, having half the footmen, and all the horsemen, will go by the plain straight to the palace. If he make resistance, then belike we must fight. If he conveyeth himself form the plain, it is like we will follow him. If he fleeth to the hills, then must your part be played, that none escapeth that cometh to you. Think you were on hunting, and that we be the hounds, and you keep the nets. Then you must remember to prevent and stop the ways before the deere be up, and they must be in covert that shall be appointed to it, that they may prevent the deer before they come. But you may not do Chrysantas, as many doth which loveth hunting; for they many times spend the whole night without sleep. But now men must have measurable rest, that they may be able to resist sleep, nor you may not wander in the mountains, as one that had no guides (except the way be much shorter) to lead you the easiest way. For an army that goeth easily, goeth speedily. Nor you may not lead your men running, though you be wont to run up the hills, but you must lead a measurable pace, that your army may conveniently follow. And it were good, that some of the best sort, and forward men, should sometime stay and encourage the other. And the forward must so pass, as all the other may seem to run."

Chrysantas hearing this, and being glad of Cyrus' instruction, took his guides, and departed. When he had told them that should go with him what to do, he went to rest. When he had rested so much as seemed convenient, he marched to the hills. When day was come, Cyrus sent a messenger to the king of Armenia, willing him to say thus:

"Cyrus commandeth you, O king of Armenia, thus to do, that with all speed you come uno him, bringing both an army and your tribute. If he demand where I am, say as the truth is, in the marshes? marches?. If he do ask, whether I will come myself, say, and that truth, that you know not. If he ask how many we be, bid him send some man and learn." Thus he sent a messenger with this commission, thinking it to be more princely, than to come upon him without warning. He being throughly appointed both to go the journey and also to fight, if need were, marched forth. He gave a commandment to his soldiers, that they should do no man wrong. And if any of Armenia chanced to meet them, to bid them be of good comfort, and every man that would, to come and fill at his pleasure, either meat or drink.

The End of the Second Book

The Institution of Cyrus

The Third Book

Cyrus thus did. The king of Armenia, hearing Cyrus his ambassage, was astonished, remembering that he had done wrong, both in withholding his tribute, and in not sending aid, being most of all in fear, because it should be espied that he had begun to edify his place, so that he was able to keep out his adversaries. Being troubled with all these things, he sent out to gather his strength and also conveyed his youngest son Sabaris, to the moutains, and the wives and daughters, both his and his sons,' with all their ornaments and jewels, of much value, appointing men to conduct them safe. He also sent forth others to espy what Cyrus did, and also made in a readiness those Armenians, that were present, and forthwith others came to him, saying that Cyrus was at hand. Then he being afraid to try it by fight, conveyed himself away. Which the other Armenians perceiving, fled every man home, intending to carry away such things as they had.

Cyrus beholding the field full of them that ran away and fled to save themselves, he sent them word that he would hurt none, which did tarry, but if he took any fleeing away, he would handle as his enemy. Whereby many stayed. And all they that privily fled were with the king. And when as they which went afore with the women, fell in their hands, which lay privily in the moutains, they made by and by great escries and fled, and were very many taken. The king hearing of these things, doubting what he shold do, fled into an hilltop. Which Cyrus seeing, did beseige the hill withthe army that he had, and sent to Chrysantas, commanding him to leave the custody of the moutains, and come to him.

And when Cryus had all his army together, he sent a messenger to the king, asking himself these questions. "Tell me, king of Armenia, whether you will remain there and fight with hunger and thirst, or come down to the plain and fight it out with us? The king answered that he would fight with neither. Then Cyrus sent again, and asked, "Why then do you lurk there and will not come down?" "You need not doubt," said Cyrus, "for you may come down and answer for yourself." "But who shal be judge," said he? "Truly," said Cyrus, "even he to whom God have given without judgment, to use you as he list." Then the king perceiving this necessity, descended.

Cyrus bringing him and all his into the middest, did enclose him with his camp, having with him all his force.

In the mean time Tigranes, the king's oldest son, which afore had accompanied Cyrus on hunting was come from a certain progress. And hearing what was done, went straight to Cyrus to know the matter, But perceiving his father, mother, brother and sisters, yea his won wife, to be captives, he could not refrain weeping. Cyrus seeing him, used none other friendly entertainment, but said, "You are come in good season, that you being present, may hear you father's cause." And straight away calling the captians together both of the Persians and Medes, and assembling also the noblemen of Armenia, which were present, and not rejecting the women being in their chariots, but suffering them to hear, when he thought it time, thus he began to speak.

"I do first give you counsel, O king of Armenia, in this cause, to speak nothing but truth, that you may be clar of that one thing, which is of all others most hateful. For to be taken with a lie, it is as you well know, the greatest impediment of men to attain pardon. Your children, your wives, and all the Armenians being present, be privy to that you have done, which hearing you speak otherwise than the truth shall think that you do judge yourself to suffer all extremity, if I do hear the truth." "Then ask what you like, Cyrus," said he, "that for the truth's sake, which you require, you may obtain what you will."

"Then answer me", said Cyrus: "did you make war against Astyages, my mother's father, and the other Medes?" "I did," said he. "Being overcome of him, did you not covenant to yield him tribute, to find him men when he should warn you, and to have no fortresses in your land?" "It is truth," said he. "Now them why have you neither paid your tribute, nor sent him aid, but have enmured? fortresses?" "Because," said he, "I was desirous of liberty, and thought it a noble thing, both to be myself at liberty, and also to leave the same to my children." "It is a noble thing," said Cyrus, "to fight, that a man may forever escape bondage. But if one being overcome by war, or made captive by any other means, should be espied to go about to revolt from his lord, tell me first yourself, would you, if you took any such, advance him with honors, as a man of price, or punish him as a transgressor?" "I would punish him," said he, "for you will not have me to lie."

"Then answer plainly to everything," said Cyrus. "If any of your officers should use himself unjustly, whether would you suffer him to be in authority still, or place another in his room?" "I would place another," said he. "If he had money would you suffer him to wax rich, or make him poor." "I would take from him," said he, "that he had." "If he would go to your enemies' part, what would you do?" "I would kill him" said he, "for why should I being reproved as a liar, rather die than showing the truth?"

The which word his son hearing, threw off the attirement of his head, and tore his garments, the women shrieked and rent their faces, as though the king had now been dead, and they all even then destroyed. But Cyrus commanding them to cease, said, "We have enough. These be rightful, you say, O king of Armenia. Now what counsel will you give us to do in the same?" The king kept silence, doubting whether he should cousel Cyrus to put him to death, or teach contrary to that he said tofore.

Then his son Tigranes, asked Cyrus, saying, "Show me, O Cyrus, because my father is like a man amazed, if I may give you counsel concerning him, what I think best for you to do?" And Cyrus because he knew, that what time Tigranes was his compainion in hunting, he had a subtle sophister attendant upon him, whom he had in great reputation, was very desirous to hear what he could say, and bade him boldly speak what he thought.

"I then," said Tigranes, "if you do allow, both that my father hath spoken and also done. I will give you counsel to follow the same. But if you think he hath done evil in all, I advise you not to follow him." Then said Cyrus, "If I will do right, I may not follow him that doeth evil." It is true," said he. "Then must I punish you father according to your sentence, if it be just to punish the unjust." "Whether think you, Cyrus," said he, "to be better for you, to punish with your profit, or with you damage?" "I should so punish myself," said he. "Yes and you should," quoth Tigranes, "much hinder yourself, if then you would kill any of your men, when it were more meet for you to have them alive." "How can they be," quoth Cyrus, "more meet for me, which be found unjust? Can I think that they will be made sober?"

"I think, Cyrus, that so it is. For without soberness, other virtues little avail. For what profit shall a man have of a strong, a valiant man, and an horseman, not being sober? What of a rich man, what of a man of power in a city. But with soberness, every friend is profitable, and every servant good." "Then thus you mean," quoth Cyrus, that your father is made in one day, of an unsober, a sober man." "Yes truly," quoth he. "Then you do say, that soberness is an affection of the mind, as dolor, not a discipline. For if he that shall be sober must be made wise, he not therefore made by and by a sober man, of an unwise man."

"What Cyrus," said he, " have you not yet learned, that one man enterprising through want of soberness to fight with his better, when he hath been overcome, hath straight way ceased from his unsoberness? Again, have you not yet seen a city moving war against another city, which being overcome, forthwith instead of fighting, would use obedience?" "But what overthrow of your father," said Cyrus, "can you show, whereby you may prove that he is made sober?"

"Truly because he feeleth it in himself, that for coveting liberty, he is made so thrall, as he never was to before. And things that he thought expedient to have been close, to have prevented or defeated, he was able to accomplish none of all. He knoweth that you, wherein you intended to deceive him, have so deceived him, as a man might deceive the blind or dumb, and not men, which had any wareness or wisdom. And wherein you thought closeness should be used, he knoweth you have so closely dealt with him, that such places as be counted most secret for his refuge, you closely had before made his prison and in swiftness you have so passed him, that you prevented him, being come with a strong army, before he could gather his power together."

"Do you then certainly think, " said Cyrus, "that such overthrows be sufficient to make men sober, and to acknowledge their superiors?" "Yea surely," said Tigranes, " much more than when a man is overthrown by fight. For he that is overthrown by strength, thinketh that his body being better appointed, he may try it again. And cities being taken, getting others' aid, think they may eftsoons renew the fight. But whom they shall judge to be stronger than themselves, them many times thy will without compulsion obey."

"Then," said Cyrus, "you think that despiteful men do not acknowledge them which be soberer than they, nor thieves true men, nor liars truth speakers, nor the unjust, them that wooeth justice. Do you not know that your father hath lied, and not performed covenants made withus, knowing that we have transgressed no point of the conditions made by Astyages?" "I do not," said he, "mean that it maketh sober men only to know their betters, without some pain done them of their betters, as now is done to my father." "As for your father," said Cyrus, "as yet, he hath felt no pain. But he is in much fear, I know well, lest he should suffer extreme pain."

"And do you think," said Tigranes, "that any thing doth more reclaim men, than great fear; do you not know, that men being striken with sword, which is counted most sharp punishment, will eftsoons fight against their enemies? But whom men do much fear, them, though they put them in good consort, they cannot look on." "Them you say," quod Cyrus, "that fear do more punish men, than to be it handled in deed."

"You know," quod he, "that I say truth, for they, which be in fear to be exiled their country, they that would fight and dare not lest they should be overcome, live most pensively. Also they that sail, fearing shipwreck, and they that fear slavery and bondage. For such can neither eat nor sleep for fear. But they that be already banished, overcome in bond, may sometime eat and sleep more than they that be in happy estate. Furthermore, it is manifest in some what a burden fear is. For some fearing lest being captives, they should be put to death, diest, afore for fear, some throw themselves down headlong, some hang, some choke themselves. So of all terrible things, fear doth most torment men's minds. And how is my father, think you, now troubled in his mind, which is in fear not only of his own captivity, but also of mine, of his wives,' and all his childrens' thralldom?"

"I can easily believe," said Cyrus, "that he is thus troubled. For it is one man's part, to be despiteful in prosperity, and soon desperate in adversity. And when he can recover, wax eftsoons proud again and stir up new trouble."

"Truly," said he, "our offense is the cause why we be out of credit. But you may both make fortresses, and retain that be already fortified, or take any other assurance or pledge what you will, you and you take our own selves we willnot greatly be grieved, remembering that we be causes of our own displeasures. But if you betake this kingdom to any tha have not yet offended, appeaering to be distrustful take heed lest you do them a pleasure, which do not take you for their friend. And if you, to avoid hatred, do put no yoke upon them to keep them under, take heed lest hereafter you shall have more need to restrain them, than you now have us."

"Be you sure," said Cyrus, "I will not gladly put such ministers in trust, as shall serve me by constraint. But such as I perceive of good will and benevolence toward me do their duties, though they do offend, then they that hate me by compulsion, doing never so well." Whereat Trgranes said, "Of whom can you get so much friendship as you now may of us?" "Of them, I think," said he, "which were never mine enemies, if I will be beneficial unto them, as you would have me now be to you."

"Can you find," quoth he, "any man at this present, to whom you may be more beneficial than to my father? Again, if you would suffer a man to love which hath done you no displeasure, what thank, think you, would he give you? What if you do not make captive his wife and children, who will for this thing love you more than he, which thinketh his deserts hath brought the same to captivity? If he have not the kingdom of Armenia, who, think you, will be so sorrowful as we? Therefore it is evident, that to whom greatest anguish shall rebound, if he be not king, the same receiving his kingdom by you, must needs give you most high thanks. And if you be desirous to leave these things in most quiet state after your departure, consider, whether you think it shall be more quiet, the kingdom being changed, or the old received manner remain still. And if you deisire to have at any time a great army, who think you, can so well prepare it, as he thta oftenest hath used to do it? Finally, if you have need of money, who think you, can better purvey the same, than he, which both knoweth, and hath all the store. Therefore, noble Cyrus, beware, lest in destroying us, you shall sustain more hindrance than my father could do you." Thus he spake.

Cyrus hearing him, was glad, because he thought all things would come to pass, which he had promised Cyaxares to do, remembering thath he had said, he would make the king more assured to him, than he was before. Then he asked the king: "If I shall give credit to you, tell me, king of

Armenia, how great an army will you give me toward this war? " Whereunto the king answered thus. "I can show you nothing more plainly nor more unjustly, than to declare unto you my whole power, that you knowing what it is, may take with you as much as you list; leaving some for the defense of this country. Likewise concerning my money, it is my part to show you all that I have, that you, knowing what it is, may take at yuour pleasure, and leave what you list." Then Cyrus said, "show me then both what power and also what money you have?" The king said, "I have now eight thousand horsemen, and forty thousand footmen of Armenia. In money, with the treasure that my father did leave me, I have numbered in silver more than three thousand talents." Then Cyrus without delay, said, "You shall then, because that the Chaldees, you borderers do make you war, send with me half your army. and for withholding of Cyaxares tribute, for fifty talents you shall pay him double. And me, you shall send one hundred talents, which I promise you, God sending me good luck, either to reapay you, if I be able, or else do you greater pleasures. But if I be not able, I trust I shall be rather thought unable, than rightly be judged unjust."

"For God's sake," said the king, "speak not so, Cyrus, for else you shall make me distrust you. But think surely thus, whatsoever you leave behind you, it shall be as certainly yours, as that you take with you." "Be it so," said Cyrus. "But what will you give me to have your wife again?" "As much," said he, "as I am able." "What, for your children?" "As much for them also as I can make." Then said Cyrus, "These be double so much, as you have. But tell me, Tigranes, what will you give to receive your wife again?" He was new married, and entirely loved his wife, and said: "I, Cyrus, would redeem her with my life, that she might not become a thrall." Then said Cyrus, "take you unto you, for I did not intend to make her captive, seeing you never fled from me. And you also, O king, take your wife and children, leaving none behind you, that they may know they depart free. And at this time sup with us, and when supper is ended go whither you list." And so they tarried.

Being set at supper, Cyrus said, "Tell me, Tigranes, where is he become, which was wont to hunt with us, whom you, as it appeared, did much esteem?" "My father," said he, "hath put him to death." "For what offense?" "He said, that he did corrupt me, which notwithstanding, Cyrus, was so good and honest, that when he should die, he sent for me, and said, 'Be not, Tigranes, grieved with you father, because he doth kill me, for he doth it not of malice, but of ignorance. And what as men offend of ignorance, that I think to be done unwillingly." "Alas, good fellow," said Cyrus.

Then the king said thus, "They that take their wives having to do with other men, do not therefore do them to death, because they do disparage their wives, but because they think, that they do quench the love, which they owe to their husbands, and therefore they use them as their enemies; even so I put that fellow to death, because me thought he made my son more to regard him than me." And Cyrus said, "Surely your offense, as I think, was a gentle fault. Therefore Tigranes, do you forgive your father." Thus talking with gentle entertainment, as meet was, after their attonement, they went gladly with their wives into their chariots, and so departed.

Being come home, some praised Cyrus his wisdom, some his constancy, some his gentleness, some, his beauty, and goodly shape. Then Tigranes asked his wife, "Did Cyrus seen so goodly to you?" "By my truth," said she, "I did not look on him." "On whom then?" said Tigranes. "Mary on him," quoth she, "which said, he would redeem my captivity with his life." So ceasing of their talk, they were at quiet among themselves, as they might.

The day following, the king sent to Cyrus and the whole army gifts of friendship, and commanded them that should go to the war, to be ready the third day, and sent Cyrus so much money as he required. Of the which Cyrus taking so much as he appointed, sent the other again. Then he demanded, whether of them should lead the army, himself or his son, which make both this answer. The father thus, "Which you will command." The son thus, "I will not forsake you, Cyrus, though I should be a drudge and follow you." And Cyrus, smiling, said, "What would you think, if your wife should hear, that you should become a drudge and slave?" "She shall not need," said he, "to hear of it, for I will do it, that she may see what I do." "It is time," said Cyrus, "for you to furnish your men." "I think," said he, "that they shall be furnished, whom my father will send you." Then gifts given among the soldiers, they went to rest.

The next day, Cyrus taking with him Tigranes and the best of the Medes' horsemen, with so many of his friends, as seemed convenient, did ride abroad to view the country, devising where he might build a fortress, and mounting to an hilltop, he asked of Tigranes, which were the hills from whence the Chaldees did use to seek their preys? Which being showed of Tigranes, he asked him again, "Be the hills now without company?" "No," said he, "but always there be spies, which do signify to others what they see." "What do they when they perceive anything?" "Every man come to the height of the hills to help that he may." Cyrus hearing these things, and beholding the country, did perceive that there was much waste ground and unprofitable in Armenia, by reason of the war. Then they came down to their camp, and supped, and went to rest. The day ensuing, Tigranes well appointed, came with four thoursand horsemen, ten thousand archers, and as many target men. While as these were gathered together, Cyrus made his sacrifice, and called the captains both of the Persians and the Medes, to whom being assempled, be spake on this wise.

"These mountains, well beloved friends, which you see, be the Chaldees, which if we may take, and in the height of them build a fortress, both the Chaldees and the Armenians, shall be enforced to be at quiet with us. Our sacrifice hath good tokens, and man's boldness shall not be so available to us to accomplish the same, as quickness and celerity. If we can prevent our enemies bofore their power is gathered and ascended, we shall get the hill top, whither without resistance, or if any be made, it shall be but small and weak. And no labor is more easy, nor more in surety, than with constant courage to make speed. Therefore harness yourself. And you the Medes shall go on the left side, and you the Armenians, being divided, shall go the half on our right hand, and the other half shall trade the foreward. And the horsemen in the rearward shall incite and provoke us foreward. and if any man waxeth faint, let him have no favor."

Thus said Cyrus. And so marched, that his bands went in length. The Chaldees perceiving the assault in the mountains, did signify it to other, and making shouts one to another, assembled themselves. And Cyrus exhorted his men, saying, "It is time, O Persians, that we make speed. For if we may prevent out enemies, they can do us little hurt." The Chaldees had every man a buckler, and tow darts, being counted the most martial men of all that region, and be ever in wages, when any need is, because they be both poor and also valiant. For their country is full of hills, and small wealth they have.

As Cyrus approached nigh the height of the hills, Tigranes being with him, said, "Do you not know, Cyrus, that you must give the onset? For the Armenians are not able to abide their enemies." Cyrus answered, that for cause he had placed the Persians next, that they might out of hand give the onset, of the Armenians should badly retire. So the Amenians had the forward. The Chaldees being ready, so soon as the Armenians were at hand, they suddenly shouting after their manner, rushed upon them. The Armenians, as they were wont, recoiled. The Chaldees chased them, and perceiving their enemies advancing up toward them, with sword in hand, some taried and were slain, some fled. some were taken. And thus shortly the hill tops were gotten. When as they were on the hills, and did behold the housed of the Chaldees, they perceived them to flee away from all the nigh habitations.

Cyrus, when his soldiers were come together, commanded them to take their dinner. Dinner being ended, and learning where the espies of the Chladees were he did by and by enmure a fortress in a place strong and full of water, commanding Tigranes to send to his father in his name, to come and bring with him all masons and carpenters that he could. Straight a messenger went to the king. And Cyrus began his building with such as he had. At which time, captives were brought unto him, some bound, some wounded. Whom Cyrus seeing, commanded the bound to the loosed, and the wounded to be cured. Then he said unto them, that he came not desiring their destruction or stirring up war, but because he would make peace betwixt the Armenians and Chaldees. "But," quoth he, "before I had gotten these mountains, I knew that you had no need of peace. For you yourselves were in safeguard, and the Armenians you did revile and rob. I therefore do dismiss you, and all other captives, giving you and all the other Chaldees space to consult, whether you will be our adversaries or friends. If that you choose war, come not hither again, if you be wise, unarmed. If you choose peace, come at you pleasure, and I will see that you goods shall be in safety, you being our friends." The Chaldees hearing this, after great praises of Cyrus, and may embracings, they departed home.

The king of Armenia, hearing of Cyrus his commandment and prupose, taking all the artificers, and other necessary things, which he thought to be good, came to Cyrus with all celerity. Whom when he saw, he said, "O Cyrus, how little is it that men can foresee of things to come, and how much is it that they will enterprise? For I now enterprising to get liberty, was made such a thrall, as I never was to before. And when I thought, that by this captivity, I should utterly have been lost, I am so preseved, as I never was tofore. For the Chaldees which have always continually molested me, I see now to be in such case as I would have wished. And this I would you should believe, O Cyrus, that I, to have driven the Chaldees from these mountains, would have given much more money than you have now of me. And all the commodities which you promised us, when you received the money, be now performed of you. Wherefore we do acknowledge our fellows to owe you yet other thanks, which if we will be honest, it will be a shame, if we do not requite. And we cannot so requite as shall be worthy for so beneficial a friend." Thus said the king.

The Chaldees came to Cyrus for peace. Whom Cyrus asked thus: Do you require peace for any other purpose than this, that you think you may live more fairly in peace than in war?" "For this only purpose," said they. then said Cyrus, "What if you have any other commodity by it?" "We would be the more glad," said they. "Do yo think yourself poor for any other thing, than for the lack of good ground?" :For this lack," said they. "Would you," said Cyrus, "pay so much tribute at the Armenians do, if you might lawfully occupy the waste ground of Armenia?" "Yes,"said they, "if we therby should sustain no damage." "What say you, king of Armenia?" said Cyrus, "will you give them to occupying of your waste ground, paying your tribute, as we shall appoint?" "I would gladly purchase this thing," said the king, "for my revenue thereby, should be augmented." "What say you, Chaldees, because you have goodly mountains, will you suffer the Armenians to use the same for pasture, paying you therefore accordingly?" "Gladly," said the Chaldees. "For we without our travail should receive much profit." "Would you, king of Armenia, occupy this as pasture to some profit of the Chaldees, to much more of your own?" "Very gladly," said he, "if I might use them without danger." "Should you not use them without danger, if you might have possession of the mountain tops?" "Yes," said the king. "But we surely," said the Chaldees, "shall not safely occupy our own ground, much less theirs, they being possessed of the mountains." "But what," said Cyrus, "if the mountains might help you?" "Then it were well," said they. "But it were not well for us," said the king, "that they should have the mountains, specially being thus fortified." Then said Cyrus, "Thus will I do. Neither of you shall have the strength of the moutains, but I will keep them in my hand, and if you vex one another, I will aid him that suffered wrong." They hearing this, did both parties praise it, affriming that by this only means, peace should be ratified. And to observe these things, they gave and took hostages on either parts, and did agree, that one should be free with the other, the one should marry with the other, they should use tillage and pasture indifferently, and one aid the other, if any did molest either of them. Thus they agreed. And at this day that league remaineth which then was made betwixt the Chaldees and the king of Armenia. These conditions being confirmed, either parts by and by did help the building of the fortress as a common defense, bringing thereunto all things necessary.

The night approaching, Cyrus called both parties as friends, to supper. Being at supper, one of the Chaldees said: "Thus concord to all other shall be acceptable, but to such only of the Chaldees, as live by robbery, which neither know the feat of tillage, nor can labor, being always wont to lear their lives inwar, seeking always their prey, being in wages and that very oft with the king of India, who is, as the say, most wealthy and many times with Astyages. And Cyrus said, "Will they not now take wages of me? I will give them as much as ever any man gave." They answered, that many would be very willing. And thus they accorded. Cyrus hearing that the Chaldees had oft recourse to the Indian king, remembering that he had sent messengers into Medea, to explore their purpose, and the same also to their enemies to espye their intent likewise, he was desirous that the king of India might know, what he there had done. Therefore he began thus for to speak.

"Tell me, O king of Armenia, and you Chaldees, if I would send any messengers to the king of India, would you send any of yours to conduct him, and help to bring to pass those things, that I would have of the king? For I would have plenty of money, that both I might give my solders good wages when they need, and also set forth and advance such as were worthy. For this cause I would have money plenty. For I think we shall have need, and it were pleasure to me to spare your money, you being friends, as I take you. But of the Indian I would gladly take if he will give me. And the messenger to whom I move you to appoint a guide and helper in the journey, shall at his coming thither say thus:"

'Cyrus hath sent me to you, king of India, saying that he hath need of money, because he looketh for another army to come out of Persia,--"for so I do indeed," said Cyrus--therefore if you will send him so much as you may well forbear, he, God giving him good success, will so behave himself toward you, that you shall think you had good counsel, when you were moved to show him pleasure.'

"Thus shall he say from me. Command them whom you will send, to do as you think good. And if we shall have money of him, we shall be the more liberal, if not we shall have no cause to thank him, but may do all things for our profit." Thus, said Cyrus, thinking that the messengers of Armenia should report of him, as he would every man should both speak and hear of him. And thus things being will stated, and the feast ended, they went to rest.

The day following, Cyrus sent forth the ambassador with such message, as he had showed before. The king and the Chaldees appointed such men to this journey, as the thought were most meet, both to do and speak of Cyrus, as should be convenient. After that Cyrus had finished his fortress and left both sufficient garrison and things necessary, appointing a Medean captain, such one as he thought would be most thankful to Cyaxares, he departed. And gathered all other army, both so many as he brought and had received of the Armenians, and also four thousand of the Chaldees, which were thought better than all the other. And being come into the inhabited places, there was none of the Armenians, neither man nor woman, but that came forth rejoicing at this peace, bringing and presenting the best jewel that any of them had. And the king was not grieved with this, thinking that Cyrus should be the most encouraged, bewig thus honored of all men. And finally came forth the queen with her daughters, and young son, offering with other gifts, that money which Cyrus before had refused. Which when he saw, he said: "You shall not make me for money's sake to do you plesures. Therefore, woman, depart hence with all thy money, and give it no more to the king to be hidden, but bestow it upon appareling of your son, and send him honorably into the host. That, that remaineth, keep for yourself, your husband, daughters and sons, that by the having thereof, you may adorn yourself the better, and live the more at quiet and pleasure. And let the earth serve to cover men's bodies being dead." Thus speaking, he rode forth. The king and all others waiting upon him, oft calling him a man of most bounty and benevolence. And thus they did, till they had brought him out of their country. After which time, the king sent him a greater army, because he had peace at him.

Thus Cyrus departed being glad, not only of the present money, which he had received, but because he had gotten such estimation, as he might have much more when he should need. And then he did camp within the borders. The day ensuing, he sent his army and money to Cyaxares, which was at hand, as he promised. And he with Tigranes and other the gentlemen of Persia, went to hunt the wild deer, and had good sport. And being come among the Medes, he gave the captains sufficient for everyone, that they might advance such of their men, as seemed most forward, thinking that if every several part did things worthy of praise, the whole should be the better appointed. And he seeing at any time any things that might encourage his host, that if he had, he would give to the most worthy, thinking that he himself was adorned with all such things, as were to the ornament and bewising of his army. After he had given them that the had received and assembled the captians and bandleaders, and whom he esteemed, he said thus:

"A certain gladness, friends, seemeth to be among us, both because we have abundance and also be able to honor them that we think worthy, and be honored of them which be advanced of us. We must always remember what feats have been the cause of these good things, and pondering with yourselves, you shall find, that to watch in time, to be painful, to make speed, and not to give place to our enemies, hath wrought this thing. After this sort, therefore, you must continue like valiant men, knowing that your obedience, your constance, your labors in convenient time, your taking pains, shall purchase you great pleasures and commodities."

Cyrus perceiving how fresh his soldiers were to endure the labors of war, how lusty their hearts to despise their enemies, how cunning to handle every man his armure, and seeing them to be well instruct, concerning the obedience to their rulers, he was desirous to do some feat against his enemies, knowing that by delays, many times good policies of princes lack their effect. Perceiving also, that in their contentions, every one was so desirous of praise that they began the one to envy the other. He was desirous that they should march foreward against their enemies, because common peril maketh common love among confederates. And in this case, they neither hate them that be more gallant in armor, nor them that be mre worthy honor, than themselves. But rather do both praise and love all such, reputing them as furtherers of a commonwealth. So afore all things, he did harness his army, and appoint them as orderly and comely as he could. And then he did call together the Pretours, the tribunes, the captains, the bandleaders, and these were free, not to be counted in the ordinary number of soldiers. Yet when it was requisite that the grand captian should know or command anything, no part was left without a governor. But if anything needed, it was appointed by captains of twelve, and captains of six. when these were come together in good season, Cyrus lead them and showed them, what was well done, and taught them how everything might be made most sure for the aid of the whole. And when he had brought to pass that they desired to do some feat, he said unto them: "Now go among your crews and teach them to do as I have taught you, encouraging them to noble feats, that every man may with prest heart vaunce forward, and the next morning to be present at the court." The next day they were in good season all about the court, and Cyrus coming with them to Cyaxares, began to speak thus,

"I know, Cyaxares, that those things which I shall speak, have heretofore been no less considered of you, than of me. But peradventure you be abashed to speak any thing of departure, lest you should be thought weary of keeping us so long. Therefore, because you speak nothing, I will speak for us both. We all think it good, that being well prepared, we should not deter the battle till your enemies invade your country, weer remaining as it were idle in our friend's land, but with all speed invade them; for now being in your country, we do against our wills cause much loss to the same. But if we were in our enemy's country, we should gladly do him the like displeasure. Furthermore, you do now vitail us to you great cost. If we were there, we should be vitailled to their pain. But if greater danger might ensue to us there than here, peradventure the most safety were to be chosen. But now they shall be equal to us, whether we tarry for them to fight here, or go against them thither. And likewise, we shall be equal to fight with them, whether we abide till they invade us, or provoke them to fight, invading them. But truly we shall have the more couragious and valiant hearts of our soldiers, if we invade them, and seem not unwilling to countenance them. And they shall be the more afraid of us when they hear that we do not linger at home beig with fear oppressed, but when we heard of their coming marched against them, that with all speed we may encounter with them, not tarrying till our own country might be endamaged, but prevent them and waste their land. Furthermore," quoth he, "if we make them somewhat more fearful and ourselves the more bold. I think it shall be to our great advantage. And by this mean, I propose that much the less peril shall be ours, and our adversary's much more. For my father ever sayeth, and you grant, and all other do accord, that fields be rather tried by the hearts of men, than by the strength of body." Thus he said.

And Cyaxares made this answer, "I would surely, Cyrus, that neither you nor any other of the Persians should suspect, that I am grieved with the finding of you, notwithstanding I think it most expedient for all thingss, that we should march forward against our enemies." Then said Cyrus, "Seeing we do agree, let us prepare ourselves. And if our sacrifice readily do assent to us, let us go on with all celerity." Then commanding the soldiers to be in a readines, Cyrus made his sacrifice, first to Jupiter king, then to other gods, praying that they being favorable and merciful, would be guides to the army, and assured succourers, confederates, and counsellors, of good affairs. He did also make petition to the avowers of Medea, inhabitors, and patrons of the same.

When he had luckily finished his sacrifice, and the army was assembled at the marches, having lucky tokens, they did invade their enemy's land. When he was soon past the borders, he pacified the lady of th earth, with liquid sacrifices, and the gods, with offered hosts, and appeased the patrons and avowers of Assyria. Which when he had done, he once again sacrificed to Jupiter father, if any of the other gods were showed, he did neglect the same. These things speedily proceeding, leading the footmen no great journey, they did encamp. The horsemen ranging abroad, did get a great prey of all things, and so continuing in camp and wasting the country, they abode their enemies.

When it was said, that they came on, and were ten days journey off, Cyrus said, "It is now time, Cyaxares, to march forward, that see seen neither to our own men afraid, to go against them but rather show ourselves to be glad that we shall fight." Which thing when it seemed meet to Cyaxares, they did set forward, always keeping array, going every day so far as they thought sufficient, and ever supped by daylight. They made no fires in the night within the camp, but afore the camp, that if any came by night, they might see them by the fire, and not be seen of them. and many times they made fires behind the campt, to deceive their enemies, whereby the espies many times fell into the scout watch, because the fire was behind, thinking themselves to be yet far of the camp. The Assyrians with their confederates, the armies being nigh together, did cast about a trench, which manner the Barbarian kings use that this day. That when they be encamped, they straight away environed the same with a bulwark, because of the huge multitude. For they knew that the host of horsemen in the night, is troublous and full of disquiet, and as I must say, most Barbarous. For they have their horses tied by the feet at mangers, to whom if any man would go, it were a pain in the night to loose them, it were pain to bridle them, pain to trap and barb them. And being on the horseback, it is not possible by any means, to ride them through the camp. For these causes, both they and the other, the Barbarians, do enclose themselves with such munitions, thinking that they thereby are in safeguard, and need not to fight, but when they list. Thus doing, they were nigh the one the other, and being distant the space of a Persian mile, the Assyrians were so campted, as we have said, in place entrenched, but plain and apert.

But Cyrus, in as secret wise as he could, did do make ramparts and mounts of earth before his camp, thinking that all shows of war being seen suddenly, should be more terrible to their adversaries. And that night, watches and wards as was expedient appointed of either parts, they went to rest. The day ensuing, the Assyrians, Croesus, and the other captains kept their army in quiet within the trench. Cyrus and Cyaxares, being in array, did tarry, looking when their enemies would come to fight. But when it was certain that they would not come forth of their camp, nor intended to fight that day, Cyaxares calling Cyrus and the other captains, said thus: "Friends, I think that as we be now appointed, so should we march to our enemy's camp, declaring that we be ready to fight. For if they will not come forth against us, our men shall be the more encouraged, and they beholding our boldness, shall be the more afraid." Thus he said. But Cyrus said: "Cyaxares, for God's sake let us not do so. For if we show ourselves as you would, and do go forward, our emenies shall view us now as we come forth, they bieng nothing afraid of us, knowing thast they be in safe place, where we can do them no hurt. Then if we doing no good, should return, and they eftsoons espye our number to be far inferior to theirs, they would condemn us, and the day following advance forthwith much more bold hearts. But now knowing that we be prest and not seeing us, you may be well assured, they will not set us light, but marvel what we mean, and not cease, I dare say, to talk their minds of us. But when the come forth, then it shall be expedient for us to show ourselves, as well to them marching straight against them taking such advantage as we heretofore have desired." So Cyrus on this wise speaking, Cyaxares and the others accorded. Then taking their supper and appointing watch and ward, and made fires before the watch, the went to rest. The next day early, Cyrus having a garland, did sacrifice, and commanded all the other noble gentlemen to have gardlands, and to be present at the sacrifice.

When the sacrifice was finished, assembling them together, he said thus:

The Oration of Cyrus

"God, dear friends, as the sacrifice expounds faith, and I also perceive, do foreshow battle, and have granted us the victory, promising health and safety in the sacrifice. Now to advertise you, what at this time you ought to be, surely I am abashed; because I know that you be fully expert as myself, and both have exercised and heard, and also hear continually of these things, as well as myself, insomuch as you may right well teach others the same. But if you be untaught, now harken. Such fellows as be come new amongst us, whom we assay to make like to ourselves, you must advertise, both for what cause we be here fournd of Cyaxares, what we have exercised, and for what purpose we have called them, that they may declare themselves to be our assured confederates. And of this also you must remember them, that this day shall declare, how worthy every man is. And marvel it is none, though in such things as men learn late, some have need of teaching. But it is sufficient, that they after adminition, can do like forward men.

And in doing of these things, you may have experience of yourselves. For he that can in such matter make other men better, he may certainly know, how perfect good he is himself. But he that hath only monition of these things, and goeth no further, he must think himself, but half perfect. For this cause I do not speak unto them, but command you to speak, that they may be in use, to please and content you; for you are nigh unto them, every man in his part. And this know you well, so long as you show yourselves to them, to be of victorious courage, so long shall you teach them and all others, not in word but in deed, to be likewise of valiant hearts."

Finally, he bade them to go to their dinner, and wearing garlands to make sacrifices, and go to their companies with their garlands. They being departed, called straight away the tailguides, saying thus, "Friends Persians, you also be made and elected to the estate of the nobility, being counted in all other things equal with the best, and for age to be more wise, for which cause you be placed equal with the best. For you being last, and marching them that be hardy, by encouraging may make them more valiant. And if any man be fainthearted, if you perceive it, you may in no wise conquer him, for it is meet for you avove any others, to get victory both for your age and sober behavior. Therefore when any of the former sort to call upon you and exhort you to follow, obey them. And that you may not be inferior to them in this thing, exhort you them agan to lead on with all speed afore, against our enemies. And how depart hence to your dinner, and being decked with garlands, go to your crews." Thus Cyrus and his army were appointed.

The Assyrians after dinner, came forth boldly and made a stout show. The king being brought in a chariot, did encourage them with this exhortation: "Friends Assyrians, now must your show yourselves men, now must you fight for your lives, for the country in which you were born, for your wives and children and for all that ever you have. If you overcome, you shall be lords of the same, as you have been before. If you be overcome, you know well, you must leave all to your enemies. Wherefore if you love victory, abide and fight; for it is a vain thing for them that would have victory, to flee away and turn to their enemies, the sightless, armless, and handless part of their body. And he is a fool which would live, and intend to flee away; knowing that they that overcome, shal be safe, and they that flee, shall rather die, than they that tarry. He is also a fool, which being desirous of wealth, seeketh his own destruction. For who do not know, that they that do overcome, save their own goods, and take theirs that be overcome. They that be overcome, shall lose both themsevles and also their goods." Thus the Assyrian king was doing.

Cyaxares sending to Cyrus, affirmed that it was meet time to set upon their enemies; saying, "though now but few be come out of the trench, yet by that time we join with them, they will be many. Therefore, let us not prolong the time, till they be more than we, but let us vance forth now, while we think we may easily overcome them."

To whom Cyrus answered, "Except more than the one half of them be overcome, be you assured, Cyraxares, they will say, that we fearing the mutltiude set upon a few of them; and not think themselves to be overcome. Wherefore a second field shall be required, when as peradventure they will use more policy, than they now do, offering themselves to try it with us, with what number so ever we will desire." The messengers hearing this, departed.

At which time, Chrysantàs, as a Persain and other of the gentlemen, brought certain runaways, of whom Cyrus having oportunity, asked what his enemies were doing. They answered that they now were come forth in harness, and the king being come abroad, did array them, encouraging always so many as came out, with a great and vehement Oration, as they say that heard it. Then said Chrysantas, "What if you, Cyrus, assembling your men, do eftsoons exhort them, that you may make them of the more courage?" Cyrus said, "Let not the Assyrian's oration trouble you, for there is no exhortation be it never so vehement that can make the hearers in one day, of cowards, valiant men, neither archers, darters or horsemen, except they have before been trained in the same feats, nor bodies able to travail, except they ahve been before accustomed to pains." "It were sufficient," said Chrysantas, "to make their hearers by exhortation the more courageous."

"Can one day's Oration," said Cyrus, "so ravish the hearers' hearts with shame, that they refraining from unfit things, will turn to that, that is expedient, and for reknown's sade endure all pain and peril, thinking this constantly in their minds, that it is better to die valiantly, than to live cowardly? If such opinions should be ingrained in men's minds and be stable, must not such laws first be given, which may pronounce to valiant men, a glorious and free life to be prepared; to cowards a base, miserable amd wretched life, everlastingly enduring?

Teachers also and governors must be appointed over them, which may rightly instruct, teach and accustome them to these things, till they amy take root in them, to think that valiant and redoubted men, be without doubt most happy, and to repute cowards and villains, of all other most misers. Thus must they be instructed, which will declare their descipline to be better than if that cometh of feat of their enemies. But if a man should go to fight with such soldiers, whereof many had forgotten their old lessons, then a man with a good exhortation, might presently make them couragious, in as much as of all others it is the most easiest thing, both to learn and to teach, that mangood is amongst men, the most precious thing. And I surely would not believe these our men, whom we have exercised with us, to be stable and constant, except I had seen you at this present, have given them example, what they ought to do and have taught them, that they were ignorant in.

But such as be untaught altogether in manhood, I would marvel, Chrysantas, if an oration being goodly pronounced, could more profit them to valiance, than a musical song, being sweetly sung, can profit them that have nothing learned to be cunning in music." This communication they had.

Cyaxares sending again to Cyrus, said that he did evil to tarry too long, and not with all speed, to march against his enemies. Cyrus made answer to the messengers, saying, "You must well understand, that they be not all come forth that must come. Thus show unto him, that all men may hear it. Nevertheless, because it is his mind, I will now set forward." Thus saying, and making prayers to God, he lead forth his army.

And so soon as he bagan to lead, he went afore apace, and they followed in good array, because they had learned and practiced afore to go in order, being courageous how the one might exceed the other, both because their bodies were accustomed to labor, and also captains were their guides, and cheerful, because of their cunning they had learned, and long afore exercized, how most safely and easily, they might encounter with their enemies, specially with archers, darters, and horsemen. And being yet without the danger of the arrows, Cyrus gave this privy word, Jupiter confederate and captain.

When it was gone through the army, he began to sing to Castor and Pollux a song of triumph, according to the custom, which all the soldiers, with devout mind, and loud voice did recount, for by such thing being made superstitious, they have the less fear of men. The song being ended, the nobles went together with lusty countenance, being well taught, beholding one another, calling by name their friends and governors, saying, and that oft, "Go to it, loving friends, go to it, valiant men," encouraging one another to follow. Which they that were behind, hearing semblably exhorted the former, to march on boldly.

Thus Cyrus' army was full of forwardness, desirous of reknown, full of strength and boldness, full of courage, soberness and obedience, which is, I think, most terrible to a man his enemies. The Assyrians being come out of their trench, when the Persain host approached nigh, lept into their Chariots, and went among their other people. The Archers, darters, and slingers, threw their weapons, much sooner than they could hit. When the Persians coming on, were within the arrow shot, Cyrus with loud voice, said, "Bold friends, let one speedily go forward showing himself, and encourage other." They told this forth to others. And some for prompt courage, for lusty heart, and haste to fight, began to run, whom the whole main battle followed, running. And Cyrus himself forgetting to go softly, led the army running and also cried thus, "Who doth follow? Who is so hardy? Who shall first kill a man?" The others hearing the same, cried likewise. And this noise, as he would have it, went through the whole army, "Who shall follow?" "Who is hardy?" The Persians after this sort, manly gave the onset. Their enemies were not able to abide the field, but recoiled and fled into their trench. The Persians pursuing them to the entrance of the same, flew many of them being thrust in heaps together, and leaping after them which fell into the ditches, killed many, both horse and man. For some of the Chariots enforced to flee, fell into the ditches. The horsemen of the Medes seeing this, set upon their enemy's horsemen, which also recoiled.

And there began a great chase, both of horse and men, and slaughter of both sorts. The Assyrians being within their trench, standing at the top of the ditch, neither had the wit nor the power to shoot or dart at them that slew so fast, partly for theterrible fight, partly for the great fear. And in short space, perceiving that some of the Persians did murder many of them at the entry of the trench, they turned their back, andfled from the front of the ditch. The wives of the Assyrians and their confederates, seeing them fight within the camp shrieked out and strayed abroad, like folk amazed, some bearing their children, some, and they young, running and tearing their garments, beseeching all that they met with, not to flee and forsake them, but to defend their children, their wives, and themselves. Then the kings in persons with their most trusty men standing at the entry, and climbing up at the height of the ditch, did both fight themselves, and exhort others the the same.

Which thing when Cyrus perceived, fearing lest if they should make irruption, a few might soon be hurt of so many, he commanded they should retreat out of the arrow shot and be obedient. Then might a man have seen the goodly education of the noble men, for they straight obeyed themselves, and straight charged others to obey likewise. When they were without the shot, they stood in their places as it had been in a dance knowing perfectly where every man should be.

The End of the Third Book

The Discipline of Cyrus
The Fourth Book

Cyrus tarrying a good while with his army, declared them to be ready to fight, if any would come forth, but when none came, he retreated his host, so far as he thought good. And when he had encamped, apppointed watch and ward, and sent forth the scout watch. Standing in the middest, he assembled his own soldiers and thus spake:

The Oration of Cyrus

"Friends, Persians, I first do give God so great thanks as I can, supposing that you all do the same, for we have gotten victory and health, wherefore we be bound to render God gifts of thanks, with all that ever we have. I truly praise you all at this time, for this present feat is achieved to all your honor, but what every man is worth, when I am certified of such as be meet, I shall be ready to reward the same accordingly, both in word and deed. But as for this captain Chrysantas being nigh me, I shall not need to learn of other; for I myself know what he is. For as he hath done all things as well as you have, even so when as I, calling him by name, commanding him to retreat, he driving his sword to strike his enemy, heard me forthwith, and leaving that he was about to do, did as he was commanded, for he both himself drew back, and very readily had others do the same. Insomuch as he brought his crew without danger of shot, before our enemies could perceive we gave back, or bend their bows, or throw their darts. And so he is both safe himself, and through his obedience, hath saved his men also. I see others wounded, of whom, when I know what time they were hurt, I shall then declare my sentence of them. But Chrysantas being valiant in manly prowess, wise, and meet both to rule and be ruled, I at this present, make a Tribune or captain of a thousand. And when God shall give me any other good thing, I will not then forget him.

And I will advertise you all, that what as you have seen in this fight, you never cease to remember the same, that you may judge always of yourselves, whether valiantness or cowardice rather saveth the life. And whether they that fight willingly, be sooner eased, than the unwilling.

Finally, what manner pleasure victory bringeth. These things, you may now best judge, having both experience of them, and the thing being so late done. And certainly, by remembering of these things you shall be the better. Now therefore, as men loved of God, and valiant and wise men, take your repast, making sacrifice to God, and singing a song of triumph, ever providing for that which is commanded."

These being spoken, he took his horse and rode, till he came to Cyaxares, and rejoicing with him for their common victory, as it was meet, beholding how it stood with him, and enquired if he needed anything, returned again to his own army. Who at that time having supped, and appointing convenient watch, went to rest.

The Assyrians, because their king was slain, and with him almost all their noble men, were in much dolor, and many that night fled out of the camp. Which thing Croesus and the other confederates perceiving, were much grieved, and as all things were dolorous, so this most troubled them all, that the chief nation of their army was of no policy nor manner, wherefore they left the camp, and departed in the night.

The day being come, and the camp of his enemies appearing to be barren of men, straight he went in with the chief of the Persians. And his enemies had left many sheep, many oxen, and many wagons full of treasure. And them came thither Cyaxares with all the Medes, and there did dine. Dinner being ended, Cyrus assembling his captains, said thus: "What and how great goodness of God is offered unto us, do we seem not to regard? For now you yourselves do see, that our enemies for fear of us be fled away, which being within a trench, leaving the same, and fled away, how can a man think they would have biden by it, if they had seen us in the plain? And if they having no experience what we be, durst not abide us, how shall they now be able to abide us, being overcome, and suffering many displeasures at our hands? And if their most valiant men be slain, how shall their cowardly dare fight with us?" Then one said, "Why do we not then with all speed pursue them, seeing so good success is evident?" "Because," said he, "we want horses. For the best of our enemies, whom it were most convenient, either to take or kill, shall be on horseback, whom we be able, with God his help, to put to flight; but to take them by chasing, we be not able."

Then they said, "Why do you not go and show these things to Cyaxares?" He answered, "Follow you all now me, that he may know we be all of one mind." Then they all followed him, and declared what they thought expedient for the things they requested.

And Cyaxares, partly envying that they should first speak of such things, partly peradventure supposing himself to be well enough, would not adventure the second time, for truly both himself was jocund, and saw many others of the Medes to be so likewise. Therefore he said unto Cyrus, "I have perceived, Cyrus, both by report and proof, that you the Persians, of all men covet never to be satisfied in any one pleasure. I truly think it is much more to be desired, to enjoy that pleasure that is greatest. And what think can show greater pleasure of felicity to men, than is now chanced to us? Therefore if now being in happy case, we soberly can retain the same, we may peradventure without danger, continue in this felicity to our old age. But if we be in this unsatiable, and study still to pursue ever new pleasures, take heed lest we suffer, as they say many have done in the sea, which, having good chance, will not leave sailing, till they be drowned. And many achieving victory, being desirous of more, have lost the first.

And truly if our enemies that be fled, were in number fewer than we, we might peradventure safely pursue them; but now remember with what portion of them we all fighting, have gotten victory. Many there be which stroke no stroke, whom if we do not compel to fight, they not knowing neither our nor their own strength, through ignorance and faintness, will be glad to escape. But if they know that they shall be in as much peril by departing, as by tarrying still, we must beware, lest we do compel them against their wills, to play the valiant men. And this know for surety, that you are not so desirous to take their wives and children, as they to conserve the same. Consider also, that wild swine, though they be many, when they espy the hunter, will flee with her pigs, but if a man hunteth any of their young, though perchance there be but one, she will not flee, but rage at him that is busied to catch the prey. Now therefore if they, enclosing themselves in a trench, suffered us to fight with as many of them as we would, and now would couple with them in the plain, and they severally shall fight with us, and shall assail us at the front as they now did, some on the one wing, some on the other, and some at the tail. Consider, lest every of us, shall have need both of many eyes and of many hands, too. Finally, I would not gladly now seeing the Medes in such joy, go further with them, compelling them to more danger."

Cyrus made this answer, and said, "You shall not need to compel any man, give them only leave to follow me that will, and peradventure we shall do such feats, as both you and your friends shall rejoice at. And we will not chase the multitude of our enemies, for how could we take them? But if we may catch any of the remant or tail of the army, we shall bring the same to you. Consider also, that we at your need, have come a long way, to do you pleasure, you therefore being just, must requite the same, that at our return, we may have some profit, not all taking for it of your treasure."

Then said Cyaxares, "Truly if any man will willingly follow you, I would also acknowledge thanks unto you." "Send one of your trusty men with me," said Cyrus, "which may declare your commandment." "Take of these whom you will," said he. "And show thou, that who they will, may go with Cyrus." Cyrus taking this man, departed. To whom he said thus, "Now shall I prove, whether your words were true, when you said you had a pleasure to behold me." "Then I will not forsake you," said the Medean, "if you say so." "And will you encourage others," said Cyrus, "to follow me?" Then he swore and said, "By God I will do so well, that you shall look merrily upon me." Then he declared effectually all the cause why he was sent of Cyaxares, and added this, that he would not forsake so noble, so bounteous a man being descended (which was a thing passing others) of God's lineage.

Cyrus being about this thing, as it were by divine chance, messengers came to him from the Hircanians. The Hircanians be borderers to the Assyrians, no great country, and therefore subject to the Assyrians. They were counted at that time good horsemen, and so be yet. Therefore the Assyrians used them, as the Macedonians used the Scirites, sparing them neither in pains nor in perils, and at thus time were charged with the defense of rearward, being a thousand horsemen, that if any danger should be in that part, these should feel it afore them. The Hircanians, because they should come last of all, had their wagons and their families last also, for the most part of the Assyrians, go to war with their households. Thus at this time, the Hircanians were used in the warfare. Then considering how they were treated of the Assyrians, how their king was slain, and themselves overcome, how great fear was in the army, and how their confederates fainted and shrunk from them.

These things being passed, they thought it good time to make defection, if Cyrus' host should still invade. And sent their messengers to Cyrus, for his name, by reason of this battle, was most reknowned. They that were sent, said unto him, that they had just cause to hate the Assyrians. Therefore, if he would go now against them, they would become his confederates, and be the forward. And beside these, they declared in what case his enemies were, that they might the rather stir him the take the voyage in hand. Cyrus asked them, "Think you, that we may overtake them, before they be entrenched? For we think it a great loss, that they have escaped so privily." Cyrus spake this, because he would have them to take good conceit of themselves. They answered that if in the morning early, they would go with speed, they might overtake them. That they by reason of their multitude and wagons, do go very slowly. And also they said, that because they had watched the night before, making how a small journey, they were encamped. And Cyrus said, "Have you anything to prove, whereby we may believe, that you do tell us truth?" "We will," said they, "ride this night, and bring you pledges, only do you make us promise before God, and give us your right hand, that we may declare the same to others, as we receive of you." Then he promised them faithfully, to use them as his friends and assured, if so be, they performed their promise, and that neither Persians nor Medes, should be in more credit with him. And at this day, a man may see the Hircanians as trusty rulers and governors, as the best of the Persians and Medes.

Supper being ended, Cyrus set forth his army somewhat before night, commanding the Hircanians to tarry and go forth with him. All the Persians, as meet was, speedily came forth, and Tigranes also with his own army of the Medeans came forth; some, which being children when Cyrus was a child, were become now his friends; some being his companions in hunting, and delighting in his goodly behavior; some to give him thanks, because he had delivered them from great fear; some for hope, because he appeared a valiant and fortunate man, which hereafter would be a man of mighty power. Some, because when he was brought up in Medea, and had done them some pleasures, would do him how some service; many because through his gentleness, they received pleasures of his grandfather; many because they saw the Hircanians, and a rumor was spread, that they should be brought to great wealth, were moved that they might have part thereof. So the Medeans almost all, came forth, except such as did accompany Cyaxares, and they that belonged to them. All others gladly and readily did set forth, not as it were of necessity, but of free heart and gentle courage.

When they were come forth, first he went to the Medeans, and both praised them and prayed with great desire, that God might be a favorable guide, both to him and them, and that he at length, might be able to give them worthy thanks, for their good heart toward him. In conclusion he said, "Let the footmen have the foreward", and commanded the horsemen to follow. And if in any place, they should rest or stop their pace, he commanded that some of them should make speedy repair to him, that they might ever know what were best to do. And then he commanded the Hircanians to conduct the host, which asked of him, "What, do you not look that we should fetch our pledges as you have commanded, that you having our true plight, might go foreward?" Who, as they say, made this answer, "I know that all we have faith and trust in our own hearts and hands, for we be so appointed, that if you be true, we shall be able to do you good. If you be false, we do not think it will come to pass, that we shall be subject to you, but you, God willing, rather thrall to us. Therefore Hircanians, because you say that your company is last, when you see them, give us knowledge that we may spare them." The Hyrcanians hearing this, led the way as he commanded. Marvelling at his so princely courage, neither fearing the Assyrians, the Lidians, nor none other their confederates, and that he did not one iota esteem, neither their absence, nor their presence.

Thus going forth, night approached, when, as it is said, a light from heaven did glitter on Cyrus, and all his army. Whereby every man conceived fear of God, and boldness against his enemies. They going forth speedily without let, made that night a great journey, and came very nigh the Hircanians' army, by break of day, which the messengers perceiving declared to Cyrus that they were their countrymen. Which they knew both because they were last, and also by the multitude of their fires. Wherefore Cyrus sent one of the messengers to them, commanding him to say, that if they were his friends, they should with all speed come and meet with him and take hands; he sent also some of his own men, commanding them to say to the Hircanians, that as they saw his men give the onset, so they also should do. Thus one of the messengers tarried still with Cyrus, and the other rode to the Hyrcanians.

And whilst Cyrus tried what the Hyrcanians would do, he stayed his army in array. Then the chief of the Medeans, with Tigranes came to him to know what they should do. Which said unto them, "This next host is of the Hircanians, to whom, one of their own messengers with certain of mine, is gone to say unto them, that if they shall come and hold forth their right hands. Wherefore if they so do, take them by the hands every man, as shall chance, and also embold them, but if they take their weapons, or go about to flee, do your endeavor to dispatch them first, that none of them escape." These were Cyrus' admonitions. The Hircanians hearing the messengers, were glad, and taking their horseback, came with all celerity, holding forth their hands, as it is said. The Medeans and Persians did likewise take them by the hands, bidding them be of good heart. Then Cyrus said, "We truly, O Hircanians, do now give credit to you, you must do likewise to us. But tell me first this thing, how far hence is the forward, and the other piussance of our enemies?"

Then said Cyrus, "Now then, go to it, friends Persians and Medes, and you also Hircanians, for I speak now unto you as to our friends. And you must certainly know, that we be in such case, that if we trifle, we shall sustain utter displeasure, for our enemies know the cause of our coming. But if we go to it with a constant courage and assault our enemies with martial and vigorous hearts, you shall see them very shortly that they shall be found as slaves fugitive. Some of them playing at us, some flying away, so for being discomfitted they shall stare on us, and neither suspecting that we be come, neither in array nor appointed to fight, we shall take them prisoners. If they we will herafter eat our meat and take our rest, and lead our life pleasantly, let us give them no respite, neither to consult, nor to prepare any good for themselves, neither to know at all, that we be men, that they may think, nothing else to come amongst them, but buckler, sword, battleaxe, and blowes. And you Hircanians, advancing toward them go afore us, that by the sight of you armor, we may the longer be in covert. When that I am come to our enemies' army, leave with me every of you a troop of horsemen, which I may use, remaining in their camp, if ought needeth. And you princes and seniors make the assault in array many together, if you will do wisely, that you fall not into the throngs, and be born down by violence. Suffer your younger force to chase and kill. For this is now most sure, that few of our enemies do escape, and least fortune, as it chanceth to many conquerors, should change her copy, beware in any wise, that you fall not to pillage. For he that so doeth, is no valiant soldier, but a vile burden bearer. And it shall be lawful for him to use such a one as his slave.

"And this also you must know, that nothing is so available as victory, for he that conquereth, do spoil all things, men, women, money, and all the whole land. Then look only to this, that we may retain our victory, for in it he that spoileth, is comprised. And in following this chase, remember that you return to me, by daylight. For the night being come, we will receive no man."

Thus Cyrus when he had spoken, he sent every man into his crews, commanding them that they should go likewise, and signify the same to their decurions, which were in the front of the battle; who hearing this precept, gave like commandment unto every one of his men. And so the Hircanians led them forward. Cyrus with the Persians went in the middleward, placing the horsemen, as it was meet, on either side.

Their enemies, when they could discern the thing, some marvelled at the sight. Some perceived the matter, some told it forth, some cried out. some loosed their horses, some prepared themselves, some threw their armor of the wagons, some did on their harness, some leaped on horseback, some bridled the same, some set their wives in the wagons, some gathered together their riches, to save the same, some hoarding their money were taken, prepared to fly away; and we must think, that they did many other diverse things, saying that no man fought, but perished without resistance. Croesus the Lidish king, because it was summer, had sent his women in chariots before, by night, that they might by reason of cold air, have the easier journey, and he taking his horsemen with him, followed them. Likewise did the Phrygian which is king of Phrygia, that is next Hellespont.

When that they had learned and heard of them that fled, and others that overtook them, how the matter stood, they themselves fled, as much as they might make. But the king of the Cappadocians and Arabians being nighest, and making resistance unarmed, were slain of the Hircanians. But the most part that were killed, were Assyrians, and Arabians. For being in their own land, they were earnest in their way. The Medeans and Hircanians bearing down as they would, continued in this chase. Cyrus commanded the horsemen being left with him, to ride about the tents, and slay as many as came forth with harness. To others that remained, he did proclaim, that so many of his enemies' soldiers as were horsemen, target men, or archers, should bring forth their armor trussed up. and leave their horses at their tents. He that did contrary, should forthwith be beheaded. They with swords, ready drawn, stood in order about the tents. The others which had armor came and brought it forth, casting it in one place as he commanded. Which he caused to be burned, by them, whom he appointed.

Then Cyrus remembering that he was come without any manner of victual, and that without it, he could neither continue his army, nor do any other feat, providing to the same, both speedily and prudently, he thought it needful for all the soldiers, that some man should have the charge of the provision, that sustenance might be ready, at the soldiers' coming. Wherefore perceiving that it was very expedient to prevent all them that had the provision of victual in the camp, he commanded, that all the commissaries should assemble. And where there was no commissary, the most ancient in the tent. To him that disobeyed, all extremity was pronounced. They seeing their lords obey, did forthwith obey themselves.

When they were come together, they first commanded them to sit down, which had in their tent more than two months' victual. And of these almost all sat down. These things thus learned, he spake unto them after this sort. "Go now, friends, if you be sick of displeasures, and look for any good at our hand, see that you do you diligent endeavor, that you provide in every tent, double so much victual for captains and soldiers, as you have done tofore for every day. And see that all other things that may be meet for the good dressing of the victual, be ready prepared. Because they that shall have the victory, shall soon be here again, and be glad of such plentiful purveyance. And know you, that it shall be for you profit, if you do entertain men honestly." They hearing this, did with all diligence, as they were commanded. He assembling his captains, said thus unto them:

The Oration of Cyrus

"I know, dear friends, that we at this present, might prevent our fellows being absent, in taking our dinner and refreshing ourselves, both with meat and drink; but me think that such a dinner cannot profit us, as to be noted careful for our fellows, nor the good cheer can make us so strong, as if we can make our confederates couragious. Therefore if now whilst they be chasing, staying our enemies, and fighting with then that resisteth, we should appear to set them so light, that before we know what they have done, we should be noted to have filled ourselves, though we be not reputed unhonest, yet we shall in our most need lack confederates. But he that will provide, that they being in pains and perils, at their return may have necessary food, these dainties, I think, should be more pleasant to us, than if we did by and by fill our bellies. Consider furthermore, that though there were no cause of shame toward us for them, yet we ought at no time, to overcharge ourselves with meat or drink, for we have not yet accomplished our enterprise, but all things have even now need of most care and diligence. We have in this camp many more enemies than we be ourselves, and then at liberty which ought still to be safely kept, and so to be kept, that there might be some to provide us necessaries. Furthermore, our horsemen be gone, making us to muse where they be, wheter they will return or tarry. Therefore friends, I think, such meat and drink ought to content us, as a man thinketh most expedient, not to be full of sleep and forgetfulness.

"I know, furthermore, that there is much money in the camp, which being common, as well to them that were at the taking of it, as to ourselves, I know we might use at our pleasure, and convert to our private substance. But I think it should not so much avail us, to take it to ourselves, as if we appearing to be just men, might by this means purchase them our more assured friends, than they now be; therefore I think it good to commit this money to be distributed of the Medeans, Hircanians, and Tigranes at their return. And to think it our advantage, though they distribute less to us. For by gains they will have the more pleasure to tarry with us. And at this time to be aforehand with them, it would minister riches to us, but a short space; but to be desirous to possess those things, whereof riches ariseth, this, I think, might purchase us and all ours, more durable wealth and riches. I suppose that we being at home do much travail to this end, that our diet might be the finer, and our gains the greater, that when need required, we might use both to our weal. Therefore surely I cannot see, wherein we might learn a lesson to our greater commodity, than of these present things." Thus he said.

Hystaspas, a Persian, and one of the nobility, confirming Cyrus his oration, said thus,

"It were an unseemly thing, Cyrus, if we many times in hunting will continue without meat, to kill a wild beast, not being greatly available to us, now in the hunt of all riches, as it were, we should suffer such a thing to be an impediment to us, as prevaileth in evil men, and is obeisant to good men, for we should appear to be slack in doing our duty."

Hystaspas thus according with Cyrus, all the others did approve the same.

Cyrus then said, "Go to then, seeing we accord, let every man send of his band, five of his most forward men, which shall go about, And whom they see preparing necessary things, them they shall praise, whom they see negligent, them they shall more straightly correct, than if they were their own masters." And they did accordingly.

Then some of the Medeans, overtaking certain wagons going away, did return and drive them, being replenished with things meet for the army. Some of them took and brought away chariots of the most noble women, part being lawful wives, part concubines which were carried about for their goodly beauty, which they took and brought away. For the manner of the warfare in Asia, is even at this day to have with them their most precious things, saying that they have the more courage to fight, their most lief things being present. For them, they say, of necessity they are enforced manfully to defend. And peradventure it is for this cause, peradventure for pleasure and volupty.

Cyrus beholding the feats of the Medeans and Hircanians, did at it were, rebuke himself, and his train that other men at that time should seem more valiant than they, in doing feats, he and his remaining in an idle place. They that brought this gear, showed what they had brought to Cyrus, riding forth again to pursue the remnant. For so they said they were commanded of their captains. Cyrus grieved with these things, when he had bestowed the prey, assembling eftsoons the captains, and so standing, as they might hear what he spake, said thus,

The Oration of Cyrus

"If we, friends, may achieve those things which we see to be evident, great profit shall redown to all the Persians, and the greatest by reason be ours, that travail for it, we all I am sure, know. But when we be lords of them, how shall we be able to retain them, except we have Persian horsemen of our own, I truly cannot see. Consider therefore we Persians have armor, whereby we may put back our enemies at handstrokes. But they being put to flight, what horsemen, what archers, what target men, what darters, can we lacking horse, either take or kill when they flee? And what fear need either archers, darters, or horsemen, have to do us displeasure, than by trees fixed in the earth by nature. And if this be so, is it not evident, that these present horsemen do think these prizes which be taken to be no less theirs than ours? Yes, and peradventure more too.

"Therefore the case standeth in this necessity, if we can prepare horsemen not inferior to theirs, may we not all plainly espy, that we shall be able to do all things against our enemies without them, which we do now with them? Yes, thereby we may have them of gentler stomachs toward us, that whether they tarry or depart, we shall little pass, being strong enough of ourselves without them. I think no man will reply to these, but that it were far better that the Persians should have horsemen of their own. But this peradventure you so must ask, how we should prepare the same. Let us then consider, if we would be furnished with horsemen, what we have, and what we lack. As for horses we have in the camp many already taken, we have bridles to ride them, and other things meet for men of arms. Furthermore, we have all things that an horseman should need, as breast plates defensive for our bodies, darts both to cast and to keep. What lack we then, be like men, but of them we have plenty, for nothing is so much our own, as we ourselves be ours.

"Yet peradventure some man will say, we be not cunning, neither any of us was cunning in that we now can do, before we learned the same. Then some will say, that they learned it when they were children. And I pray you, whether be children more prudent to learn those things that be taught and showed, than men? Whether when the things is learned, be children more able in body to practice the same or men? Furthermore we have such opportunity to learn, as neither children nor other men have. For we shall not need to learn to shoot, as children, for we do know the feat; nor to dart, for we can do it already. And it is not with us, as it is with other men, for unto some tillage is a let, unto some, occupations, to other domestical matters. But us, not only time or opportunity, but also necessity enforceth to study the feats or policies of war.

"Furthermore, it is not in these things as in many other warlike affairs, which as they be difficult and hard, so be they profitable. For is it not more pleasant to ride our journeys, than to go them on foot? And for speed, is it not more pleasant to be, if need requireth, straight with a man his friend? And when need is, straight to chase, either a man or a wild beast, and overthrow the same? And is not this also a great ease, that when a man must bear harness, the horse must help to bear the same? For truly is it all one to wear and to bear? But if any man do fear, lest we enterprising the feat of riding, and not attaining to it, should prove neither good footmen nor good horsemen, he feareth in vain. For we may, when we list, soon fight afoot, neither shall we, in learning to ride, forget our cunning on foot." Cyrus thus said.

Chrysantas agreeing with him, spake on this wise:

The Oration of Chrysantas

"I truly am so desirous to learn the feat of riding, that being once a horseman, I would think myself a winged man. Now I am content, when I contend to run with any man on even ground, only to pass him by the head. And when I see a wild beast outrunning me, if I came to aim mine arrow or dart, that I may prevent and hit it before it be very far off. But being a horseman, I may kill a man as far off as I may see him, I may in chasing deer, overtake and kill, some at hand, some with dart strike, as though they stood still. For if two things be swift and draw nigh together, they be as though they did stand.

"Wherefore of all creatures, I do most desire to counterfeit the Hippocentaurs, if any such were, which in forecasting used man's prudence, and in working that required man's hands, but to overthrow it that fled, and drive back it that tarried, they had the swiftness and strength of an horse.

"Therefore if I were an horseman, I would translate all these things to myself. For I shall be able to foresee all things, having reason as a man, and with my hands I would use mine armor, and with the strength of my horse, I would overthrow that as did resist me. But I would not be so compact of an horse and man, as Hippocentaurs be, for this is better than to be so concorporate. The Hippocentaurs, as I think, lack many commodities, which men have found how to use, and many pleasures, which horses by nature know how to enjoy. But if I learn to ride, being on horseback, I shall do the feats of an Hippocentaur, alighting from my horse, I shall eat, I shall be clad, and take my rest as men do. Therefore what other thing shall I be, than a divided and united Hippocentaur. In this also, shall I pass a Centaur. He seeth with two eyes and heareth with two ears, but I shall foresee with four eyes and forehear with four ears; for an horse, they say, forseeing with his eyes, do warn a man of many things, and advertise him no less forehearing with his ears. Therefore write my name as one most willing to be an horseman."

"And us also, for God his sake," said all the others. Then Cyrus said, "Seeing we be fully accorded, what if we make a law for ourselves, that it shall be villany for any man to be seen on foot, to whom I shall give horses, whether our journey be little or great, that men in all things may take us to be creatures made of horse and man." Thus Cyrus did ask them. They all accorded to the same. Wherefore from that time, till this day, the Persians have followed this decree, insomuch that none of the noble and honorable men of Persia in no wise willingly will be seen abroad on foot.

Thus they debated their matters, and the day being more than half past, the horsemen of the Medeans and Hircanians came riding to them, bringing many prisoners both horses and men. For so many as would deliver their harness, they did not kill. Being come, Cyrus asked them first, if they were all safe, which thing affirmed, he asked what they had done? They declared everything, setting it forth to the utmost.

He heard them gently, whatsoever they would speak, and praised them thus:

"Truly friends, you have declared yourselves to be right valiant men, and surely you seem now far more lusty, couragious, and warlike, than you did tofore." Then he asked them, how much ground they had gone over, and whether it were inhabited or no? They said, that they had passed through a great ground, and that every place was inhabited, and replenished with sheep, goats, neat, horses, victual, and all good things. "Then must we," said he, "look for two things, the one to be their lords that have these things, the other, that they may remain still, for a place inhabited is a rich possession. And a place desert of men, is also desert of other good things. I know well that you have slain all such as did resist, and rightly, for that doeth chiefly establish victory, but such as yielded themselves, you have brought prisoners, whom if we deliver, we shall, as I think, do right well. For first it is not meet, that we at this time should beware of them, or keep them, or find them victual. And with hunger truly we will not kill them. Then setting them at liberty, we shall have the more subjects, for if we can achieve the lordship of their country, all the inhabitants of the same shall become our captives, and the others shall the rather tarry, if they see these delivered and left alive, and shall rather choose to be obedient, than to make resistance. Thus I think if any man judgeth otherwise, let him say his conceit." They hearing, did agree these to be done.

Cyrus then calling the prisoners, thus said:

The Oration of Cyrus

"Friends, because you have been obeisant, you have saved your lives. Do so herafter, and you shall sustain no damage, saving that he shall not be your king that was tofore. Yet you shall have the same houses, you shall till the same land, you shall accompany with the same wives, and rule the same children that you do now. Neither shall you fight against us, nor none other, but if any man offer you wrong, we will defend you. And that no man should command you to go to war, bring in your harness to us, and to them that do bring forth the same, peace is given, and other things which we have spoken, without deceit. But as many as will not deliver their warlike weapons, against them we must out of hand make war. If any of you will come to us as a friend, to do or show us anything, him will we entertain as a fellow and friend, not as a slave. These things persuade yourselves, and declare them to others. If any will make resistance to you, being willing to do thus, bring us to them, that we may rule them and not they us." Thus Cyrus said. They kneeled on their knees and said they would so do.

Being departed, Cyrus said:

"Now it is time, O Medeans and Armenians, that we all sup, we have prepared you the best we could get. Therefore go you and send us half you bread, that is journeyed, for it will suffice us both, but meat and drink send us none, for of them we have sufficient. And you, Hircanians, bring these men to their tents, the chief, to the best. For have regard of it, and all others, as you shall think most seemely. And yourselves sup, where you shall most delight, for your tents be yet untouched, you being as well provided for as they. And this know you both, that such things as be abroad, we will keep and watch this night, to them within your tents look yourself, and bestow your harness well. For they that be in the tents be not yet our friends."

The Medeans and Tigranes' men washed, for all things was ready, and changing their garments, went to supper, their horses likewise lacked not forage, and they sent to the Persians' half their bread, but sent neither meat nor wine, thinking that Cyrus and his company had had enough, because, he said, he had plenty of them. But he meant, for meat, hunger, for drink, running water. Cyrus causing the Persians to sup, and the night drawing nigh, did send many bands of five and ten, commanding them to lie in coverture round about the tents, thinking watch to be needful, both lest any man should assail them without, and lest also if they within would flee and convey forth their money, that the same might be taken, and so it chanced in deed. For many fled, and many were taken. Cyrus suffered them to have the money that took them, commanding the men to be killed, insomuch that afterward you could not, though you would, have taken one going away by night. Thus the Persians did, whilst the Medeans were drinking, banqueting, and using their minstrels.

Cyaxares, king of the Medes, that night that Cyrus went abrode, was drunk as well as his fellows, for their good fortune, thinking the other Medes to have been in their tents, except he, because he heard so great a noise, for the Medes' servants, their masters being absent, did riotously drink and make revel, specially because they had taken of the Assyrians's camp, wine and many other like things. Day being come, no man repairing to his pavilion, but such as supped with him, and hearing say, that the camp was void of the Medes, and other horsemen, he came forth and saw it was even so in deed. Then he was sore displeased, both with Cyrus and the Medes, that by and by for (as they say) he was a cruel and inexorable man, commanded one of his men being at hand, to take the horsemen that were about him, with all haste, go to Cyrus' host, and say thus: "I thought that neither you (Cyrus) would so rashly have dealt with me, nor that you Medeans, though Cyrus were so minded, would have left me thus desolate. Now therefore whether Cyrus will or not, come you with all speed to me." Thus he commanded.

The messenger that was appointed to go, said, "How shall I, sir, find them? How shall I know where Cyrus and his men be become? For I hear say that diverse of the Hircanians being fled from our enemies and come hither, be now gone, being their guides in this voyage." Then Cyaxares hearing this, was much more moved with Cyrus, because he would not show him of it. And therefore with much more haste, sent for the Medeans, as though he would leave Cyrus alone, and with greater threatenings than before, accused the Medeans' fact and threatened the messenger, if he did not make bold declaration thereof. This messenger went forth having a hundred horsemen, being angry with himself, because he went not forth with Cyrus.

And going their journey, by reason of diverse ways and paths, they wandered they wist not whither and could not come to Cyrus' host, till they chanced upon some of the Assyrians, whom they compelled to be their guides. And so went till they espied the fires about midnight. Being come nigh the camp, the watch, (as they were commanded) would not give them passage before day. Day appearing, Cyrus calling his clergy, commanded them to choose out the most precious things to make sacrifice to God. They being about the same, he assembled the nobility and said:

The Oration of Cyrus

"Friends, God foreshoweth much good, but we, O Persians, at this present be very few to achieve the same. For when we have achieved it, if we be not able to retain it, it must return to other again. And if we leave part of us, for the custody of that we have now won, we shall be taken shortly to be of little power or none. Therefore I think it good that one of you should with all celerity, repair into Persia, declaring what I say, and commanding them with all speed, to send an army, if the Persians desire the dominion of Asia and commodity thereof. Go thou then which are most ancient, go, I say, and thus declare that so many soldiers, as they send, when they be come to me, I will care for the finding of them. What we now have, you well know, whereof see you keep no secret. And what I may send of these things into Persia honorably and lawfully belonging to God, inquire of my father concerning the commonwealth; inquire of the princes and let the send some to see what we have done, and to make answer to our requests. And you being well appointed, take a band of men to accompany you."

Then he called the Medeans, at which time, Cyaxares his messenger, and in presence of them all, declared both his anger toward Cyrus and his menacing toward the Medeans. In conclusion he said, that he had commanded the Medeans to depart, though Cyrus would have them tarry. The Medeans hearing the messenger stood in silence, being in perplexity, how they might disobey his commandment, and afraid how to obey his threatenings, specially knowing his cruel conditions.

Therefore Cyrus said, "I, messenger and Medeans, do not marvel, though Cyaxares seeing our enemies them to be many, and not knowing what we did, be troubled both for us and for himself. But when he shall know, that many of our enemies be slain, and all put to flight, first he shall ease of his fear, then shall he know, that he was not left desolate, because his friends have destroyed his foes. And how can we be worthy accusement rightly, doing his pleasure, enterprising nothing of our own brain. For I desired him to license me to take you with me, and you as men not desirous to go forth, asked of him if you should go. Now you be come hither indeed, but being commanded of him, to go so many of you as were not unwilling to the same. As for his anger, I know well, being appeased with our well doings, it will relent and vanish away, with his vain fear. Now therefore you messenger, rest you, because you have travailed. And you, O Persians, because we look for our enemies, either to fight or yield, prepare, that we may be in good appointment, for so appearing, we must needs much rather accomplish our purposes. You the prince of the Hircanians, tarry, commanding your captains to see their soldiers harnessed."

The Hircanians going about the same, Cyrus said, "I have great pleasure, O Hircanians, perceiving you not only to declare you assured friendship, but also wit and policy, which at this present shall, I am certain, much avail us. The Assyrians be mine enemies, but now more hateful to you, than me. Therefore let us consult for both parties, that none of our present confederates, do forsake us, but that we may, if we can, get more. You have heard how the Medean calleth home his horsemen, whch if they depart, than how can we, only footmen, remain? Therefore both you and I must do our devors, that this messenger may be desirous to abide with us. You therefore preparing a tent well apparelled with all necessaries, shall appoint him to the same. I shall devise to occupy him about some such thing, which he had rather do, then depart. And declare you unto him what hope of great avail all our friends may conceive if our emprises have good success. When you have thus done, repair eftsoons to me."

The Hircanians departed and brought the Medeans to his tents. He that should go into Persia, was there present. Cyrus commanded him to say unto them, as he in his former words had declared, and that he should deliver letters unto Cyaxares. "And I will," said he, "that you shall be privy to that I write, that you may know how to make direct answer, if he make any demands." The epistle was thus written:

The Epistle of Cyrus

"Cyrus to Cyaxares greeting. Neither did we leave you desolate, for no man that is superior to his adversaries, is then destitute of friends, nor we did not depart from you, thinking you to be left in any danger. But the further we be distant from you, the more we think we work for your profit. For they which remain nighest their friends, do not most provide their friends security, but they that drive their enemies furthest off, they rather see their friends in safety.

"Consider therefore, what I am towards you, and you toward me, and then appeach me. I brought your confederates, not so many as you thought, but so many as I was able. You granted me being among my friends, so many as I was able to allure, now being among mine enemies, you do call home not him that will, but every man generally. Truly I thought then, that either of us had ought thanks to other. But now you enforce me to put you out of mind and do my part to tender all the thanks I can to them which have accompanied me. Yet truly I can not be like unto you: for sending now into Persia for an army, I do command that so many as shall repair to me, if you have need before they come to us, you shall command them to do you service, not as they will, but as it pleaseth you. And I will counsel you, although I am of less years, that you will not revoke your gifts, lest for thanks, emnity shall be due unto you. Nor when you say you are left alone, then do not menace many, lest you reach the same to set little by you. Fare you well. We shall be ready to come to you, when we have with speed accomplished those things which being achieved we think, shall redound to both our public weal."

"Deliver this to him, and if he do ask you of any of these things being written, affirm the same. And concerning the Persians, I have given you precepts tofore mentioned." Thus speaking to him and delivering him the letters, he dismissed him, charging him so to make haste, as he knew speedy repair to be profitable. Then he did see, that all were in harness, both Medeans, Hircanians, and Tigranes' men, and the Persians were also harnessed. And at this time certain of those marches, brought forth their harness, and he commanded the darts to be thrown into that place before appointed and to be burned of them which were assigned, chiefly such as were not needful. But the horses he commanded the bringers to keep and remain, till he did otherwise signify unto them.

And assembling the captains of the horsemen, and Hircanians, he said thus:

Cyrus his Oration

"Do not marvel, friends and confederates, though I do oft assemble you: for new matters being in hand, be commonly in no due order. And things out of order must needs make business, till they be well placed. We have much treasure taken, we have many men likewise. And because neither we know, what is properly ours, nor they what was severally theirs, a man cannot see very many of them doing that they should do, but all, almost doubting, what they ought to do. Therefore that this may be redressed, you shall divide the same. And what tent any man hath taken, being furnished with victual, ministers, and apparel, with other sufficient implements for a warlike tent, hereafter he must put not more to it, than the receiver may know, because he ought to be as circumspect in these, as in his proper possession. He that hath chanced on a tent unfurnished, seeing to them that be in it, shall relieve the lack of the same. For I know that there be many things superfluous, for our enemies had all things more abundantly, than our number can spend. The treasurers of the Assyrian king and of other princes came to me, declaring that they had coined gold, making mention of certain tributes.

"Therefore proclaim that they bring forth all such things to you wheresoever you sit, affraying them that do not obey your commmandment; you receiving it, give to an horsemen double, to a footman single, that you may have to buy such things as you lack. Proclaim a market place in the camp, where no man do other wrong, suffering victuallers and merchants to sell every man his chaser, and these things being uttered, to bring others, that our camp may be inhabited." And they forthwith proclaimed the same. But the Medeans and Hircanians said thus: "How shall we without you and yours make division of the things?"

Cyrus to these words thus replied, "Do you friends think that when any thing is to be done, we all must be present at every matter, and that I am not sufficient to provide for your wants and you for ours? And how can it be, but we shall have more matters to do, bringing fewer to pass than we do, but consider, we have kept these things for you. You making us believe they have been well kept. Therefore, divide you them now, and we will believe that you have divided well. And so in this matter let us endeavor to do somewhat else for the commonwealth.

"First consider how many horses we have, and how they be brought to us, if we suffer them to be unridden, we shall have no profit by them, but trouble in keeping of them. But if we appoint horsemen to them, we shall be both delivered of business, and they shall augment our strength, if you have any other to whom you would give them, with whom you could have more pleasure to adventure when you need than with us, let them have them. But if you will rather have us to help at a pinch, give them us. For when as late you went forth and did adventure without us, we were in great fear, lest you were not well. And you made us much ashamed, that we were not where you were. But if we take horses, we shall follow you.

"If we seem to do more good being horsemen, we shall lack no couragious diligence, to aid you, but if we seem to do more good afoot, we shall alight among you, and straight become your footmen, taking our horses to be kept of some, appointed to the same." Thus he said. And they made this answer. "We, O Cyrus, have neither men to let upon these horses, nor if we had, we would prefer any man to you, you being willing to occupy the same. Therefore now take the horses, and do with them as you think good." "I take them," said Cyrus, " and with good fortune be we made horsemen. Divide you the common spoil, and the first select for God, as the sages shall think good. Then divide for Cyaxares, in every thing, as you think you may most gratify him." They then smiling, said, "That the fair women must also be divided." "Divide," said he, "both women and other things as you list, when you have made division for him, see that these, O Hircanians, which willingly have followed me, have no cause to complain. And you Medeans, honestly esteem these our first confederates, that they may think to have done well, in allying friendship with us, and distribute part of everything to Cyaxares his messenger, and to them that came with him, exhorting them to abide with us, saying that I would have it so, that Cyaxares may be the better ascertained of everything that is done. To these Persians and my train, that that is superfluous, yoursevles having honest position, shall be sufficient. For we, I tell you, be not much brought up in delicates, but very homely. Therefore you peradventure, shall laugh at us, if you give us any precious thing. And I know well, that setting on horseback we shall be the cause of much laughter to you. For I think surely that we shall have many a fall."

Then they went to make division, having good sport at the riding matter. Cyrus calling the captains, commanded them to take horses, horseburdens, and horsekeepers, and that in number each man by lot, should equally receive them to his array. He commanded also to be proclaimed, that if there were any slave of the Assyrians, Syrians, Arabies, Medes, Persians, Bactrians, Carans, Cilicians, Grecians' army, or of any other place, they should show themself. They hearing the proclamation, very many showed themselves straight away. He, choosing the best favored, said, that if they would be free, they must be harness bearers which he delivering to them, affirmed he would provide, that they should have things necessary. Whom leading to his captains, straight away he bestowed, commanding bucklers and short sword to be delivered them, that they, having the same, might follow the horses. And that themselves, haing curettes and spears, should ever be on horseback. And he began the feat, and to the footmen of the nobility in his place, he appointed another captain of the noblemen.

Being busied about these things, Gobryas, an Assyrian and ancient man on horseback, with a company of horsemen, having all barbed horses, came at that instant. And they which were appointed to receive harness, commanded him also to deliver his lances, that they might burn them as they did other: Gobryas said, he would first see Cyrus.

The ministers leading the other horsemen behind, conveyed Gobryas to Cyrus, who, seeing Cyrus, said thus: "I am, O Lord, an Assyrian born. I have a strong fortress and am lord of a large land. And having a thousand horsemen, I served the Assyrian king, with whom I was in high favor. After that he being a noble man was slain of you, and his son my mortal enemy succeedeth him in the empire, I am come to you, and kneeling on my knees, I recommend myself to you, as captive and confederate, beseeching you to review my cause. And that you may the better do it, I adopt you to my son, for of the male kind I am childless. For the only son which I had, O Lord, both good and goodly, so reverencing and loving me, as a child might cause his father to be happy. This my sovereign lord, father to him that now reigneth sent for my child, intending to give him his daughter in marriage. I, looking too high, sent him forth, thinking to have seen my son espoused to a king's daughter.

"The king now seeing, calling him to hunt, and permitting him to range at large as one that was counted his most excellent horseman, friendly in the hunt entertained him. A bear being put up, they both followed the chase. The prince picked his dart, alas the while, and missed. My son in evil time, let drive and overthrew the bear, whereas the other disdaining, kept this hatred secret. A lion again aroused, he eftsoons missed, which as I think was not a strange thing. My son again, O unhappy chance, hit the loin, and slew him, and said,' Twice have I in order driven one dart, and at each time killed a deer.' At that word that wicked man no longer dissembling his hatred, but cruelly taking a spear from one of his men, stroke him through the heart, and beraught my only and lief son, his life. And I poor miser instead of espousal, did bring the dead corpse away.

"And being thus in age buried my most good son, growing to man's estate. This murderer as though he had vanquished an enemy, neither showed any token of repentance, nor did him any honor for his wicked trespass at his funeral, but his father truly both rued for me, and showed evidently, that he was in anguish for mine so great dolor. I truly if he had lived, should never have come to you to the hurt of the other, for he was especial good lord to me, and I as faithful servant to him. But the kingdom being revolved, to the murderer of my son, I can never be faithful to him, nor he can never be friendfull to me, for he knoweth my heart toward him. And as before I lived a pleasant life, so now being dispoiled of my son, I waste mine age with pain and pensiveness. If you therefore will take me to your clemency, I have some hope, that through you, my dear son's death shall be revenged, and my self revive again, neither living with ignominy and reproach, nor dying with sorrow and lamentation." Thus he spake.

Cyrus answered, "If you, Gobryas, think in heart, as you have spoken with tongue, I receive your humble suit, and promise you, God being my good lord, the avenging of your son. But now tell me, if we do you this pleasure, suffering you to retain your city, your country, your armor and power as you have heretofore, what service will you do us for these benefits?" He said, "My fortress is at your commandment, I deliver my house as your house, and the tribute and land that I pay now to him, I will translate to you. When you go to war, I will go awarfare with you, I will aid you with the force of my country. I have also a daughter, a virgin, and dear damsel, being now marriage worthy, whom heretofore, I thought I had reserved a wife for this new king. But now my daughter oft kneeling on her knees, hath made humble request unto me, not to give her to her brother's killer, which thing I myself approve. Now therefore I give her to you, so to be provided for, as I shall appear to provide for you."

Then Cyrus said, "In confirming the truth of these things, I give you my right hand, and take yours, God being witness betwixt us." These things being done, he commanded Gobryas to depart to his men in harness, asking him how long the way was to his country. He answered, "If you set forth tomorrow in the morning, you shall the next day lie with me." Gobryas then departed, leaving a guide behind him.

Then came the Medeans, saying that they had given the sacrificers such things, as they could choose out for God his part. And they had selected a most goodly tent for Cyrus, and a Susian woman, being reputed the most goodly creature in all Asia, and two most excellent musician women, and secondarily to Cyaxares the next in price. And furnishing themselves with such like things, that they should want nothing in the time of war, for there was great abundance of all things. The Hircanians also took that they needed, dividing equal portion, with Cyaxares his messenger. And certain superfluous tents they gave to Cyrus to the use of the Persians. They said also there was a coin, which being collected, should be distributed. And so it was. They thus did, and said. Cyrus commanded them to take the custody of Cyaxares' portion, whom he knew to be most familiar with him. "And whatsoever you give me, I take it," said he, "thankfully, and he hath most need among you, he shall use the same."

Then one of the Medes, a great esteemer of music, said: "I truly Cyrus, hearing this night past, these women minstrels whom you now have, I was greatly delighted. Therefore if you would vouschafe to give me one of them, I would think it greater joy to war, then to remain at home." Cyrus said unto him, "I give her thee with all my heart. And I think I ought to give thee more thanks for thy request, than thou, me for my gift, so desirous am I, to do you pleasures." And he that asked the woman had her.

Thus endeth the Fourth Book.

THE SCHOOL OF CYRUS
The Discipline of Cyrus,
The Fifth Book.

Cyrus calling Araspas a Medean, which was his playfellow being a child, to whom also he gave the Medean robe off his back at his departure from Astyages into Persia, commanded him to take the custody of the woman and the tent. She was the wife of Abradatas, king of Susa, which was not present at the taking of the Assyrians' camp, being gone of embassage to the king of Bactria, being sent thither of the Assyrians to treat of confederacy betwixt them, and of entire friendship with the king of Bactria. Cyrus commanded Araspas to take the custody of her. Who being so commanded, asked of Cyrus if he had seen her, whom he commanded him to keep. "No surely," said Cyrus. "Indeed," said he, "I chose her for you. And at our first coming to her tent, we could not know her, for she sat on the ground with all her women about her, being apparelled like her handmaids, we being desirous to know which was the mistress did avise them all forth with, and she although she did sit muffled and beholding the earth, did far exceed the other. Wherefore commanding her arise, all the others did arise about her. She far did pass them all, as well in feature, and lineaments of body, as nurture and comeliness of the same, although she was clad in coarse array, and the tears did distill evidently from our eyes, some on her attire, some down to her feet.

"Wherefore the most ancient of our company, said, 'Be of good cheer, Lady, we hear that you have a goodly valiant man to your husband, but now know you for certain, that we have chosen you for a man, which neither in beauty nor in valiantness is inferior to him, but as we think, if there be any man, Cyrus is the man most worthy of admiration, whose, from this time you shall be.' When the lady heard this, she did tear that tirement of her head, and cried out, and all her maids together shrieked with her. At which time her face the greater part did appear, likewise her neck and hands.

"And be you assured, O Cyrus, that to us all that did behold her, it seemed impossible, that such a creature could be born of mortal parents in Asia. Therefore, sir, see her in any wise." Then Cyrus said, "Truly so much the less, being such a one as you do report her." "And why so," said the young man. "Because," quoth he, "hearing you declaring her beauty, if I should be moved to go and see her, having almost no time, I am afraid lest she should soon allure, to come eftsoons to behold her: whereby I might perchance wax negligent in my weighty affairs, sitting and vising her."

The young man smiling, said, "Think you Cyrus, that the beauty of a mortal creature, could enforce an man unwilling, not to do for the best? If nature be of such power, she should enforce every man alike, for the fire burneth every man alike, because it is his nature. But of beautiful things, some with some be had in price, some not so, some esteeming thus, some that. For it is a voluntary thing, and every man loveth what he list. The brother is not in love with the sister. Another is. The father not with the daughter. Another is. For fear and law is sufficient to restrain love. But if there were a law which should enjoin that men should not eat, and yet not be hungry, should not drink, and yet not thirst, and that no man should be cold in winter, nor hot in summer, law truly could compel no men to obey these things. For by nature they be conquered of the same, But to love is a voluntary thing. Every man loving his own things, as his apparel, and other garments."

Then said Cyrus, "If love be voluntary, how can it be, but a man may leave it when he list? But I have seen men weep for sorrow, because of love, and to the loved would bcome bound, and thrall, and yet before they loved, reputed none evil so great as bondage; they giving away many things which had been better for them to have kept, and have desired of God to be delivered of love, as of any other thing, from the which they could not be released, being bound with stronger durance, than if they had been tied with chains, yielding themselves to the loved, serving them with all obedience, and being in such distress, do not once attempt to make an escape, but be rather the jailers of the loved, that they should not escape them."

Then the young man said, "They do thus," quoth he, "and therefore they be very misers; and as I think wishing continuance of their woe, would so die. And whereas there be a thousand ways to be rid of this life, they do not rid themselves, but some of them fall to stealing and robbing of other men; yet when they have robbed and stolen, you with the first do see, that theft is not necessary, and accusing the thief and robber, do not pardon, but punish him. Semblably the beautiful do not compel men to love them, or covet that is not lawful. But the vile shadows of men be inferior to their affections, and they do accuse love. Honest and good men, although they desire gold, good horses and fair women, yet they can easily refrain from all the same, not being more subjects of them, than they ought to be. For I did behold this woman, which seemed to me a most goodly creature, and yet I am now with you, I am on horseback, doing such things as my duty requireth."

"Peradventure," said Cyrus, "you came sooner away, than love could fasten in a man. For the fire touching a man, doth not straight burn him. And wood is not straight in flame, yet would not I willingly neither touch the fire, nor behold beautiful persons. And I would counsel you Araspas, not to be busy in beholding beautiful people for the fire burneth whom it catcheth, and fair folk so enflameth them, that they burn in love."

"I warrant you, Cyrus," said he, "though I never leave looking, yet will I not be overcome, whereby I should be any thing that I ought not." "You speak well," said Cyrus, "therefore keep this woman as I bid, and see well unto her; for peradventure this woman is taken in good time."

Thus they talking, departed, the young man noting both the singular beauty, and perceiving the great honesty of this woman, and having the custody of her, thought he would do her pleasure, and by continuance understanding that she was not unthankful, but very diligent on her part, to cause her servants that all things at his coming should be ready, and if he were by chance sick, lacked no keeping, he through all these occasions fell in amours with her, and peradventure there was no marvel in the matter. Thus these things stood.

Cyrus being desirous that the Medes and others his confederates should be wiling to abide with him, assembled all the chief of them, and said thus.

The Oration of Cyrus

"I certainly know, O Medeans, and all other here present, that you come not forth with me, neither for lack of money, nor in this behalf, minded to please Cyaxares, but for the desire to gratify me herein, and seeking mine honor, you came forth to travel by night, and to adventure yourselves with me. For the which things, I thank you. If I did not, I should do naught. But to recompense you accordingly, I am as yet of no power. And so to say I am not ashamed. But to say, if you tarry with me, I will acquit you, I might well be ashamed, for I think I should seem to say for this purpose, that you might be the more willing to tarry with me. But instead of it, thus I say. If you depart, obeying Cyaxares, I having good success, will do my devour that you shall have cause to praise me. For I will not depart, but keeping my promise with these Hircanians, to whom I have made an oath, and joined hands, I shall never be found untrue to thee. And I will attempt to do so much for this Gobryas, which of late hath given us his towns, country, and power, as he shall not repent him of his repair to me. and most of all, God so manifestly giving us good chance, I should be in fear and dread if that I left that thing and did depart unadvisedly. I therefore will thus do. Do as you shall think good, and declare unto me what your mind is." Thus he said.

He that once said he was his kinsman spake first in this wise: "I truly, O king, for a king, you seem to be no less by nature, than a master be in a swarm of the same, for to him always bees willingly be obedient, insomuch that if he remaineth at home, none goeth abroad. If he goeth forth, none tarrieth behind. Such vehement love is engrafted in them, to be governed of him. I say that men be semblably affected toward you, for when you departed from us into Persia, whom was there of the Medeans, that did forsake you, that did not wait upon you, till Astyages did return us? And when you came from Persia to aid us, we might perceive that incontinent, all your friends willingly followed you. And now thus we stand that being with you in our enemies' land, we dare be bold: But without you, even to return I should be afraid. Therefore let other men show what they will do;

for I truly, O Cyrus, and all mine, shall remain with you, and by the sight of you, abide all brunts, firmly trusting to your benificence."

Then spake Tigranes thus: "You, O Cyrus, shall not marvel though I say nothing, for my mind is not appointed as a counselor's, but as a performer of things that you do command." Then the Hircanians said: "I, O Medeans, will think if you depart, that it is the workmanship of God, not suffering you to enjoy so great felicity. For who is well with himself, that will recoil, his enemies being fled, and will not receive, they delivering their harness, and will not take, they yielding themselves and theirs? Especially having such a captain as this is, who I think, God being my record, hath more delight to do us pleasure, than to enrich himself."

After him all the Medeans said, "You, Cyrus, have brought us forth, and you, when you think it time to return, shall bring us home." Cyrus hearing these words, thus made his prayer: "O Jupiter immortal, grant me I beseech thee, that I may be able in doing them pleasures, to surmount their doing me honor." Then he commanded all others to have their appointed garrisons about them.

And the Persians to take tents seemely for horsemen, and sufficient for the footmen, and so to order that all the ministers should bring all necessary things to the Persian crews and to see that their horses be well trimmed. And the Persians should have nought else to do, but attend upon warlike affairs. And thus they spent this day.

Rising early in the morning, they marched toward Gobryas. Cyrus being on horseback and the new made horsemen of the Persians, about two thousand. Others having shields and swords followed, these being equal in number, and the residue of the host, set forth in array. He commanded every one to say unto their new servants, that as many of them as be seen behind the guides of the tail of the army, or before the front, or were taken on either side divided from them that were in array, should be punished. The next day about twilight, they were at Gobryas' fort, and saw a strong trench, and all things prepared within the walls to make strong resistance and many oxen and sheep, to be gathered within the trench. And Gobryas came to Cyrus, willing him to ride about, and see if the entrance were very easy, and that he should send some trusty men to him within, which viewing what there was, might make relation to him.

So Cyrus being willing to see at that present if the town might be taken, or Gobryas appear vain, he rode about and saw everything too strong for him to enter. They whom he sent to Gobryas, did report to Cyrus, that there was such plenty within, as was able to their judgement without want, to suffice a man's life them that were within. Cyrus mused what this matter should man. Then Gobryas himself came out, and brought forth all that were within, some bringing wine, barley meal, wheat meal, some driving out sheep, neat, goats and swine, and all other vitail, and brought forth abundantly, that Cyrus with his whole army might sup well. Some being appointed did distribute and serve the supper.

Gobryas as when all his men were come forth, moved Cyrus to enter in, that he should think all to be in surety. Cyrus sending in afore espies, with power, entered in himself being entered the gates which were opened, he desired all his friends and captains about him to do so.

When all were in, Gobrays brought cups of gold, lavers, and flagons, with all other kinds of ornaments, and a coin called darickes innumerable, and all things wondrous bountifully. Finally bringing his daughter, a maid of marvelous goodly hue and beauty, clad in mourning apparel for her brother's death, said thus, "I give you these riches, and this my daughter. I do recommend to be bestowed as you shall please. We beseech you, I tofore for my son, she now for her brother, that you would be his avenger."

Cyrus thus answered, "I promised you to avenge your quarrel to my power, if you were true. Now finding you so to be, I am bound to keep it, and her I will also promise, that with God his help, I shall perform no less, and this treasure I also accept, rendering the same to this your daughter, and him that shall be her mate; one gift if I have of you when I depart, I will more joyfully accept, than all the treasure of Babylon, which is much, and of the whole world, which is infinite."

Gobryas marvelling what it should be, and suspecting he would name his daughter, said, "what is it, Cyrus?" And Cyrus answered, "I think, Gobryas," said he, "that there be many men which by their will, would neither displease God, nor hurt man, nor be found false. But because no man will prefer them to great riches, to dominion, to strongholds, to dear beloved children, they do die before they have declared what they were. But you giving me now strong towns, infinite riches, your whole power, and most dear daughter, have manifestly declared to all the world, that willingly I neither would be cruel toward strangers for money's sake, nor vain of my covenants. These things shall I never forget be you sure, so long as I shall embrace justice, and be thought worthy of the praise of men, but shall do my diligence to reacquit your honor, by all honest ways.

And be not afraid that you shall lack a meet man for your daughter, for I have many honorable friends, of the which some shall marry her, having so much money as you have given, or other much more than it, I can not truly say. And know you well, that some of them, for the money which you have given, will not a little the more esteem you. But me now they entirely love, desiring of God, they may have once occasion to declare that they will be no less loyal and faithful to their friends than I am to mine. And toward their enemies never to be remiss, while they love, except God worketh the contrary. But they do not so much esteem all your riches, being joined with all Syria and Assyria, as they do virtue and noble fame. Such men set even here, I would you should well know."

And Gobryas smiling, said, "For God his sake, Cyrus, show me which they be, that I may request of you, one of them to be my son." "You shall not need," said Cyrus, "to request of me, but if you accompany with us, you shall be able to show any of them to other." Thus much talking and taking Gobryas by the hand, he rose up and departed, taking all his men with him.

And after much desire of Gobryas' part, to sup within, he would not, but supped in his tents, taking Gobryas with him as a guest, thinking most assurance for them in the army, that he should be present, no many knowing better how to do, if any danger should chance. And setting upon seats of grass, thus demanded of him: "Tell me, Gobryas, have you more carpets than any of us?" To whom he answered, "I know well that you have many carpets, and many resting places, your house is far larger than ours, which for your houses, use earth and heaven, your resting places be so many, as there be caverns on the earth. And you take for carpets, not so many as be made of the wool of sheep, but so many as the field and mountains do send of the branches."

And Gobryas this first time supping with the Persians, and seeing their thin fare, thought his more liberal than them. But when he had advertised their moderateness in diet, for there is no Persian of good education, that in meat or drink appeareth to be moved in eyes, or, with ravening, nor in the mind, but be of as foresight, as though they were not at meat. And as horsemen not being troubled with their horses, can both hear, see and speak on horseback as they ought, even so they at meat, think they ought to appear both prudent and moderate, and to be moved for meat or drink, they think it very gross and brutish. He perceived also that they demanded one of another, such questions as were more pleasant to be demanded, than not. So jested one with another, as was more pleasant to be jested, than not. And so joyed, as was far void of despite, far off from doing hurt, far off from offending one another. And the greatest thing among them, seemed to him, that being in warfare, no man should think he ought to be better provided for than others, that came to like adventure by chance, thinking that feasting to be the best, if they may make their confederates best instruct to war.

Therefore, Gobryas rising to go him, thus, as it is reported, said, "I do no more marvel, Cyrus, though we have more plate, apparel, and treasure than you, were being less worthy than you. For all our care is, to have most possessions, all yours as I perceive, to be best men." Thus he said. Cyrus answered, "Then Gobryas, be here tomorrow betimes, bringing your men of arms, that we may see your strength, and that together you may convey us through your country, that we may know which we should take for our friends, which for our foes."

Thus communing, they departed, the one and the other to his business. When day was come, Gobryas brought his horsemen and led the way. Cyrus as was the part of a wise captain, did not all only mark the way, of the voyage, but in his way considered if he might impair his enemies, and increase his strength.

Calling the Hircanians and Gobryas, for them he thought to have most knowledge in those things that he would learn, said, "I think, dear friends, that I should not do amiss to debate with you, my most assured friends, concerning this war. For I see it to be more to be regarded of you than of me, that the Assyrians do not overcome us. For I peradventure not going well to work, may have some other refuge. But if he subdue you, I see all that you have, shall be another man's. He is mine enemy, not hating me, but thinking it is his detriment, if we be strong. And for this cause, he maketh war against us. But you he hateth, and thinketh he hath injury at your hands." To this they both answered, that every of these things did warn them to be careful, because they knew it belonged to them, and also were in great study, how this present enterprise should succeed.

Then he began thus, "Tell me, doth the Assyrian think, that you only make him war, or knoweth that he hath also another adversary?" "Surely," said the Hircanian, "his greatest enemies, be the Caducians, a nation very great and valiant. The Sacans also our borderers, have sustained much displeasure by the Assyrian, be going about to have them thrall, as he hath us." "Think you not, the," said he, "that they both would gladly take our part against the Assyrians?" "Yes very earnestly," say they, "if they might confeder with us." "And what letteth them to join with us?" said he. "The Assyrians' whole country," said they, "through the which you now go." When Cyrus heard this, "What Gobryas," said he, "do not you accuse this young and new made king of proud and haughty behavior?" "I," said he, "have so found him." "Is he so," said Cyrus, "only to you, or to some other likewise?" "Certainly to many other likewise," said he. "But to show of his outrage toward poor men, what should it need. For a much more noble man's son than I am, being his companion as mine was, and banquetting with him, he did make an eunuch, for because as some men say, his harlot praised him for his goodly aport, saying, 'She should be happy, that might be his wife.' But as the king himself now sayeth, because he would have disparaged his woman. And now he is an eunuch for his labor. But come to his dominion his father being dead."

"Do you not think," said Cyrus, "that he would be glad to see us, if he thought we might do him any good?" "Yes, I know that certainly," said Gobryas, "but is is hard to see him." "Why so?" quoth Cyrus. "Because," said Gobryas, "he that will join with him, must pass by Babylon itself." "And what difficulty is in that," said Cyrus. "Because I know," quoth Gobryas, "that a more puissant power shall issue out of it, than you have, and this you must know, that for this cause the Assyrians yield you less harness, and bring you fewer horses, than they did at the beginning, because your power seemed but weak to them that saw it. And thus rumor is very much dispersed. Therefore I think it best, that we go forth early."

Cyrus hearing Gobryas so say, spake thus unto him: "I think, Gobryas, you say well, moving me to make my jouney most circumspectly. Therefore raising the matter, I cannot see what way to be more safe and sure, than to go the right way to Babylon, where our enemy's power is most puissant. And there be very many as you say. If they be in courage, they will as I think declare it to us. If they see us not, but think we vanish for fear of them, you know well they shall be delivered of the fear which now they are in, and shall for it gather greater courage, so long time as they see us not. But if we march straight against them, we shall find some yet lamenting their death whom we slew, some wrapping their wounds which they had of us, and all yet remembering the manhood of this our host, and the miserable flight and calamity of theirs. This know also, Gobryas, that a great multitude endowed with boldness, be very stout and fierce in hearts. The same being in fear, the more they be, the fear fuller and more amazed be the minds, for of many and evil rumors, of many and evil chances, their fear augmenteth. Likewise of many cowardly hearted and amazed men, it is increased. Therefore for the vehemency of it, it is hard for us to be extinguished with words of a captain, for for him to work courage, marching against his enemies, or by recoiling to stir up their manhood; and the more that a man exhorteth them to be bold, the more in peril they think they are. Therefore let us thoroughly debate this matter, as it is. For if hereafter the victories in chivalrous affairs shall be theirs, which may number most men, then you do not fear for us without a cause. And we at this time be in danger. But if as here to before, so now also the battles shall be tried by the good fighters, you may be bold and not be deceived yourself, for you shall, God being our help, find more among us that will fight than among them.

"Therefore be more bold. And furthermore consider this with yourself: our enemies be very much fewer, than they were before we gave them their overthrow, very much fewer than when they fled from us. But we be more now after our victory, and stronger through access. Do not therefore dishonor yourselves, being now with us, for with conquerors, Gobryas you know, that even they that hang on, be of bold heart to follow. Nor you may not be ignorant of this, that it is expedient that our enemies should now behold us. And you know well that we can seem no way so terrible to them, as to go against them. Therefore my sentence being thus notified, lead us the straight way to Babylon." So they went on, and came the fourth day to Gobryas his country's end. Being in his enemy's land, he took and appointed to be in array about him, both footmen and men of arms, so many as he thought good. The other horsemen he willed to range abroad, charging them to kill so many as did wear harness, the others to bring to him with all the cattle they could take. He commanded also the Persians to range with them. And many came again, thrown off their horses, many bringing great prey.

When the prey was brought in, assembling the princes of the Medes and Hircanians, and the honorable Persians, he said thus:

"Gobryas, loving friends, hath entertained us all after most honorable fashion. Therefore if we appointing God his part and the residue of the army sufficient, would give him the whole prey, we should do very well, showing ourselves so shortly, that we in doing pleasures, do our most endeavor to surmount them that have done us the same." When they all heard this, they all praised him, they all extolled him, and one said thus:

"We all, O Cyrus, will do thus, for Gobryas as I think did disrepute us as beggars, because we came not full of money, and because we drink not in golden cups. But if we do thus, he shall know that men may be liberal without gold."   "Go, therefore," said Cyrus, "giving the sages that is due to God. And choosing out necessaries for the army. That as remaineth, call Gobryas and give it him." So they taking that was meet gave the other to Gobryas. Then marched toward Babylon itself, being in array.

And when of the contrary part, the Assyrians came not forth, Cyrus commanded Gobryas to ride and say, "If the king will come forth in defense of the enemy, that he would fight with him, if not to defend his country, or else it must forceably give place to the conquerors." Gobryas rode thither whereas he might be most safe, and uttered the same. The king sent him this answer: "Thy Lord sayeth, O Gobryas, that it repenteth him, not because he hath slain thy son, but because he hath not slain thee also. But if you will needs fight come thirty days hence, for now I have no leisure, being about purveyance for the same." Gobryas said: "I pray God this repentance never leave thee, for it is manifest, that I do vex thee, seeing thou art troubled with repentance."

Then Gobryas showed the Assyrian's answer, which being heard, Cyrus withdrew his army. And calling Gobryas said: "Did you not tell me that he whom the Assyruan did geld, would as you thought take our part?" "I know well he will," said he, "for we have many times very freely devised together." Then said Cyrus, "Seeing you think it for the best, go unto him, and first so do as you know he will show you, then after more familiarity, if you perceive he will be our friend, devise how he may be our covert friend, for no man doth so much avail his friend in war, as if he be counted his enemy, nor none doth so much endamage his enemy, as he that is counted his friend." "Truly," said Gobryas, "I know that Gadatas would give largely, to do this present king of Assyria some great displeasure." "Tell me," said Cyrus, "do you think that the captain of the fortress, which you say was built both for the Hircanians and Sacans, as a defense of the country in all war, will suffer this eunuch to come with his power to the fortress?" "Yes, certainly," said Gobryas, "if he unsuspected, as he is now, did come unto him." "Should he not," said Cyrus, "be most unsuspect, if I did beseige his holds, as though I would take them, and he to make resistance, as much as he might, and I to take some of his, he contrary wise to take some of ours, to send as it were messengers from me, to them which you say be enemies to the Assyrian. And the captains, should say, that they were going to the army to fetch ladders to seal the castle, which the eunuch bearing, should aim to be that cause of his coming to reveal these things." "I know well," said Gobryas, "that if the matter be thus handled, that he will be ready and desire him to remain there, till you be past." "Think you not, then," said Cyrus, " that being overcome, he might cause us to get the castle?" "Yes, surely," said Gobryas, "he going about the same within, and you sharply assailing it without." " Go your way, them" said he, " and in declaring these things, do what you can, that he may be prest. And as for assurance, utter you nor declare no more to him, then you have received of us."

Thus Gobryas went forth, the eunuch was glad to see him, granting to all things, faithfully promising to do his endeavor. When that Gobryas had reported, that the eunuch unfaintedly had taken in hand all that Cyrus willed, the day following he did make assualt. Gadatas did resist, the ground which Cyrus took was so much as Gadatas suffered.

The messengers which Cyrus sent being to fore instructed whither to go, Gadatas suffered some of them to escape to get ordinance and fetch scaling ladders. They whom he took were examined before many others. When they had showed the cause of their coming, he straight away being well appointed, went that night as it were to reveal the same. Finally being credited, he entered the castle as an aid. And the while with the captain, made such preparation as he could. When Cyrus was come, with the help of them that were captives, he took the castle.

This done, Gadatas the eunuch staying out of hand all things within, came forth to Cyrus, and doing his homage according to the law, said thus, "Rejoice, noble Cyrus, even so I do truly," quoth he, "for you with God do not only command me, but also compel me to rejoice. And this you shall know for certain, if I do much esteem to leave this castle as an help to my confederate friends." "The Assyrian as it appeareth, Gadatas, hath beraft your giving of children, but he cannot bereave your getting of friends, for know you well, that by this feat, you have made us so your friends, that we will to our power, do our parts to be no less your assured friends, than if you had sons and nephews natural." Thus he spake.

The Hircanians straight rejoicing at this fact, came to Cyrus and taking him by the right hand, said, "O noble Cyrus, thou great comfort to thy friends, how much thanks makest thou me to won to God that hath allied me with thee." "Go therefore," said Cyrus, " and taking the castle which you now do so rejoice to be mine, so appoint it, that it may be most seemly for your friends and other confederates, most of all to this Gadatas, which hath taken and yielded it to us." "What," said the Hircanian, "shall I when the Cadusians, Sacans, and my countrymen come, call him that we may use common consultation of matters needful, and of the good governance of the castle?" Cyrus assented, he should so do.

And they being assembled, which should have to do with the castle, did devise by common assent for the guard of it, that it might be no less commodious, than friendfull unto thee, and an hold of resistance against the Assyrians. This being done, the Cadusians, Sacans, and Hircanians, went on this warfare more in number and lustier in courage. And then of the Caducians, were assembled twenty thousand footmen, and four thousand horsemen. The Sacans ten thousand archers on foot, and two thousand archers on horseback. The Hircanians sent more, so many footmen as they could, and increased their two thousand for tofore many horsemen were left at home, because the Caducians and Sacans were at debate with the Assyrians, all the time that Cyrus sat about the provision of the castle. The inhabitance of the Assyrians, adjoining to those places, many brought their horses, many delivered their harness, fearing their borderers on every side.

Then came Gadatas, showing Cyrus that messengers were come, declaring unto him, that the Assyrian hearing of the loss of this castle, and being grieved with it, was prepared to invade his country. "Therefore, Cyrus, if you will suffer me, I will do the best I can, to save my forts: for of other things, I do not greatly pass." Cyrus said: "If you do depart now, when shall you be at home?" Gadatas answered, "The third day I shall sup in my country." "And do you think, said he, to find the Assyrian there?" "Yea, I know surely," quoth he, "for he will make haste, so long as you seem to come to far off." "In what time," said Cyrus, " might I be there with mine army?" To this Gadatas answered, "you have now, O lord, a great army, and you cannot get to my land in less than six or seven days." "Then go you with all speed," said Cyrus, "and I shall come as I may." So Gadatas departed.

Cyrus then assempling all the princes of his confederates, who were present at that time very many noble and martial men, said thus:

The Oration of Cyrus

"Friends confederates, Gadatas hath done feats, which we all ought much to esteem. And that before he had any pleasure showed him of us. And now the Assyrian, as it is reported, invadeth his land. Wherefore it is manifest, that he will be avenged of him, because he thinketh he hath sustained great displeasure by him. And peradventure he thinketh after this sort, that if such as make defection to us, be not hindered by him, and they that be with him, be so destroyed of us, that shortly none will abide with him. Therefore friends, I think it shall be a noble act, if we cheerfully do aid Gadatas, being so beneficial a man to us, doing but right in requiting thanks. And truly as I think, we shall do a feat profitable for ourselves, for if it be apparent to all men, that we do intend nothing more than to subdue and displease them which do us hurt, and to exceed in doing well, them that do us good, it is like that by this means, many will desire to be or friends, and none court to be our enemies. but if we seem to forget Gadatas, how can we, I pray you, but other means, allure men to do us good? How can we be bold to praise ourselves? How can any of us look Gadatas in the face, if we being so many, be overcome in doing well of one man being in such case?"

Thus he said. Every man accorded, that this thing should be done. "Go to them," said Cyrus, "seeing you all assent. And let every man now leave for our beasts and carriage, such as be most meet to go with the same. Gobryas shall be captain and have the conveying of them, for he both is expert in the way, and strong for other occasions. We will set forward with the best, both of our horses and men, having vitail for three days. The less and homlier, we provide now, the pleasanter shall we dine, sup and sleep heraefter. Now then let us march forward. Chrysantas, first take them that be harnessed with breast plates, and lead the way which is plain and broad, placing all the centurians in the front. Let every crew follow you, one after another, for being thick together, we shall go both more speedily, and the more surely. Therore I will that the curette men shall lead the way, because they be the slowest part of the army. And the slowest going before, the lighter must needs easily follow. But when the lighter leadeth the way in the night, it is not to be marvelled, though the army be dispersed. The same dispersed, be soon put to flight. After these, Artabas shall guide the tergate men and archers of the Persians. Next them, Abramas the Mede, the Medean footmen. Then Thatamas the Caducians, and all these so shall order, that the Centurians may be in the front, the tergat men on the right side, the archers on the left, after a quadrat battle. And thus going, they shall be the readier to do their feats.

After them all the carriage shall follow whose captains shall so oversee them all, that all things be in order, before they rest. And that early in the morning, they with their carriage be ready in due order, that they may follow in array. After these carriages, the Persian horsemen shall follow, having likewise the captains of the horsemen in the front, and every captain of horsemen, shall lead his troop by itself, as the captains of the footmen. Then Rambacas the Medean, with his own horsemen likewise. After, you Tigranes with your men of arms, and so forth all other captains of horsemen, with such as you came to us, with the same set forth. Last of all, according to their coming, the Caducians shall go, you Alceuna leading them see that you at this time be last of all, and that none be behind your horsemen. And remember that you all go with silence, both captains and other sober men: for in the night all must be perceived and wrought rather by ear, than by eye. And disarray in the night is more troublous and harder to stay, than in the day. Therefore silence must be used, and order must be kept. And the watches of the night, when we shall rise by night, must be both short and many, that none in the watch, the lack of sleep being long, be hurt in the way. Therefore the hour of departure must be warned with a horn. Thus having every man that is necessary be present at the way that goeth to Babylon. He that marcheth, must always follow straight at the tail."

After this, every man went to his tent, talking by the way thus together: "What a memory hath Cyrus! How many hath he set in order? How many commanded by name?" Cyrus did this through great diligence, for it seemed very marvellous to him, if artificers should know the names of every instrument, pertaining to their occupation, and a physician know the names and tools of medicines which he useth, that a captain should be so dull as to have no knowledge of the names of his inferiors, whom he must use as instruments, when he will prevent anything, when he will eschew, when he will encourage, and when he will frighten. And when he will set forth any man, he thought it a seemly thing to call him by his name.

He was also in this opinion, that they which supposed they were known of their chief captain, should the rather desire to be seen doing well, and the more refrain to be seen doing evil. It seemed also a foolish thing unto him, if he would have anything done in the army, to command it as some masters command in their families, let one go fetch water, let another go for wood, for he thought if they were so commanded, every man would look other in the face, no man doing that was commanded, every man being in fault, and no man ashamed of it, none fearing the displeasure for it, because it was generally every man's fault. Therefore he called by name, whom he commanded to do any thing. And this was Cyrus' opinion in these matters.

The soldiers when they had supped, appointed watches, and prepared everything accordingly, they went to rest, and about midnight, warning was given with an horn. Cyrus willing Chrysantas to tarry in the way, before the setting forth of the army. He with his ministers went forth, shortly after Chrystanas was present with the curette men, to whom when Cyrus had appointed leadmen, he commanded him to set forth quietly, till one should come and show him that all were in the way. He standing in the way, did set forth in order him that came well; to him that slacked, he sent to call him forth. When they were all in the way, he sent horsemen to Chrysantas, to show him that all were ready in the way. Then he did set forth faster, he himself riding quietly to the former part, did behold the array, and whom he saw goin in good array, and without noise, to them he would ride and demand what they were, which thing being known, he would praise them.

If he saw any disordered, the cause thereof being considered, he would labor to appease their tumult. One thing only was left in his night's purveyance, that before the whole army, he did send few expedite footmen, which should both see Chrysantas, and he them and give good ears, if by any other means they could perceive anything, they should signify that same to Chrysantas in meet season.

And one there was chief and governor, which did order them and show what was met, and without rebuke what was not so. Thus by night he went on.

The day being come, because the Caducian footmen came first, he left with them the horsemen of the same that they should not be destitue of men of arms. The other he commanded to go to the foreward, because his enemies were in the front, that if any should come against him, he being stong and in array, might couple with them. And if any flee, they might the more speedily chase the same. For he had always in array, some to chase if need were, some to remain with him, never suffering the whole array to be broken. Thus Cyrus led forth his host, himself not using always one place, as the battle required, espying and considering what ought to be done. Thus Cyrus' army marched forth.

One of Gadatas' horsemen, a man of power, seeing that he had forsaken the Assyrian, thought if Gadatas might be destroyed, that he should have all his land. He therefore sent one of his trusty sevants to the Assyrian, commanding him that went if he found the Assyrian army in Gadatas' land, he should declare unto the king, that if he would lay in ambushement, he might take Gadatas and all his company, commanding him also to show plainly what power Gadatas had, and that Cyrus did not follow. Declaring also which way he should come, charging his servants within, to yield to the king his castle, with all his good which he had in Gadatas' land; saying also, that he would come himself after he had slain Gadatas, if he could do it; if not, from hence forth he would he on the King's part. He that was appointed to this thing, riding past, came shortly to the king, declared the cause of his coming. Which being heard, he straight away took the castle, and having many horsemen and chariots, laid ambushments in every village. Gadatas being nigh these villages, sent certains spies afore; the king perceiving that espies were coming, commanded two or three chariots and a few horsemen to flee, as though they were but few and afraid. The espies seeing this, fell to chasing, making a token to Gadatas. He being deceived, pursued with all his power.

The Assyrians perceiving that Gadatas might be taken, came straight forth of ambushment. Gadatas' company perceiving that, fled: the other pursued. He that privily watched Gadatas, stroke him, but he missed, and gave him no deadly stripe, for he wounded him in the shoulder. That done, he rode till he came among the chasers. Being known what he was, and joining with the king, he spurred his horse and freely fell to the chase. Then such were taken of the light horsemen, which had but show horses, and Gadatas' horsemen were in danger all, being tired with their long journey. But when they saw Cyrus coming with his army, a man may think that they were as glad and joyous, as it were from a storm to arrive at an haven. Cyrus at the first fight, marvelled. But perceiving the matter and his enemies all making against him, he led his army in order, against them: which his enemies perceiving, recoiled and fled. Cyrus seeing that commanded them that were appointed, to follow the chase. He with the residue went on as he thought good. Then chariots were taken, some their drivers being overthrown, some in the return, some by other means, some being enclosed of the horsemen, which slew very many, and him that hurt Gadatas.

The Assyrian footmen that beseiged Gadatas castle, being many, some fled into the castle, that had forsaken Gadatas, some got away afore, to a certain great city of Assyria, whither the king was also fled, with his chariots and horsemen. Cyrus when this was done, entered Gadatas' land, and appointing what should be done with things taken, went straight to see how Gadatas did with his wound. As he was going, Gadatas, his would dressed and bound up, met with him. Whom Cyrus seeing, was glad, and said, "I was coming to see how you did." "And I," said Gadatas, "was coming to behold and see your visage again, which hath such a mind, that having no need of me, I now well, neither making me promise, have done thus for me, never receiving any private pleasure at my hand. But because I seemed to you to further my friends, you have so lovingly helped me, for now by myself I was perished, but by you, I am saved. I swear by the God immortal, O Cyrus, if I were as I was once, and had gotten children, I think I should never have had such a child as you have been to me. For I know many other children and this king of Assyria, have wrought his father more grief, than it is able now to do you."

Cyrus said to him, "Gadatas, yourself being a greater marvel, do now marvel at me." "O," quoth Gadatas, "what meaneth it that so many Persians, so many Medes, so many Hircanians, and all the Armenians, Saces and Caducians being present, study to do you pleasure?" Then Gadatas thus prayed: "O Jupiter, O gods all, grant these men all weal and plenty, and specially him, which is cause that they be such. And that we may reward them, O Cyrus, whom you praise, take gently these gifts, that I am able to give you." And so brought forth very many, both, if he would, that he might make sacrifice, and also to reward the whole army worthily, for this good feat and happy chance.

The Caducian being governor to the reward not being at the chase and being desirous to do some notable feat, making no man of counsel nor showing anything to Cyrus, did range the country toward Babylon. His horsemen being scattered, and the king of Assyria coming from that city whither he he before fled, met with them having his army well appointed, and perceiving, set upon them and slew the prince of the Caducians, and many others, taking many horses, and defeated them of the prey which they so drove. And the Assyrian chasing so far, as he might with surety, returned. The foremost of the Caducians were saved at the camp, a little before night. Cyrus hearing the thing, met with the Caducians, whom he saw wounded, he comforted, and sent to be cured as he had done Gadatas, and the other to be received into the tents, being careful that they should have all necessaries: taking the other honorable men of Persia to be jointly overseers to the same. For good men in such things be willing to take pains.

And then Cyrus was grieved and it did evidently appear, for when the time came that other went to supper, he still tarried with his ministers and surgeons, and with his will, leaving no man uncured, but either presently saw the doing himself, or if he could not intend it, every man might see, that he did send other to cure them. And so at that time they went to rest. By the break of the day warning was given to the captains, to be assembled, he said thus:

The Oration of Cyrus

"Friends and confederates, it is an human thing, that that is chanced, for men to err as men. I think it no marvel, yet it is seeming that we of this thing that is chanced, enjoy some commodity, that is to learn never to disperple, from the whole power, it being weaker than our enemies, yet I do not speak thus, as though a man might not sometime, the case so requiring, go forth with less power than the Caducian now did, for though a man deviseth to him that is able to help, and do set forth, yet he may be deceived. It may chance him that tarrieth, to deceived his enemies, to change his way from them that be already gone. There may be other things to work our adversary's trouble, and our friend's surety. And so be separate, that he shall not depart, but shall augment his strength. But he truly that departeth, makng no man privy, he doth not differ from him, that adventure alone.

"But for this, God willing, we will be avenged of our adversaries, or it be long. For when you have made a short dinner, I will bring you where the deed was done, and we shall both bury the dead, and also show to our enemies, that where they think they have overcome, there, God willing, others shall overcome them, and shall have no great lust to behold that place, where they have slain our friends. If they will not watch with us, we will burn their towns, and waste their countries. That beholding what they have done to us, theyshall not rejoice, but beholding their own displeasure, they shall be sad. Therefore all others go to dinner, you Caducians first choose you a prince, according to your law, which with God his help and ours, may see unto you in all your lacks. And when you have dined, send your elect to me." They did so.

Cyrus after he had led forth his army, did appoint him that was elected of the Caducians, to his crew, commmanding him to lead the same next him, "That we," quoth he, " may encourage our men." Thus they went forth and coming to the place, they buried the Caducians, and wasted the land. This being done and getting much vitail of their enemy's country, they marched to Gadatas' land. And considering that they which did yield unto him, inhabiting nigh Babylon, should suffer displeasure, if he were not present, he commanded all the prisoners, that he delivered, to say unto the Assyrian, and sent an herald to the same that he was ready to suffer his husbandmen to occupy the earth, doing them no harm, if he likewise would suffer the tillmen of them which had yielded to him, to occupy their ground also. "And although you can let, yet shall you let but few. For it is a small country that is given over to me, but I may suffer much of your ground to be occupied. As for reaping of the fruit, if it be war, he shall reap it, that hath the victory; if it be peace, it is plain, it shall be yours. For if any of my soldiers ariseth against you, or any of yours against me, we both shall be able to punish the same." Thus instructing the herald he sent him forth.

The Assyrians hearing these things did the best they could, to persuade the king to accord the this request, because very little should be void of war. and the Assyrian whither it were thought the persuasion of his countrymen, or that he was desirous, he assented to it, and these conditions were made that the husbandmen should have peace, and the soldiers war. Thus Cyrus brought to pass concerning tillage. And as for pasture of cattle, he commanded his friends, if they would, to use and lay them in their dominions still. They brought praise from their enemies, so much as they could, that the warfare might be the sweeter, to their confederates. For the perils is no less, without receiving of necessary victual. And the sustenance taken of their enemies, seemed to make the labors of war lighter. Cyrus being appointed to set forward, Gadatas came, and brought many other and diverse gifts, as it was meet from a noble place. He brought also many horses which he took from his horsemen, whom he suspected of treason.

When he was nigh, he said thus: "I have brought you, Cyrus, these things, that you at this present may bestow them as you think good. And count, that all that ever I have beside, to be yours, for I neither have nor shall have of my body begotten, to whom I may leave mine inheritance. But with me, all my stock and name must decay. And I take God to witness, Cyrus, which see and hear all things, that I have neither done nor said any wrong, or evil, wherefore I should so be served."

And this speaking, he bewailed his fortune, and could no more speak. Which things being heard, Cyrus having pity of his distress, said thus: "I receive your horses, whereby I shall do you pleasure, giving them to your more assured, then they which as it seemeth, before had them. And I shortly shall supply the Persian horsemen to that number of ten thousand which thing I have long courted, your other treasure, take and keep it yourself, for it might else be that I in the reacquital, should be inferior to you. And if at our departure you should give more to me, then you receive of me, by the gods, I could not but be ashamed."

Then Gadatas said: "Truly I believe you in this thing, for I see your gentle nature, therefore I am ready to keep them. For so long as we were in friendship with the Assyrian, my father his possession, was most princely, the great city Babylon bring so nigh. And what commodities might redound of so noble a city, that did we enjoy; and what encumbrance, we departing him again, did not feel of them. But now that we be at discord, it is evident when you be departed, that all my friends and family, shall be in danger of deceit, and as I can perceive, we shall lead a pensive life, having our enemies so nigh, and seeing them stronger than ourselves. And peradventure some man will say, why did you not consider so much before you made defection? Because, Cyrus, my mind through despair done me and anger in me, could never consider what was best for me. But I always was as it were with child, after this sort: Shall I not be revenged on him which is enemy both to God and man, which mortally hateth, not only if a man do him displeasure, but if he suspect any man to be better than himself. He therefore I think being bad, useth their help that be much worse than he, be you of good cheer, Cyrus, you shall not need to fight with any good man, for he is able to provide for this, and take the pain to kill him, that is of more price. This is it that grieveth me, and I dare affirm among the evil, he far exceedeth."

Cyrus hearing him, thought he spake matter worthy to be weighed, and therefore said: "Will you not them Gadatas, fortify your hold with strong garrisons, that you may use the same safely, when you repair to them yourself, and going this expedition with us, as he now is, that he shall fear you and not you him. And in as much as you delight to see your own, take such with you, with whose company you delight. And go forth with me, and you shall do me as I think, much pleasure, and I will do for you the best I may."

Gadatas hearing this sighed and said, "May I prepare all things before you depart? For I would have my mother with me." "You may prepare," said Cyrus, "and I will abide on you, till you say that all is well. Then Gadatas departing, with Cyrus help, did guard his forts, which were strong, furnishing them with all things, wherewith great manors may be inhabited, and took with him both his faithful friends, in whom he delighted, and also many whom he distrusted, compelling them to lead their wives and sisters, being yoked, that by them he might detain them. Cyrus having Gadatas and his retinue, which should both declare the way, waters, forage and vitail, that he might always camp in plentiful places, marched forth.

And so going till he espied the city Bablyon, and perceiving there was a way that led to the very wall, he called Gobryas and Gadatas, asking them if there were any other way, which did not lead so nigh the wall. Gobryas answered, "Sir, there be many ways. But I thought now you would have gone nigh to the city, that you might show them your army, which is now both great and goodly, seeing that when you had fewer, you came to the wall, and they did see us to be not many. And though the king be now prepared, as he said to you he would be ready to fight, yet I know if he saw your power, he would think himself still unprepared."

Cyrus to this thing answered, "I think you marvel, Gobryas, that what time as I, having much less power, yet vanced even to the city wall, why now having more power, I do not march to the same. But marvel not, for it is not all one to march straight and to march about. For all men march straight, which being well appointed, think it best to fight. They march about, which being forecast, consider how they may march most safely, not most shortly. For we must needs compass by reason of our longer going, chariots, and other very much carriage, contained in our army. These things must be closed with harness men, and none of our carriages to appear to our enemies void of harness, wherefore going after this sort, it must needs follow, that the strong shall encounter with the weak and feeble. Therefore, if they of the city would rush out by throngs, and join with us, they should more fiercely encounter with us, passing by, and where men go in length, there be the help continueth the longer. But being nigh, all they of the city, might easily assail us, and retreat when they lift. But if we march being no further distant than they may see us, and keep the same length that we now do, they shall see our multitude, and because of the glittering, all our whole company shall seem more terrible. And if they come orderly against us thus marching, espying them far off, we shall not be taken tardy, but rather good friends, they shall attempt nothing, if they be enforced to range far from their walls, except they think they be more puissant than all we; for to depart far, is full of fear."

When he had said thus, he seemed to them that were present, to say well. Therefore Gobryas did lead, as he commanded, the army thus passing by the city, he retired back to strengthen it, that was behind. When he had so travailled a certain space, he came to the borders of the Assyrians, and Medeans, from whence he marched, whereas were three castles of the Assyrians and assailing one, being the weakest, he took by force. The other two, Cyrus assaying and Gadatas persuading, the captains did yield. This being done, he sent to Cyaxares, requesting him to come to the army, that he might devise with him, concerning the keeping of these castles, that he had taken, and that he should see his host, and be a counsellor in other things as shoud be thought meet to be done, and say, if it be his pleasure, that I will come to him, there to encamp.

The messenger went to show him these things. Cyrus commanded Gadatas to deck very gorgeously the Assyrian tent, which the Medes had selected for Cyaxares. And beside all other ornaments, to bring the women into the parlor of the tent, and with them the women musicians, which were chosen for Cyaxares. And they did as they were commanded.

He that was sent to Cyaxares, after he had declared his message, Cyaxares hearing him, thought it better that the army should remain in the borders, for the Persians were come which Cyrus sent for, being in number forty thousand archers and tergate men, perceiving that they also did hurt the Medean land, he thought it better rather to be rid of these, than to receive a new multitude. He that conducted the Persian army, demanding of Cyaxares, according to Cyrus his epistle, if he had any need of the army, who denying the same day hearing the Cyrus was at hand went and led the host to him.

Cyaxares the day following, with the residue of the Medean horsemen, went forth. When Cyrus heard that he was coming, taking the Persian horsemen which were many, all the Medeans, Armenians, Hircanians and other his confederates, being best horsed, and cleanest armed, went to meet and show Cyaxares his power. Cyaxares seeing so many goodly and brave men, accompanying Cyrus, and so few,(and them very base) waiting upon him, he thought it should be much dishonor to him and was very pensive. Cyrus lighting off his horse and coming to kiss him, as the manner was, Cyraxares lighted off his horse, but turned his back, and would not kiss him, but wept that all men saw it.

Then Cyrus commanding all others to stand back and stir not, taking his uncle by the hand and leading him out of the way under palm trees, commanding the ground to be covered with carpets, and caused him to sit and sitting with him, said thus: "Tell me on God his half, uncle, why are you angry with me, and what it is, that you with so displeasant countenance take so grievously?" Cyaxares answered thus, "Because, Cyrus, I am reputed by the ancient memory of all men, to be lineally descended of old progenitors' kings, and that being a king his son, and taken as a king myself, and now considering how vile and base I am appointed, and with how brave a company both of my retinue, andwith other power, you be with honors present. It would I think have grieved a man thus to have been served of his enemies, but so to be entreated of them that have least cause, it is, God wot, a pressing pain. I had rather ten times be buried quick in the earth, than to sustain such villany, and be and laughed at, of mine own servants. I know this, that you are not only of more power than I, but that my servants also which come to meet me, be more mighty than myself, and so appointed that they may do me more hurt, than I can do them." Which words speaking, he wept much more than he did before, insomuch that he enforced Cyrus to fill his eyes with tears, staying therefore awhile.

Cyrus said thus: "Neither do you speak these things truly, O Uncle, nor take them rightly, if you think that in my presence the Medes be appointed as they were able to do you any displeasure. I marvel not though you be angry and in fear. But whether you be rightly or unrightly displeased with them, I will pass over, for I know if I shoud excuse them you would take it grievously. And I think it a great err, that a man in power, be offended with all his subjects at once, for he must needs in fearing many, be hated of many. And because he is in indignation with all, he causeth all to be of one mind. For the which cause be you assured, I would not send you your men, till I came myself, fearing lest something might chance through this anger, that should repent us all.

"But of these things, I being present and God willing, you be clear out from all danger. But whereas you think that you be unjustly handled of my part, it grieveth me very much, that I employing my pains, to the uttermost part of my power, to do my friend most pleasure, should seem to work the contrary. But let us not thus accuse one another, but try if we can, what mine offense is, and I will avouch that case which in friendship is most narrowly required. And if I be thought to have done evil, I will confess the wrong. But if it shall appear that I have done no fault, nor intended the same, you must confess that you have had nor wrong at my hand. And if it shall be evident that I have done you good, and have been willing with all my power to the same, shall I not seem to you to be worthy rather praise, than to be accused? It is but right. Let us then examine everything, particularly that I have done, and so it shall plainly appear which is good, which evil. And we will begin from the first original, if you think it good.

"When you understood that many enemies were assembled, and they ready to invade you and your land, you sent straight to the common counsel of Persia, requiring aid, and to me privately, to labor to be captain, if any Persians should be sent. I was persuaded with your words, and came, bringing you men to my power, both many and very meet." "It is true," said he. "Then show me first," quoth he, "whether in this thing you do take any displeasure by me, or rather friendship?" "It is manifest," said Cyraxares, that by these I have had pleasure." Then quoth he, "When our enemies came, and you must needs match with them, did you in that thing, perceive me either eschewing labor, or fearing peril?" "No surely at all," said he. "When the victory with God his help was ours, and our enemies were fled, did not I desire you that we should with common force pursue them, and with common courage avenge them that if good for harm did chance, it might be commonly born? In these things can you accuse me of any avarice?"

At which words, Cyraxares held his peace. Cyrus saying unto him again, "Seeing in this thing you had rather keep silence, than make answer, yet show me, if you thought yourself to have injury, when as you thinking it dangerous to follow the chase of our enemies, and I not sufering you to be in any part of that danger, desire you to send some of your horsemen. And if in this request I did you wrong, in especial doing you the pleasure of a just confederate, I would you would declare the same.

And when Cyaxares said nothing to this, Cyrus said, "Seeing it is not your pleasure to answer, show you now, wherein I have done you displeasure. When you did answer me, that perceiving the Medeans to be in joy, you would not cease that joy and enforce them to any more danger, if that I seem to have done you displeasure, because not passing of your anger, I did require eftsoons, that thing which I knew you might easily grant me, and as easily command the Medeans to it, for I requested you to give me him, that would willingly follow me, which thing being obtained of you, my travail was to persuade them. Then I went and persuaded them. When I had so done, I took them with me, you being well contented. If you think this worthy to be accused, nothing that you give us and receive, as it appeareth, shall want accusement. Well, we thus marched forth. When we were gone, what feat did we that is not evident. Did we not take our adversary's camp? Be not many of them dead that came against us? Be not they that be alive hereafter, many their horses, many their harness, yea and their money, which tofore spoiled and bare away your goods. Do you not see now, your friends having and bringing the same, part for you, and part for them, that be under you. And that that is the most noble and high feat, you see your land augmented, and your enemies impoverished, you see their fortress taken, you see yours which before were in your adversary's possession, to be contrary wise now returned to you. If any of these things be good or if any be evil, I being glad to learn, I know not how to say, yet I would be glad to hear." Thus being spoken, Cyrus ceased. Cyaxares made this answer.

"If these things, Cyrus, that you have done be well done, I know not what I ought to say, for you know well that these good things be of such sort, that as the more they appear to be, so much the more they do aggrieve me. For I had rather you had augmented your own land by my strength, then see mine so enlarged of you. These things to you the doer, be honorable, but to me, the very same bring dishonor. And as for money, I think I give you more freely, than I take of you, that you have given me for being enriched with them by you, I perceive the rather how I am made the poorer. And if I did perceive my sujects to have had a little injury at your hand, it should I think grieve me less, than it do now, to perceive that they have received great pleasure by you. If you think that I unjustly do weigh these things, turn them all from me, to you. And then consider what they seem to you. If a man should so handle your hounds which you keep for yourself, and your friend's pleasure, that they be made more obedient to him, than to you, should he delight you with such service? If this seemeth but a trifling thing to you, yet consider this: If a man should so train your servants, whom you keep for your service, and attend upon your body, that they had rather be his, than yours, would you give him any thanks for his benificence? Let us come to that which men do most love and embrace, as their chief propriety. What if a man should so attend on your wife, that he could make her more in love with him, than with you, would you thank him for this attendance? I think you should have great cause. But this I know well, that he that did thus, should of all other do you most injury. And to speak a thing most like to my anguish, if a man would so handle these Persians, that you have brought, that they had rather obey him, than you, would you count him your friend? I think not, but rather your enemy, than if he had slain many of them. If you should lovingly thus say to any of your friends, go and take of mine, all that would go, and he hearing, take all that ever he could, he being enriched with your goods, you not having sufficient for your need, could you think him an unreprovable friend? So Cyrus, I think, that I now have sustained, though not the very same, yet the like by you. Yet truth it is that you say, that I granting you them that were willing, went forth with my power, leaving me alone. And whatsoever you have now taken with my power, that you bring to me, and, and do enlarge my land with my power, I being no cause of these commodities seem to show myself as it were a woman, you doing pleasures both to other men, and also to my subjects. So you appear to be a man, I not worthy to be a king. Do these seem benefits unto you Cyrus? You know if you had esteemed me, you would have been well ware, to beraft me anything rather than mine authority and honor. For what am I the better to have my country dilated, and be myself dishonored. Nor I did not rule the Medeans because I was better than all they, but because they thought me in all things better than themselves."

He thus still speaking, Cyrus did interrupt him, saying: "For God his sake, uncle, if I have done you any pleaure, now, at my request, cease of your complaint, and when you have full experience, how it be toward you, and if any doings shall appear to your, to be done for your profit, I embracing you, and you me, take me as your friend. But if they appear other wise, then accuse me."

"Peradventure," said Cyaxares, "you speak well. And I will do so." "What," said Cyrus, "if I kiss you?" "If you will," said he. "Will you not turn from me as you did alate?" "No," said he. Then Cyrus kissed him; which thing when the Medeans, the Persians and other many beheld, being all in suspense, whereto this matter would ensue, were straight glad, and rejoiced.

Then Cyaxares and Cyrus taking their horses, rode afore. The Medeans, as Cyrus winked to them, followed Cyaxares; the Persians, Cyrus; them, all others. When they were come to the camp, and they had placed Cyaxares in a tent well apparelled, they that were appointed, did minister all things necessary unto him. All the time that Cyaxares was unoccupied, before supper, the Medeans went to him. Some of their own minds, many commanded of Cyrus, presenting their gifts: one a goodly cupbearer, another, a cunning cook; some a baker, some a musician; some cups; some a gallant garment. Everyone for the most part gave him the most precious things that they had gotten; insomuch as Cyaxares did repent him, both because Cyrus had not withdrawn himself from him nor the Medeans were any less loyal unto him, than they were tofore.

When the time of supper came, Cyaxares called Cyrus, desiring him because he had not seen him long before, to sup with him. "Do not desire me, Cyaxares," said Cyrus. "Do you not see that these which be present do all tarry on us? Therefore I should do vile, if I seem to seek my own pleasure, little regarding them. For soldiers thinking themselves to be condemned, if they be good, be made much the less couragious; if they be evil, they be the more despiteful. But you which have come so far, go now to supper. And if any do you honor, embrace and feast by the same that they may have the more assurance in you. I will depart, going about these things which I have spoken. Tomorrow early, all the chief men shall be ready at your gates, that we may devise with you, what is hereafter to be done, you being present, show your sentence, whither you think it good to continue this war, or to discharge our army." Then Cyaxares went to supper.

But Cyrus assembling his especial friends both in wisdom and valiantness at a need, said thus:

The Oration of Cyrus

"Loving friends, that that we first have wished, that, by God his help, we have. For so furious we invaded, so much land have we conquered, that we may see our enemies impaired, and ourselves augmented both in number and courage. Now if our friends lately gotten, will remain with us, we shall be the more able to accomplish both when time requireth force or policy. Now that the most part of our friends, may have the mind to abide with us, it must be as well your feat as mine to compass it. And as he which in fighting taketh most men, must needs be counted most chivalrous, so when policy must be had, he that can make most men to accord with him, seemeth worthily most eloquent in tongue, and valiant indeed. Yet do not muse in this matter as though I would show you a form of Oration, which I would every one should follow, but so handle them, that they may be persuaded by the feats, that every of you do. And let this be your study and care. I will diligently see that the soldiers having necessary things, so much as I may, their advice may be known, concerning this war."

Thus endeth the Fifth Book.

The Discipline of Cyrus

The Sixth Book

This day being thus spent, and supper ended, they went to rest. The day following early, all the confederates came to Cyaxares' doors. And in the time that he apparelled him, and heard so much people to be at his gates, even that time Cyrus' friends brought unto him, some the Caducians, desiring him to tarry, some the Hircanians, another Sacan. Hystaspas brought Gadatas the eunuch desiring Cyrus to tarry.

Cyrus perceiving that Gadatas was in great fear lest the army should be dismissed, smiling, said, "I know well Gadatas, that you being persuaded by Hystaspas, do think as you have said." Gadatas holding up his hands to heaven, swore that he was not so moved to think by Hystaspas perusasion, "But I know well," said he, "that if you were departed, all that I have should utterly be lost. And therefore am I come to him demanding if he knew your pleasure, concerning the dissolving if the army." "Then by like," said Cyrus, "I do wrongully charge Hystaspas." "Yes, surely," quoth Hystaspas, "very wrongfully, for I did speak to Gadatas, that it was not like that you would tarry, affirming that your were sent for of your father." "What say you," quoth Cyrus, "durst you be bold to utter so much, not knowing my mind?" "I by my truth," said he, "for I see that you be desirous to go and show yourself to the Persians, and declare to your father what you have done." "Are not you desirous," said Cyrus, "for to go him?" No truly," said he, "but I will tarry so long, as a captain, till I have made this Gadatas, Lord of the Assyrian."

Thus they in sadness boarded one with another. Then Cyaxares being honorably arrayed, came forth and sat in a Medean throne. When all were come that were appointed and silence made, Cyaxares said thus, "Dear friends, peradventure because I am present, and ancient to Cyrus, it is seemly that I should speak first, and opportunity, as I think now serveth first to consult of this, whether it is meet still to continue our war, or to discharge the army. Let every man therefore say, what he thinketh in this matter."

Then first spake the Hircanian, saying, "I think, loving friends, that there is no need of words when the very deeds declareth what is best, for we all know, that abiding together, we shall do our enemies much more damage than receive. But if we be disperpled, they shall deal with us to their most pleasure, and to our most pain." After him, the Caducuan said, "What should we speak of departing home, and to be discovered? dissevered? though we continue the war. For we being warlike and scattering but a while from our company, were surely beaten." Next him Artabasus, which sometime said he was Cyrus' kinsman, spake thus, "I, Cyaxares, do much dissent from them which have tofore spoken. For they say that we ought to tarry and continue this war. But I say that when I am at home, I am in war. For I have helped many times, when our goods be driven away, and many times I had business about our forts, being fearful and ware of their trains. This I did of my own cost. But now I have their castles, and am not afraid of them. I feast with their goods and banquet at mine enemy's cost. Therefore, seeing that to be in war, partly is domesticall and as a feast, I do not think that this common joy should be dissolved." Then Gobryas said: "I, friends and confederates, hitherto have cause to praise Cyrus' fidelity, for he hath not failed in anything that he hath promised. But if he did depart out of this land, it is evident, that the Assyrian will not so cease, but be avenged, both as he intended to do you wrong, and as he hath already done to me. And I shall afresh be punished, because I am confederate with you."

After all these, Cyrus said, "I am certain, friends, that if we now dissolve our army, our state shall be feebler, and our enemies again stronger. For all they from whom harness hath been taken, shall shortly make new. They whose horses were bereft them, shall shortly get others. And for them that be slain, others shall grow and be gotten. Therefore no marvel it shall be, though they efsoons be able to molest us.

"If it be so, what meant I to move Cyaxares to propound the case of the dissolution of the army? Know you well, that I feared after collapse. I see our enemies able to march with us, with whom if we use this trade in war, we shall not be able to fight, winter also is at hand, if we had houses for ourselves, yet surely we have none for our horses or ministers, nor for the multitude of our soldiers, about the which we cannot proceed in war; the victual where we have come, is consumed of us; where we have not cxome, it is conveyed, for fear of us, into their holds, so that they have them and we cannot come by them. For who is so painful or who is so hard, that striving with hunger and cold, can endure to war.

"Therefore if we should use this trade of war, I truly affirm, that we should rather willingly discharge our army, than afterward for want of provision be compelled unwillingly. But if we will continue the war, thus I say we must do with all celerity, our endeavor shall be, to take so many of their holds as we can and build of our own so many and strong as we may. If this be done, they shall have most victual which be able to take most, and lay it up. They shall beseige others which be more strong, and now we do not differ from them that sail in the sea, for they always sailing, and yet that that they have sailed is no more their own, than that that they have not sailed, but if we can get the holds, the same shall put our enemies beside their ground, and for the quiet, be to us in all things more available.

"But if any of you peradventure doeth fear to be in garrisons, far from his own country, let not this trouble you. For we being furthest from our country, will take in hand to keep those holds that be next to our enemies, you shall keep and maintain those which be in the borders of you and the Assyrians. And if we keeping those that be next our enemies, can save the same, you being so far off, shall live in much quiet. For they cannot, as I think, set light the harms being so nigh,and intend to work any wiles with you, being so far."

When the things were spoken, as well all the other as Cyaxares himself rose up, and said, they were ready so to do. Gadatas and Gobryas both, the one and the other, said they would defend their holds, where their confederates should determine that they might be helpful to their friends.

Cyrus seeing all to be pressed to do as he had said, thus concluded: "If we then will accomplish all that we have said, we must with all celerity provide such things as we have used, as engines to beat down our enemy's holds, and workmen to build fortresses for ourselves." Cyraxares promised to provide one engine, Gadatas another, Tigranes another. And Cyrus said he would do his diligence, to make one himself. When these things were thus agreed upon, they prepared engine matters. And every man did purvey things meet for the engines, and such men were appointed, as seemed most meet to such purposes.

And Cyrus perceiving that long tarrying must needs be in this matter, did encamp in a place which he thought most wholesome and most commodious for things needful. And whatsoever needed defense, he finished it, that they might always remain safe, if at any time with their force they did camp far off. Furthermore inquired of them, whom he thought to have most knowledge in the country, from whence they might best provide for the army, and always encamped nigh pastures, both that the army should have things needful, and also be the more in health and strength, to endure the labor of their voyage, that in their carriage to keep their order.

Thus Cyrus was occupied. Many of the renegades and captives of Babylon, said, that the Assyrian was departed into Lidia, conveying many talents of gold and silver, with other riches and treasure infinite. Wherefore the commons of the solders reported, that he removed his money for fear. But Cyrus considering that he was gone, to make all sure that he could, contrary wise prepared to be ready to join with him, as though he should go to battle, and did furnish the Persian horsemen, taking some horses of the prisoners, some of other his friends, receiving all men, rejecting nothing, whether any man gave him good harness or horse. He also prepared chariots some of the captives, some otherwise, as he could, and did destroy all cars with two horses, being the faction of the Trojans, and also that manner of driving chariots which the Cyrenians yet useth. For afore time the Medeans, Syrians, Arabians, and all in Asia, did use their chariots so, as the Cyrenians now do.

He thought it most expedient that they which were best in the fight in chariots, should be in that part where the light harnessed men were, which to attain to the victory, have not very great power. For chariots three hundred bring three hundred men, and have horses a thousand and two hundred governors of the chariots be such, as the noble men do think most trusty, to the number of the three hundred and such as do not hurt to their enemies. Therefore he did banish this kind of chariots, and for these he did prepare more warlike, with strong wheels, which should not soon be slit, and long axeltrees, for all things being large the the harder to overturn. And he made for the drivers a seat, as it were a tower of stong timber, the height whereof is five cubits, that the horses may be rule about the seats. And he did harness the cart drivers, with helmets all save their eyes; he did also fasten such picks of iron round about the wheels, two cubits in length, and other under the axeltree, declining toward the ground, as though they should assault their enemy's chariots. And as Cyrus then devised them, to they at this day use their chariots, which be under that kingdom. He has also many camels, so many as his friends could provide, and all the other that were taken.

Thus these things were finished. Being desirous to send a spy into Lydia, and learn what the Assyrian did, Araspas the which had the keeping of the fair Lady, seemed most meet for this purpose. But Araspas had this chance, being caught with the love of the Lady, he was enforced to break to her of his last. Which she denied being faithful to her husband, although he is absent, whom she loved entirely, yet she did not accuse Araspas to Cyrus, being afraid to set variance betwixt two friends. But Araspas thinking it a villany not to obtain his lust, menaced the Lady, that is she would not willingly, she should do it against her will.

Then the woman fearing violence, kept the thing no longer close, but sent her eunuch to Cyrus, commanding him to declare all the whole matter, which when he heard, laughing once again at him, which said he was superior to love, sent Artabasus to the eunuch commanding him to say unto him, that he should not enforce the woman, but if he could assure her he would not hinder him. Artabasus being come to Araspas, did rebuke him, calling the woman a things committed to his fidelity, declaring his untrust, his unrighteousness, and untemperance, insomuch as Araspas wept for sorrow, being oppressed with shame, and confounded with fear, for Cyrus' displeasure.

Which thing Cyrus understanding called him, and privily thus said unto him: "I see, Araspas, that you be afraid of me, and are much troubled with shame. But let it go. For I have heard that gods have been conquered of love. And I know that men being reputed most prudent, have been sore tormented with love. And I have accused my self, because I could not contain, being in company with beautiful persons, little esteeming them. And of this your fear, I am the cause. For I enforced you to this invincible feat." Araspas making answer, said, "You be in this things, Cyrus, even the same man that you be in all others: that is, merciful and pardoning men's offenses.

But truly other men do oppress me with pensiveness, and seeing the rumor of my mishap is dispersed, insomuch as mine enemy's rejoice, my friends counsel me to make as escape, lest I should be grievously punished of you for my guilt." Cyrus said, "Know this well, Araspas, that by this opinion, you may do me high pleasure, and greatly profit ourconfederates." "How can it be," said Araspas, "that I can any ways do you acceptable service?" "If now," said he, "you would fain to make an escape from me, and go to our enemies, I think you might be credited of them" "By God," said Araspas, "I am sure that I and my friends, might so raise a rumor that I were departed from you." "So may you," said Cyrus, "return to us, knowing all our enemy's secrets. And I think they will make you privy to all their counsel and devices, because you shall be in credit with them, so that nothing shall be hid from you that we would know." Then said he, "I will even now depart, for you know that this shall be an argument of truth, because it shall be thought that I flee for fear of your punishment."

"Can you so forsake fair Pantheia?" said Cyrus. "Surely, Cyrus," said he, " I have two minds, and with the one I have now played the philospher, with this unjust sophister Love. For thee is not one, both good and bad, nor loveth at one time, good and evil things, and yet at one time will and will not do one thing. Therefore it is manifest, that there be two minds, and when the good is superior, it worketh well; when the evil, it enterpriseth evil. And now because the good hath you his confederate, it doth subdue, and that very mightily."

"Well," said Cyrus, "if you will now go, you must so do, that your credit may increase among them, you shall show unto them, what we are about. But so show as our doings may be lets to their emprises. And this shall be a let unto them, if you say, that we be appointed to invade their land. For hearing this the shall the less gather together their whole power, every man fearing his private part, and you shall tarry with them a good while. For that that they do being next us, that to know shall be most convenient for us, and counsel them also to be in array when you think they be most strong. For when you shall be departed and thought to know their order, they must needs keep the same, and be afraid to change it, and if they do change, they shall be troubled with the sudden change." Thus Araspas departing, taking his most assured servants and uttering to some of them what he would have done in this matter, went his way.

Pantheia hearing that Araspas was gone, sent to Cyrus, saying, "Be not sorry, O Cyrus, for Araspas his departure to your enemies, for if you will suffer me to send to my husband, I will promise you, that he shall come and be a much more assured friend, than Araspas was, bringing you so much power, as he is lord of. For the father of the king was his friend. But this king attempted once, to have made divorcement betwixt me and my husband. Therefore knowing that this king doth despite him, I am sure he should gladly incline to such a man as you be." Cyrus hearing this, commanded her to send to her husband, and so she did.

Abradates knowing his wife's tokens, and perceiving how other things stood, speedily came to Cyrus, having two thousand horsemen. They that were the Persian espies, sent to Cyrus, declaring what he was. Cyrus straight commanded, that he should be brought to his wife. When the wife and husband saw the one the other, they did embrace each the other, as it was like, after such despair. Then Pantheia declared the goodness, the temperance, and the clemency of Cyrus toward her. Abradatas hearing it, said: "What shall I do, Pantheia, to render thanks to Cyrus, for you and me?" "What other thing," said Pantheia, "but to endeavor yourself, to be such a one toward him, as he hath been toward you."

Then Abradatas went to Cyrus, and when he saw him, he took him by the right hand and said, "For the pleasures that you have done me, O Cyrus, I have no more to say, but that I betake myself to you as your friend, as your servant and confederate. And whatsoever I see you desire, I shall do my devor to the uttermost of my power, to aid and help you in the same. And Cyrus said, "I accept you. And now I dismiss you, to go and sup with your wife. Then you shall again be placed in my tent, with your and my friends."

Afterward, Abradatas perceiving Cyrus very studious about forked chariots, and varied horse and horsemen, he intended to provide him an hundred chariots of his own, and men of arms like unto his, and appointed himself to be in a chariot captain to the other. And he yoked in his own chariot, eight horses in four teems. His wife Pantheia had made of her treasure, a coat of gold, and an helmet of gold, and likewise his vambraces, and had apparelled the horses of the chariot, with harness of brass. Abradatas thus had done. Cyrus seeing his chariot with four teams, though he might as well devise one with eight teams, in the which a place of engines made very low, might be drawn with eight yoke of kine, and this was three paces at the most above the ground, wheels and all. Such towers following in order, might be great succor to his footmen, and great hurt to his enemies array, he made in these houses, circles and pinnacles, and placed in every tower ten men. When all his provision was finished, concerning his towers, he did practice experience how they would draw, and the the eight yoke did more easily draw a tower with all the men in it, than every yoke one load of carriage. For the weight of the carriage was twenty-five talents: And the weight of a yoked tower, like a tragical tent, made of the heart of trees and twenty men and harness, the burden being less than twenty-five talents to every yoke. So when he perceived this carriage to be expidite and ready, he provided that these towers should go with the army, thinking that the advantage of war, was health, justice, and felicity.

There came at this time from the king of India, one bringing money, and showed Cyrus that the king did thus greet him: "Cyrus, I am glad that you have declared to me your want, I will be your friend, and send you money, and if you have more need, send unto me, for I have commanded my men to do your commandment." Cyrus hearing this, said, "I command that certain of you tarry here in our tents, for the custody of the money, and to live at your lust. But thirty of you shall go at my request to our enemies, as it were from the king of India, to treat of confederacy. When you have learned what they say and do, you shall with all speed, declare the same, as well to the king, as to us, in the which things if you do me faithful service, I will give you more hearty thanks for it, that for the money that you have brought me. For common spies, being like slaves, can know nor report nor more, and the common sort; but such men as you be, do many times explore, the most secret counsels." The Indians hearing joyfully these things, and being rewarded presently of Cyrus, went forth the next day, promising when they had learned all that they could of their enemies, they would return with all the speed they might.

Thus Cyrus had provided all things for the war, very princely, as a man intending no small enterprise. And was not only studious for the good doing of his confederates, but also moved emulation among his friends, that they might show themselves most clean in their armor, lusty on horseback, and painful in labor. This feat he devised, causing them to show themselves abroad, rewarding such as were most forward. And the princes whom he saw careful to have their soldiers most warlike, them he would with praise provoke, beneficing them with such gifts as he could. When he made sacrifice, kept awake, then would he appoint such exercise, as might serve in war giving royal rewards to them that did best, so that much joy was in all the host.

Now Cyrus was finished all things as he would for this expedition, engines except. The Persian horsemen were the full number of ten thousand; and the picked chariots, which he had prepared, were a just hundred; and those which Abradactes the Soufian counterfeited like Cyrus, were also as many. And Cyrus caused Cyaxares to change the Medean chariots, from the Trojan and Lydian fashion, after this form, and they also were an hundreth. And on every camel there were appointed two men, being archers; and the most apart of the army, was now in such courage, as though they had had already the victory, and their enemies could do nothing. These things being thus furnished, the Indians which were sent of Cyrus in especial, came and declared that Croesus was elected captain and and conductor of all their enemies. And that it was declared of all the kings being confederated, that every man should be present with all his puissance, and to bring so much men as could he, which should serve both to hire so many for wages, and to reward so many for need, as they could, and that many were already in wages of swordfighters, and that the Egyptians were sailing toward them, being in number one hundred and twenty thousand with shields as low as their feet, and great spears such as they now use, and short swords, also that an army of the Cyprians was coming by ship, and that all the Cilician were now present, both Phryians and Lycaonians, Paphlagonians, and Capadiocans, and Phonicians. And with the prince of Babylon the Assyrians, and the Ionians, Eolians, and almost the Grecians inhabitants of Asia, were enforced follow Croesus. And that same Croesus had sent to the Lacedemonians for aid. And that this army was assembled at the river Pactolon, and that they would go in Thymbraia, where as now the assembled of the Barbarians of neither Syria being under the king, be made, and thither every man was commanded to bring his chaser and ware.

And the captives did show almost the same things, for Cyrus devised that such might be taken, as he might learn somewhat of them. Wherefore he sent espies like unto slaves, as they had been runaways. When Cyrus his host heard these things, every man was in muse, as they had good cause, that they went abroad more discouraged than they were wont, few appearing to be merry. They flocked together, being full of questions of these late tidings. Cyrus hearing such fear to be conceived in his army, called together the princes of the armies, and all others, by whose discouragement he thought damage might ensue, and by their good courage, profit, commanding also his servants, that is any other of the men of arms would come to hear what was said, they should not prohibit him. To the which being assembled, he said thus:

The Oration of Cyrus

"Friends, I have assembled you, because I perceived some of you, after that report was made of our enemy's power, to be very like fearful men. I marvel truly that any of you is in fear, because our enemies do gather together, seeing we be much more increased now, than we were when we did discomfit them. And now thanks be to God, we be far better appointed, than we were tofore. Seeing these things, O good Lord, should you not be bold? If you be now afraid, what would you do, if the rumor were that all the things which maketh with you, were all gainst you? What if you heard that they which first had victory upon us, did eftsoons come against us still retaining their victory; or that they which tofore did defeat the shot of the archers and darters, did now come, both the very same, and other many like unto them?

"Furthermore, if they which so appointed the footmen that they got the victory, be now so furnished in horsemen, that they dare encounter with men of arms, and haberdowning bow and arrow, having every man a strong spear, intending so to come and fight at hand, also vancing with chariots which be not made as afore, easy to be driven away, but have the horses barbed, the drivers standing in towers of timber, being armed their uppermost part with breast plate and helmet, with sithes of iron fastened to the axeltrees, able to disturb in a moment, them of the contrary part. Besides forth, they have camels, with which they give the onset, every one of the which, a hundred horses dare not abide to look on. They have also towers to break the ray, with which the guard and defend theirs, and with their darts, drive you from fighting with them in equal ground. If any of you would report that all these things our enemies had, being now afraid, what would you then do? Seeing that now you be in fear, when it is told that Croesus is chosen grand captain of our host which was so much more cowardly than the Syrians, that when they were discomfitted and fled, Croesus seeing them, vanquished, instead of succoring his confederates, fled himself away. This also is told, that our enemies not being sufficient of themselves, are compelled to have other in wages, which would better fight for them, than they for themselves, if any man be if this opinion, that these be puissant, and ours feeble, I think it meet for such friends, that they depart to our enemies. For being there, they shall do us more good than if they were still with us."

When Cyrus had thus said, Chrysantas, a Persian stood forth, and spake on this wise:

The Oration of Chrysantas

"Do not marvel, O Cyrus, though some fearing this news be of discouraged countenance, for it is not of any fear, but of grief: as when men be desirous and in hope to made good cheer, then if any business is showed, which must of necessity be done afore the same, no man, I think, is glad to hear such news. So we likewise, thinking now to have been in wealth, and hearing that there be yet things undone, which must needs be done, we have heavy countenance, not for any fear, but because we would satisfy our former desires. But seeing we shall not only fight for Syria, whereas is plenty of coin, cattle, and fruitful date trees, but Lydia also, whereas is abundance of wine, figs, and oil, the sea flowing to it, through the which more goods cometh, than any man hath ever seen. Remembering I say these things, we be no more grieved, but rather encouraged, that we with all speed, might enjoy these Lydian commodities." Thus he said.

All other the confederates being delighted with this oration, praised the same. Then Cyrus said, "I think, friends, it were best for us to go against them with all celerity, that by our speedy coming, we may prevent them in such places, as they have provided their victual. And the sooner that we go, the fewer shall we find present, and the more absent. Thus I think if any of you be of other judgement, either for our safeguard or expedition, let him show his mind."

When as many did accord that it was best to march forth with all speed against their enemies, and no man did reply, then Cyrus began after this wise:

The Oration of Cyrus

"Loving confederates, our hearts, bodies, and harness which we need to have, be abundantly, God be thanked, provided for us. Now we must provide victual for our voyage, both for ourselves and for our beasts; and that no less than for twenty days. I accounting, perceive that we shall have a journey of fifteen days, in the which we shall find no victual, for all is wasted, partly of us, partly of our enemies so much as they could. Therefore sufficient meat must be provided, for without it, we can neither fight nor live. And as for wine, let every man have so much as may suffice, accustoming ourselves to drink of water, because much of our journey lacketh wine, and though we could provide very much of it, yet it should not suffice. Therefore that we for lack of wine, do not fall into sudden diseases thus must we do. Let us straight away begin to drink water with our meat, which thing now doing, it shall be no great alteration. For he that eateth meal cakes, eateth dough mixed in eater. And he that eateth bread, eateth it tempered with water. And all boiled meat, is dressed commonly with much water. Then after meat if we drink wine, nature being well contented, shall rest. And yet we must leave that after meat, till we have learned to drink water. For mutation by little and little, causeth nature to abide every change, and God teacheth us the same, drawing us by little and little from cold to endure vehement heat, and from heat, to vehement cold. Whom we following, must accustom to assay the way, before that we may come to our purpose.

"As for the burden of your bedding, bestow it upon necessary victual; for excess of victual, shall not be unprofitable. And though you lack bedding, fear you not but that you shall sleep sweetly, if you do not, then blame me. As for garments, the more plenty that a man hath present, the more shall he help both the whole and sick. And we must provide such victual, as is for the most part, sharp, tart, and salt, for such both be good meat, and of long continuance. When we become to plentiful places, whereas it is like, we may get coin, there must we prepare bakehouses, to bake us bread, and the instruments of baking be but light.

"We must also prepare such things, as sick men shall have need of, for the burden of them is very little, but if there shall happen any such chance, great shall be our lack. We must have also collars, for they be much occupied, both in horse and men; which being worn and rent, must needs cause tarriance, except a man have other bindings. And if any man hath learned to plane a spear, he must not forget a chipaxe, and it is also good to have with him a file, for he that sharpeth a spear's head, he also sharpeth his heart. For a certain shame cometh to him which sharpeth his spear, and is himself a coward.

"We must also have very much timber, both for chariots and wagons, for in many affairs, many things of necessity shall be painful and onerous. And we must have also necessary instruments, for all these things, for craftsmen are not to be had in every place. But to do as chances shall require, a few and they not very cunning, shall suffice. We must also have in every chariot a pickaxe and a fork, and on every bearing beast, a basket and an hook: for these be necessary for every man his private use, and also many times profitable for common causes.

"And what need is of necessary victuals, you the leaders of harness men, inquire of the soldiers that be about you. For it must be regarded that they lack not, for we shall have need of them. The drawing beasts which I command to have, you captains of the carriage, fetch and provide. And him that lacketh compel you to prepare. You also captains of the forward, you have set out by me whom I have rejected both of darters, archers, and slingers. They that be darters in this soldierfare, must be compelled to have an ax to chop wood. They that be archers, a fork. They that be slingers, a pickaxe. They which have these things must go before the wagons as wings, that if need be to make way, you may readily perform the same. And that I lacking anything may see where to provide and use the same. I will also have of meet age for war, blacksmiths, carpenters, and shoemakers with their instruments, that if anything requireth their art in the army, we shall not lack the same. And they shall be dismissed from the trade of soldier, and doing service in their craft, to him that requireth for money, they shall have their appointed place.

"And if any merchant will follow for to sell anything, let him have victual for the days tofore spoken, if he be taken selling otherwise, he shall be spoiled of all. But when those days be expired, then he may sell what he will. And what merchant, we shall know to bring most victual, he shall be rewarded and advanced both of me and my confederates. And if any thinketh he shall need money for his occupying, let him bring such as will depose for him, and be his surety that he shall follow the host, and he shall have part of our treasure.

"Thus I have pronounced my mind in these things. If any man perceiveth any other thing to be needful, let him make declaration to me. And go you forth to make preparation. I will make sacrifice for our setting forward. And when our sacrifices shall be well finished, we shall signify unto you. And let every man be present with these things tofore rehearsed, at a place appointed, with their captains, you the captains every man his men being set in array, shall all come to me, that every one may know his several place.

"They hearing these things, prepared themselves. He made sacrifice, which being lucky, he marched forward with his army, and the first day encamped so nigh as he could, that if any man had forgotten anything, he might go for it, and if any man knew any thing to be wanted, he might prepare it. Cyaxares with the third part of the Medeans abode at home, that the country should not be destitute of help. Cyrus set forward so speedily as he could. The horsemen being in the forward, sending afore them outriders and espies, to have through knowledge of former places, next then he placed the carriage, and where it was plain ground, he made many several bends of wagons and carriage. In the reward the footmen's host followed. If any the carriage were left behind, such captains as chanced to be there, did see that they were not stopped in their voyage. Where the way was straight, the carriage being divided, harnessed soldiers went on either sides of it. And if any thing did stop, such soldiers as were appointed, did see remedy for it. And every hundred for the most part, went with their carriage by them for it was commanded that all the carriage should go every one next his crew, except some necessary chance did let them. And every burden bearer had a token of a captain, and did go first, that the thing might be evident to them of his hundred. In so much as they went round together, and every man very circumspect to his own things, that he left none behind. And thus doing, they needed not to inquire one of another. For every thing was in more safety, and things necessary more ready at hand, throughout the whole host.

The espies going forward, thought they saw men gathering forage and wood, and they did see other beasts drawing such matter, and feeding. And looking further, they thought to espy a smoke or dust araised, of all the which they did gather, that their adversary's army was at hand. Wherefore the captain of the espies, sent one in haste to declare the same to Cyrus. Who hearing of it, commanded them to abide in the same places, signifying to him, when they saw any new things. And did send a troop of horsemen to outride, commanding them to do their endeavors, to take some of the men, that were in the plain, that he thereby might have some certain knowledge. They did as they were commanded; he separated another crew of his men, to provide such things as he though should need before they did join. And first he willed them to dine, then to remain in their array, foreseeing to things commmanded. After dinner he called the chief of horsemen, footmen and chariots, and the captains of the engines, carriage and wagons, and there came together. They that did course the plains, brought certain men that they had taken; who being demanded of Cyrus said that they went before the camp, and came beyond the scoutwatch, to provide forage and fuel. For by reason of the multitude, all things were very scarce.

Cyrus hearing this, asked how far off the army was. They answered two Assyrian miles. Then Cyrus thus demanded: "Is there any talk of us among them?" "Yea, surely," said they, "and that very much, of your nigh approachment." "And be they glad to hear it?" said Cyrus. Thus he asked, because of them that were present. "No surely," said they, "they be not glad, but rather very sad." "And what are they now doing?" said he. "They do array themselves," said they, "and so have done these three days." "Who doth embattle them?" quoth Cyrus. "Croesus himself," said they, "with another Grecian, and one Medean which as they say, fled from you." "O immortal Jupiter," said Cyrus, "that I might take him as I would." Then he commanded the captives to be had away, and rose as though he would say somewhat to them that were present.

In the mean time came another from the captain of the espies, saying that a great troop of horsemen did appear in the plain, and "we think," quoth he, " that they be sent to view your army, and before this troop, there be thirty other horsemen riding together, which if they could, would peradventure take us, being espies, and we but ten in this mission." Then Cyrus commanded the horsemen which were always attendant upon him, to ride to the post, being quiet and secret from their enemies. "And when," quoth he, "our men leave their espiall, arise you, and resist the pursuers of our espies. And that you may not be oppressed with the great troop, go you Hystaspas with a thousand horsmen and show yourself against our enemy's troop, and see you do not pursue them in any covert, but providing that your espies may keep their place, go forth. And if any declaring token of love, come unto you, receive them gently." Hystaspas departed, and armed himself, the others went forth as they were commanded.

And Araspas with his servants being come with in the mission, chanced to meet with him, who was afore sent as an espye, being keeper of the woman of Susa. Cyrus hearing of it, leaped from his chair, and running to him, did lovingly embrace him. Others not knowing the thing, were much amazed at the matter, until Cyrus said, "Loving friends, this man most truly is come unto us. Therefore it is convenient, that all men should know what he hath done: he neither disdained with any offense, nor afraid of any punishment, did depart, but was sent of me, that knowing our enemy's secrets, he might reveal the same to us, Therefore, the promise that I have made unto you Araspas, I do remember, and I with all these, will perform it. It is meet friends, that you also honorably do entertain this honest man, for he for our weal hath adventured himself, and sustained the infamy of an odious crime." Then they all did embrace Araspas, taking him by the hands.

Cyrus said, "Enough of this. Now what the time requiteth we should know, that Araspas, declare, diminishing nothing of the truth, nor impairing our enemy's puissance, for it is better that we thinking it more, should find it less, than hearing it less, should find it more." Araspas answered, "That I might know the more certainly their power, I was one that did appoint their array." Then said Cyrus, you do not only know their number, but also their order." "Yea, surely," said Araspas, " and how they intend to make their fight." "But first," said Cyrus, "declare us briefly their number." "They be all appointed thirty a rank, both foot and horsemen, except the Egyptians which be separated, as it were forty furlong off. For I was very diligent to know how much ground they did contain." "Then show," said Cyrus, "how the Egyptians be appointed, because you did except them." "The captains of very ten thousand divide the thousand into several hundreds, for this form of array, is their country fashion. And Croesus was very loath to grant them this array, for he did covet to exceed your army in the main battle of footmen." "Why should he covet that?" said Cyrus. "Because," quoth he, "he might envision you with the greater multitude."

"But they should first know," quoth Cyrus, "whether they could enclose other as they intended. But we have heard of you, what we for the time needed to learn. You therefore, friends, must work accordingly. Therefore departing hence, look well to the armor both of your horses and yourselves, for many times the want of a trifling thing, doth make both man, horse, and chariot to be unprofitable. In the morning early when I have made sacrifices, I will that both horse and man be refreshed, that when the time shall require, the travel of both neither shall for lack of good be insufficient. And you Araspas, shall guide the right wing as you are appointed. And you the other captains of ten thousand, continue as you be already placed, for when the fight shall join, it shall be no time to change horses from one chariot to another. And enjoin the centurans and bandleaders to be placed in the man battle, every band being divided in two parts. And a band did contain four and twenty men. Then one of the captains of ten thousand said, "Do you think, Cyrus, that we being thus appointed, shall be able to match with so main a battle, being so many a rank?"

Cyrus said, "When the battles be so thronged together that they cannot conveniently encounter with their enemies, do you think that they shall do their enemies hurt or confederates good? I rather would that for every hundred, ten thousand were set in a rank for so should we fight with the fewer. I will appoint my main battle, that the same, I think in every part, shall avail and defense itself. I will place the darter, next the curette men. After darters, the archers, for these may not be placed first, which themselves confess, that they can endure no fight at hand. But being forefenced with curetines, they do endure. And some darting, some shooting before all the rest, may annoy their enemies. And when a man doeth endamage his adversaries, it is evident by the same, that he doth relieve his friends. Also I will place hindermost, such as be called sure behind. For as there is no profit in an house, without strong building of stones, and wise workers of the roof, even so there is no profit in an army, except both the first and the last be good and forward men. Therefore do you order yourselves as I do proscribe, you captains of the tergate men, place your bands after this sort. And you captains of the archers next the tergat men, likewise. And you which are captans of them in the rearward, command that every man have eye to other, encouraging them that do their duties and menacing them that be slow in the same. And if any man would shrink and be traitorous, let him be punished with death. They which be foremost, must embold the followers by word and deed. And you which be placed after all, must cause that cowards be more in fear of you, than of our enemies.

"And thus do you: You Abradatas being master of the ordinance, so do that the teams and carriers of the towers may follow immediately next the main battle. And you Daochus, being captain of the carriage, next the towers, conduct all that part of the army. And let your officers sharply chastise them, which go or tarry out of time. And you Carabucus, being captain of the chaiots that carrieth the woman, appoint the same last next the carriage, for all these things following, shall both cause opinion of multitude, and also be apt matter for us to work policies. And our enemies if they will enclose us, shall be enforced to fetch the greater compass. And the more ground that they compass, the weaker must they needs be: you therefore thus do. And you Artabasus and Artagersas, have each your thousand footmen with us next these. And you Pharuncus and Asiadatas, do intermedle neither of your thousand horsemen in the main legion, but behind the chariots severally appoint your army, and then repair to us, with the other captains, for you must so appoint yourself, as you may fight with the first. And you which are captains of the men on camels, place them behind the cars, and Artagersas shall appoint: you that be elected leaders of the chariots, let the chief of you be placed with his chariots, before the main battle. Every other hundred chariots, one warding the right side of the army, shall follow the legion, on the wing, and another the left side." Thus Cyrus did embattle them.

Abradatas the Susian king, said, "I promise you Cyrus, I would be right willing to be placed against the face of the contrary battle, except it seeeth otherwise to you." Cyrus rejoicing and commanding him, demanded of the Persians being in other chariots, if they could suffer the same. Whom answered that it should be their dishonesty to grant it. Wherefore he caused them to cast lots. And the lot fell on Abradatas, according to his request, and was placed against the Egyptians. Then they departing and providing the tofore said things, went to supper. Then watch and ward being apppointed, they took their rest.

The next day early Cyrus did make sacrifice. The residue of the army dining and making oblations, did harness themselves with many and goodly cote armors, with many and goodly helmets and breastplates. They did also harness their horses with shaffons and cremets and barbed as well their coursing horses, as them that did draw the chariots. Insomuch as the whole army did glitter with harness, and shine with orient color. And Abradatas' chariot with four teams and eight horses, was wondrous brave and martial. And he being about to put on a put on a breastplate after his country fashion, his wife Pantheia brought him an helmet and vambrances of gold, large bracelets about the joints of his hands. And a purple gown down to the foot, after robe, sarion, and a scarlet crest. This had she privily wrought for her husband, knowing the measure of his harness. He marvelled to see it, and asked of Pantheia: "Wife, have not you defaced your jewels in making me this armor?" "Truly," said Pantheia, "I have a more precious jewel yet, for if you appear to others as you sem to me, you shall be my most sovereign jewel." Thus speaking, she did enarm him and would no man should have seen her, for the tears did distill upon her cheeks.

Abradatas being in the front of the army, a goodly man to see, now harnessed with this armor, seemed a most galiard and clear gentleman, his nature being correspondant to the same.

Then taking the reins of the chariot governor, he prepared to ascend into the chariot. Then Pantheia all others being commanded to stand back, said, "Truly Abradatas, if any other do more esteem her husband, then her own life, I think you know, that I am one of them. Therefore what need I to rehearse every thing severally, for my faces I think persuade you more than my words. And thus endeavoring myself toward you, as you know I profess to by love toward you, and yours to me, that I had rather be buried quick together in the earth with you being a noble man, than live in villany. Thus I esteem you with the best, and myself not with the worst. And I know that we owe great thanks to Cyrus, which deigned to entertain me being a captive, and chosen for him, not as a thrall with villany, nor free with the disparagement of mine honor, but kept me as I had been his brother's wife. After that Araspas departed from him, which had the keeping of me, I promised him, that if he would suffer me so send unto you, that you should become more loyal and assured to him than ever Araspas was."

Thus she said. Abradatas being delighted with her, and tenderly touching her head, looking up to heaven, made this prayer: "O mighty Jupiter, grant me to appear an husband meet for Pantheia, and a friend worthy Cyrus, who hath so honorably dealt with us." Thus speaking at the entering of the chariot seat, he went up to the same. He being ascended, and the governor making fast the seat, Pantheia having none other thing to embrace, did kiss the chariot seat. And he went forth. Pantheia followed him privily, till he turned and espied her, and said, "Be of good comfort, Pantheia, farewell and now depart." Then her eunuchs and women conveyed her to her own chariot, and so bestowed her, that she was covered with a curtain. Other men, although Abradatas and his chariot, was goodly to behold, yet they could not behold him, till Pantheia was past.

When Cyrus had made oblation, and the army was furnished according to his commandment, appointing espies one before another. He assembled the captains and said thus:

The Oration of Cyrus

"Dear friends and confederates, God hath expressed in our sacrifices, the same tokens, as they did, when they gave us our former victory. I would you should record things which I think if you remember, you shall the more couragiously go to the battle. You have been exercised in martial prowess much more than your enemies; you have excelled one another; your enemies have impaired one another. Of both parties there be that have not fought. They that leans to our enemies, know that their chief captains will soon think: you that be with us, know that with willing confederates, you adventure to fight. And it is like that they which trust one another, will abide and fight with one accord. They which be in distrust, must needs devise, which of them soonest may escape. Then, friends, let us go against our enemies, having harnessed chariots against our enemy's unharnessed; and likewise being harnessed both horse and man, let us fight with them unharnessed. And with such footmen you shall fight, as you did tofore. For the Egyptians have like harness and keep like array. And shields they have greater than they either can do or see anything. And being disposed into hundreds, it is evident, that one shall hinder another, except very few. And if they think by the throngs to oppress us, we must first resist them with horses, and the weapon of defensed horses. And if any of them abide by it, how can he fight at once with our horsemen, with or footmen, and our turrets? For they in the turrets shall defend us, and so hurt our enemies, that they leaving fighting, shall not know what to do. And if you want anything, declare it unto me, and with God's help, we shall lack nothing. If any man will say ought, let him speak his mind, if not, returning to sacrificing and prayer, to God, to whom we have already sacrificed, repair unto you men, every man so exhorting his, as I have you. And let everyone declare to his men, that he is worthy to be a ruler, expressing himself to be manly, both in behavior, countenance, and words."

The Seventh Book of the School
of Cyrus' institution, containing
the overthrow of Croesus, the
taking of Sardis and Babylon,
and the beginning of Cyrus'
civil regiment.

Having made their prayers to God, they went to their ensign, and for Cyrus and his company meat and drink was brought, they being yet about the sacrifice; he standing still as he was, made a small repast, and always gave to him that wanted. Then the prayers and ceremonies of tasting made, he drank, and so did they that were with him. This done, beseeching Jupiter to be companion and guide, he mounted on horseback, and commanded the others to do the same, being all armed as he was, with coats of purple, corselets of brass, headpieces with white crests, sword and spear, and dart; this only difference was, that their armor shone like gold, and his glittering like glass; and the horses were likewise barbed with brass. Being on horseback, and musing which way to take, it thundered on the right side; at which as a lucky token, he said, "We follow the most mighty Jupiter," and so marched, having on the right hand Chrysantas, and the horsemen; on the left hand Arsamas and the footmen: commanding to have good eye to the ensign, and to follow in order. The ensign was an Eagle of gold, displayed up on a long spear, and this standard do remain with the king of Persia; his army rested thrice, before he had sight of the enemies.

Then having gone two miles and a half, they began to see their enemy's camp, which they perceived to be much greater than theirs, and saw how they stayed their main battle to fetch a compass and enclose them. Cyrus seeing this, stayed never the more, but went on; and considering how much they did stretch alength the wings of the battle, he said, "Do you mark, Chrysantas, what a compass our enemies make?" "Yea," quoth Chrysantas, "and I much marvel, for me think they draw their wings too far from the battle." "Yea, and from ours too," quoth Cyrus. "And why do they so?" quoth he. "Because," quoth Cyrus, "they fear we would give the onset ontheir battle, they being so far from it." "And how can they help one another, being so far asunder?" quoth Chrysantas. "Their purpose is," quoth Cyrus, "so much to environ us, as they may in all places give us the onset at once." "And do they well?" quoth he. "For some part they do well, for some, evil," quoth Cyrus.

Then he commanded Arsamas to lead the footmen softly, and Chrysantas to follow with the horsemen in order, and that he would go see where were best to begin the battle, and consider for all the army; and when he had found the place, he would sing a song of praise, which he willed them to follow; because of the noise and escries that should be made at the giving of the onset, which should be, when Abradatas did enter with his chariots, whom he commanded the rest to follow, that they might assail the enemies being in disorder, and that he would not be long from them. This said, he gave the privy word, that was, Jupiter favor and guide, and marched, going betwixt the Chariots and the pickmen, and spake to them all according to their quality. To some he would say, "It doeth me good to see your faces;" to some, "Remember, this day's fight is not only for the time present, but for the victories past, and the felicities to come." To some, "From hence forth we can have no cause to blame God, having given us so great advantage, but we must be valiant men." To some, "How could we ever exhort one another to more profit than now? For it we do well, we may greatly help ourselves." To some, "You be not ignorant what rewards be propounded; to them that conquer, glory, praise, advantage, freedom and rule; to them that be conquered, the contrary. Therefore, he that loveth himself, let him do as I shall, for I will give none example of cowardice." To them that had be proved before, he said, "What day the valiant men have in battle, and what the cowards?"

Then going toward Abradatas, who seeing him, left his chariot, and came running to him, and so likewise the other, that had charge of the chariots, to whom Cyrus said, "The immortal God hath given you your request, that is, to have the forward; you must remember to do well, for the Persians shall behold you, we shall follow you, and not suffer you to be succorless." To whom Abradatas answered, that for his part he was well enough, but for the sides of the host, he stood in doubt, seeing the enemies defensed with all kind of strength, and they only with his chariots. Insomuch as if he had not taken the charge upon him, he would have been ashamed of it, considering the danger of the rest, and safety of himself. "Well," quoth Cyrus, "if you be well yourself, for the rest take not thought. For I trust with God's help to order the matter so as you shall give the onset when they shall flee; and then think me to be at hand, and set upon your enemies." Thus he said with lusty words, being otherwise no great bragger, and then he said he should have the enemy coward, and the friend valiant. And whiles he had leisure, he should exhort his men to be of good courage; and that they might do it the better, to set a contention among them. For by that, every man would endeavor to do better than his fellow, and all affirm, that nothing is so available as virtue. Abradatas departed, and did accordingly.

Cyrus went to the left wing, where Hystaspas was with half the Persian horsemen Whom calling by name, he said, "O Hystaspas, now you see we need your quickness, for if we can get the advantage of our enemies, we shall without danger of ourselves overthrow them." To whom Hystaspas smiling, said, "Let me alone with them that be in the front; as for the sides, give the charge to other." "I will myself do it," quoth Cyrus, "and which of us honest by gods help have the victory, let him come to that place where most danger is."

Then coming to the carts, he spake with the captains of the same, saying, he was come to succor them. And when they shoud hear that he had given the charge, they should do there devor, because they should fight more in safety without at the side, than being within at the front. Then he commanded Pharnucus and Artagecia, that with a thousand footmen and as many Persian horsemen, they shoud set upon their enemies, when they saw him enter the right wing, and force themselves to break the ray, which they might well do, being strong and on horseback, and the enemy's fresh men in the rearward, against whom they should set their camels, and be assured that before they came to the stripes, they should condemn their enemies. Cyrus having spoken thus, went the the right wing.

Croesus supposing to be nigh enough, gaven token that they should no more go forward, but turn against the enemies, and gave the sign to battle, and at once broke in at three places, the front, and both sides, at the which Cyrus' host was in great fear; and as a little stone is enclosed in a great circle, even so was Cyrus army, with all generation of enemies, the hindermost band only except. Which thing Cyrus hearing, gave token that they should join to the enemies, a great silence being among them because of the peril that was present. Therefore he began the song of praise, the which the whole army followed. then they crying to the martial God Mars with the men of arms, he gave the charge upon the wing, which by the might of the battle that followed, was soon sparpled.

Artagerias perceiving that Cyrus had given the onset, with the Camels set upon the right wing, according to Cyrus' commandment. The horses could not abide the camels a great way off, but, as their nature is, so rove as they felt them, turned back, leaping and flinging here and there over all the fields. But Artagersas keeping order, was continually at their backs, and with good courage troubled them on both sides with his cars, insomuch, as some flying them, were dispatched of the horsemen that followed; some avoiding the horsemen, were killed with the cars.

Abradatas, without envy longer tarrying, came on, crying with loud voice, "O friends, follow me, and with his spurs took up his horse, and broke in with the rest of the chariots, and went to far, that he came to the Egyptian band, and a small company of his trusty friends with him. Where by it was evident, that as in many other places, no battle is so strong as a band of faithful friends; so that day it was proved by him and his assured friends, who never shrank from him, but were always about him without fear. The other chariotmen, seeing the Egyptian battle so strong, withdrew themselves and forsook him. He and his little company not being able to break the Egyptian battle, with extreme violence beat some down, and caused some to retire, whom with their hooked carts they broke apieces, both horses and man, and everything. Abradatas in this wonderful revolution and tempest of war, passing with his car over the heaps of so many dead bodies, fell from his cart to the ground, and so did the rest of his companions, who freely fighting as was meet for noblemen, died most valiantly.

The Persians seeing this danger of Abradatas, came whole together and broke upon them that had slain him, and slew many of them, notwithstanding the Egyptians did valiantly, being many in number, and well armed with strong and large pikes, and shields bigger than the Persian tergats that covered their whole bodies; being also good to punch at hand. And so fiercely coming on, that the Persians gave back, still fighting till they came to their towered chariots, with which the Egyptians were afresh so handled, that there began a new fight, cruel to behold, with the murder of so many men, with the noise of so many cries, and fall of so many weapons, as was pity to hear.

Cyrus being come, and seeing the Persians put back, was grieved and perceiving none other way to win, but by coming upon them at the back, with his hand he gave a turn, and unlooked for came upon them behind, and did so much harm as the poor Egyptians, amidst the wounds and blows, were fain to turn back to back, to resist their enemy; and with a cry that enemies were on their back, they fought so manfully, that Cyrus himself was unhorsed, his horse being wounded in the belly with a sword, at the grief thereof being in a rage, fell and threw Cyrus to the ground.

There might a man have seen, how worthy a thing it is for a prince to be beloved of his subjects, for by and by, making a great shout altogether, manly fighting for to save Cyrus. After much murder on both parts, one alighted off his horse, and set Cyrus on the same, who seeing the Persian hands of Hystaspas and Chrysantas to be come, and the Egyptians beaten down on every side, he went up to one of the chariot towers, where he saw all the enemies flying away on every side, saving only the Egyptians, who, being determined to die in the place, covered themselves with their shields, and resisted to the death.

Wherefore marvelling at their virtue, and pitying their calamity, commanded them that fought against them, to withdraw, and set a trumpet unto them, demanding whether they had rather die for them that had forsaken them, for be saved of him, and be reputed valiant men. The Egyptians said, "How can we be saved, and reputed valiant?" Cyrus answered, "Because we see you only remain and fight." Then the Egyptians, "And what honesty shall it be to us to be saved?" And Cyrus, "In that you do not betray your friends, but yield to us, that rather seek your life than death." The Egyptians asked, "If we become your friends, what service will you have of us?" And he said, "To be his true liege men, and receive benefit." "And what benefit?" quoth they. "In giving you," quoth Cyrus, "greater stipend than you now have for the time of war; and in peace, if you will remain with me, I will give you land and cities to inhabit." Then the Egyptians desired they might not be compelled to fight against Croesus, and to the rest they consented and gave their faith; and remained ever after trusty people, and have given them two cities beyond the Cyme at the sea coast, Larissa and Cyllene, which be still possessed of their offspring, and called the Egyptians' cities. In this fight, the Egyptians had the price of the Assyrians; of Cyrus' camp, the Persian horsemen; whereby the duty of the service remaineth in price with the Persians. The hooked carts were also much praised, and remaineth also in estimation. But as for the camels, because they did only frighten horses, and did none other hurt, and no gentle man used to keep any for to ride, they were restored to their kind and used only for burden.

After this victory, Cyrus hearing that Croesus was fled to Sardis, and the other nations gone as far as they could, he took his viage toward Sardis, where being arrived, encamped and set his artillery against the town, and the night following, with the Caldes and Persians, by the help of a Persian slave, servant to a captain of the castle, knowing a way through the gate, he got the fortress. Which thing being known, the Lidians forsook the wales. Cyrus abiding till day, entered with the rest of his army, commanding every man to keep array.

Croesus was fled into the palace, and cried for Cyrus. He leaving a guard about him, went to see the castle, which the Persians kept; and seeing the harness of the Caldeans being on the ground, they being gone to sack the town, he called their captains to him, commanding them to depart the army; for he in no wise would that they had broken order and been disobedient, should get the spoil from them that were obedient and in order, and that he had proposed to make them notable above all the Caldeans, which they through their greediness, had lost. The Caldeans were in great fear, and besought him to cease his anger, and that they would render every thing. He answered, he had not need of them, but if they would have his favor, they should deliver to the Persians the things that they had got. For thereby his army should be made the more obedient. The Caldeans did accordingly.

When Cyrus had set things in order, he commanded Croesus to be brought before him, to whom Croesus said, "All hail, my Lord, fortune having granted you so to be." "And you also," quoth Cyrus, "for we both be men." Then Cyrus asked him, if he would give him any counsel. Croesus answered, with all his heart, if it might be good counsel, for it should be good for himself also. "Then," quoth Cyrus, "you shall understand, that whereas my soldiers have taken great pains in my service, and I hitherto not rewarded them it seemeth a thing of congruence, that I should give them this city to be sacked, which next Babylon, is the most rich in Asia, loath I were to have them disobedient, and sorry to see so noble a city sacked." Croesus thus answeed, "Give me leave to say to the Lidians that I have obtained of you , that the city shall not be spoiled, neither women nor children hindered, and that they for this benefit, shall present to you the chief jewel that they have, and so shall you have riches infinite, and the city still in good case; whereas if you sack it, you shall destroy all arts and sciences, which be fountains of all good things, and when this is done, you may consult fo the sack hereafter. And as for my treasure, send your officers, and let them take possession of it." Cyrus liked his advice, and followed the same.

Then Cyrus willed him to tell what answers he had of Apollo and Delphos, because he had great affiance in them, and was in great credit with Apollo. "I would it had been so," quoth Croesus, "but it came other wise to pass." "And how?" quoth Cyrus, "for me think you speak strangely." "When I came first to Apollo, I did but to prove him. And not only God, but man also cannot abide to be discredited; wherefore when I sent unto him concerning my sons, he would give me none answer. But after I had pleased him with gifts of gold and silver, and purging myself of my former mistrust, he said I should have children, and it was true, but without any consolation to me, for the one died in the flower of his age, and the other never spoke. Being oppressed with the calamity of this misfortune, I sent again to him, to know how I might live the rest of my life in felicity. He answered: 'If I knew myself, I should live happily.' By which answer I was greatly comforted, thinking it to be an easy matter for a man to know himself, but to know another man I thought it an hard thing, and so I lived without mischance till this time. Then being persuaded by the Assyrian to come against you in camp, I fell into all kind of peril, and yet am saved, I cannot tell how, without any evil, and cannot be angry with God. For knowing myself to be weak to meddle with you, I went my way and had no hurt, but now wearing proud by my riches, and being allured by the persuasions of them that comforted me to take the matter in hand, affirming that I should be lord of all, and they my subjects, I took it upon me, not knowing myself, in that I did not consider how far unlike I was to march with you being of the line of God, and of most noble virtues, whereas the first of my ancestors was at one time made a king and a freeman; wherefore of right and skill I am for my ignorance punished, and now I know myself indeed, and confess the answer of Apollo to be true, humbly beseeching you to have pity upon me, for only you may make me happy."

Cyrus answered, that he himself knew best what was to do, and that for his part, he was sorry for his misfortunes. And in some recompense he restored him his wife, children and familiar friends, and only forbade him the use of arms. Croesus answered, if he did so, he should make him have that happy life, that he was wont to attribute to others. "And who be they?" quoth Cyrus. "My wife," quoth Croesus, "who being in continual pleasures and delicacies with me, doth not taste the cares that I find in war and other governments, but I, hereafter shall life as she doth, through your benefit; and therefore and bound once again to give great thanks to Apollo." Cyrus, hearing his talk, much marvelled at his modesty, and from that time forth, had him always with him, either for to have profit by him, or to be the more in safety for him.

The day following, he gave the money to some to keep, and appointed some to take the treasures that Croesus should deliver them, and give the clergy to offer as much as they would desire, and lay up the rest in his coffers, and appoint wagons to bear it from place to place, that they might have the use thereof at their need. This being done, Cyrus asked when any of them saw Abradatas, marvelling that he had no sight of him, being wont most diligently to report unto him. One of the servants answered, that he was slain, valiantly fighting with the Egyptians; and how he was forsaken of themost part of his men, and that his wife had taken him into her chariot, and brought him to the flood Pactolus, accompanied with her maid and eunuchs, being about to make a grave to bury him there, his wife sitting on the ground dressing the dead body, having his head in her lap.

Which when Cyrus heard, he struck his thigh, and by and by mounted on horseback, and took with him a thousand horses, commanding Gobrias and Gadatas, that they should prepare so rich ornaments as they could get to honor the body of so worthy a friend, and provide herds of cattle to sacrifice at his funeral. Being come where he saw the sorrowful wife sit by the corpse of her noble husband, he wept and said, "O faithful and good heart, wherefore hast thou forsaken us?" and took him by the right hand, which being cut off of the Egyptians, dissevered from the body, whereat he was much more grieved.

The wife shrieked pitifully, and took the hand of Cyrus, kissed it, and set it again in the place, saying, "The rest of his body is in like case, but to what purpose should I show it to you? And this hath he done and suffered, as well for your sake as for mine. For I always comforted him to do so valiantly, as he might appears a worthy friend for you. And hath done no less, not to obey me, but to serve you. And he now is dead, and I that was occasion thereof, am alive." At the which words Cyrus not being able to keep him from weeping, after a certain space, when he could speak, said, "O Pantheia, your husband being victoriously dead, hath gotten an immortal name. And now you shall take these ornaments for his funeral, which Gobrias and Gadatas have brought; and I promise you, that in other things, nothing shall be wanted to do him honor, for every one of us shall leave some monument in his memory. And as for yourself, you shall not be abandoned, for I will honor your wifely chastity and virtue, and bestow you upon whom you request me."

Pantheia answered, "I will not hide from you, upon whom I will be bestowed." This being spoken, Cyrus went his way, having pity of the woman that was bereft of such a man; and the man, that should no more see such a wife. Then she commanded her eunuchs to depart, that she might bewail her fill; and had her nurse abide, and when she was dead to fold her and her husband in one cloth. The nurse besought her, not to commit any such folly, but when she saw that would not prevail, she sat her down and wept. Then Pantheia took a sword that she had prepared for the purpose, and killed herself, and reposing her head upon her husband's breast, she did. The nurse cried out, and wrapped them together as she was commanded.

Cyrus hearing of the woman's act, returned with speed, to see if there were any hope of life. The three eunuchs, knowing their lady to be dead, drew their swords, and killed themselves. And there was made a monument for them all, that remaineth to this day; and letters in the Syrian tongue set upon the high pillars and the statues of Abradatas and Pantheia. Cyrus hearing no remedy, marvelled at the stoutness of the woman, and weeping at her calamity, departed, and caused sepulchres to be made according to every man's degree, with letters on the lower pillars, of them that bare the sceptors.

In this mean time a discord arose between the Carians, being a civil debate, and keeping the forts of the countries, and both parts called to Cyrus for aid, who being at Sardis about artillery to batter the walls of them that would not obey, sent Cadusius a Persian, a man skillful in war, and of great humanity, with an army appointed unto him, with whom the Cilicians and Cyprians went on their voluntary will, wherefore he never sent Persian governor over them, but suffered their natural kings to rule, and pay him a tribute, and find him men at his need. Cadusius came into Caria, and both parts came unto him, promising to receive him into their town, if he would be enemy to the enemies. Who answered that either parts had reason to lament of their adversary, and that they should so order the matter, as the adversaries should not know that they had conference with him, that the devise might have the better effect Then they gave their faith on both sides, the Carians, to receive him without fraud to the weal of Cyrus and the Persians, and he to enter without guile for the weal of them that received him. Thus devisng with both parts, he, that same night entered their castles and forts.

That done, the day following, he called both parts before him, thinking themselves deceived, and thus said, "O Carians, I did swear to enter into the weal of them that should resent me, now if I should destroy you both, I think I should be entered to both your hindrance, but if I make peace, and cause you to till your land, I think I am entered to both your profits; therefore from this day forth, you shall have friendly conversation together, you shall without fear labor your lands, you shall make parentages and matrimonies, and if any of you goeth about any injury, Cyrus and we shall be his adversary." From that day forth, the ports were opened, the ways full of people, the fields full of laborers, feastful days celebrated, and all things with peace and joy replenished. In this time, messengers came from Cyrus, demanding if he had need of any army or artillery. Cadusius answered, that he might spare his own army. And having finished those things, he left garrisons in the forts, and departed with his army. The Carians besought him to tarry, which refusing it, sent to Cyrus, requesting him, if he did appoint them any governor, it might be Cadusius.

At this time Cyrus sent Hystaspas with an army against Phrygia, that joineth with Hellespont, and willed Cadius to accompany him, that they might the rather obey Hystaspas. The Grecians that inhabit the sea, gave many gifts, and agreed to go where Cyrus should appoint, to pay tribute, and receive no barbarian soldiers into their towns. The king of the Phyrygians prepared himself to stand at his defense, but being abandoned of his captains, he rendered himself to be judged as Cyrus would. Hystaspas left many garrisons and departed, taking away with him many Phrygian horsemen. Cyrus gave comission to Cadusius, that he should suffer those Phrygians to bear armor, that had been obedient; the others he should spoil of their horse and harness, and make them slingers.

This done, Cyrus leaving great garrisons in Sardis, he removed his camp toward Babylon, having many carts of treasure and Croesus in his company, who had the just account of the treasure, and gave the same in writing to Cyrus, that he migh know who did faithfully, and who no. Cyrus took the writings, and said to Croesus, he had done very warely notwithstanding they that did take any of the money should take their own, for he had it for the use of all, and gave the bills to his friends, that they might know who did well, and who not. The Lidians that went willingly with him, he received them in the army; they that did the contrary, he took their horses from them, and gave them to the Persians, and burned their harness, and compelled them to bear slings, which is esteemed most vile service. But yet with other company, they do good, whereas being alone, they be worth nothing.

In his trip to Babylon, he subdued great Phrygia, Cappadocia and Arabia, and increased his camp forty thousand men, and gave many horses to his confederates. So he arrived at Babylon with an huge puissant army, and environed the city with his army, he with certain horsemen viewing the city about, and having considered the walls, he intended to withdraw the army, when a runaway of the city came and told him, that they within would set upon him if he returned, for they thought his battle very small, and it was not marvel, because the compass was so great, the host seemed very little.

Which Cyrus hearing, commanded the soldiers that were about the walls, and seemed very weak, because of the length, to return into their places, and both ends to repair to him that was in the middest, and by doubling their ranks, they that went were the bolder, and they that stood, the less in fear, and so united, approached the walls within a bowshot, and went with courage, beholding their enemies the best being on both sides, and the worst in the midst, which order is best to fight and worst to flee. And so they retired at their pleasure without damage of the enemy, and camped about the city.

When they had well considered the same, then he called the captain and principal men of the army, and said, "Companions, having considered the quality of this city, I cannot see how it can be got by force, the walls being so strong and high, but by seige, I think it the more sure and easy way to win it, there as be so many forts of men, the shall the sooner be oppressed with hunger; therefore they must either fight it out, which thing we desire, or perish by famine, which I think will prove. This is mine advice, if any of you can show me better way, I will follow it. If not, I will begin the seige."

Chrysantas answered that it was best so to do, because the city was not only strong by the walls but also by the flood Euphrates that ran through the midst of the city, and was a quarter of a mile broad, and two men's height deep. Which opinion Gobryas confirmed, being practiced in the city. Then Cyrus made a great trench and deep for the more safety of his host, and with good measure of the ground, left so much space as might serve to build a tower, compassing the city with a great ditch, and did cast the earth toward his camp, and erected towers over the flood, of an acre of bigness every way: that is, forty feet in height, and the half in breadth, making the foundation of palm trees, which in that place be very great, and their nature such, that if they be pressed down, they rose up again, and this he did to made the Assyrians to understand, that he would endure the seige, and though the flood did bear down the trench, yet it should do not hurt to the towers.

The Babylonians having victual for twenty years, made a mock of all this gear, which when Cyrus understood, he divided his army into twelve parts, that every part might serve one month in the year; which when the Babylonians heard, they made eftsoons a greater mock at the matter, considering that if the Phyrigians, Lycians, and Arabians, and Cappadocians did serve their course, the would be more enriched to them than to the Persians. The trench and towers being furnished, Cyrus had learned that there was a feast in the town, at which the Babylonians used to revel and riot all night.

Wherefore when night was come, he opened the trench, and suffered so much water to pass, as the flood might be washed over, which being done, he commanded the tribunes of the Persians that they should bring their bands two in a rank, and the rest of the army to follow in like order. Then he commanded certain to proved, whether it were passable.

Which being known, he called the captians and conductors, and thus said, "Friends, seeing we may with commodity enter the city by the flood, let us boldly do it, and fear nothing, for having overcome them when they were well friended, watchful, sober and in good order, now being the more part oppressed with sleep and wine, and all without armor, what shall hinder or stop our victories? Which hearing that we be entered the city, shall not only not be able to fight against us, being astonished and amazed, but scarcely able to stand upon their feet. Now peradventure some men may think, that at the entry of the city, we shall suffer a sharp assault, being beaten with stones and times that shall come from the houses' tops upon us. But this is not to be weighed, for we have Vulcan the god of fire for our devor, because the porches of their houses be overlaid with sulphur, and their gates made of palm tree, plastered with rosen, and we have flax and pitch and fire brands enough to made sudden and great fire, so that with little labor we shall made them either forsake their houses, or be burned in the same. Therefore with lusty heart and courage take your armor and follow me, who, with God's help will conduct you into the city, and by the help of Gobyras and Gadatas, who can guide us well the way, and they shall bring us straight to the palace." "That," quoth they, "shall not be hard to do, the gates of the court being open, and the keepers drunken as the rest of the city is." Cyrus said, the thing was not to be delayed, but to go on with all speed, to take their enemies tardy. And this said, they entered in, and of them that they met, some they killed, some fled into their houses, some made shouts and cries, to the which they that were with Gobyras answereing with like noise, because they might seem to be drunk as they were; they together with the band of Gadatas, went to the palace, where finding the gate shut, they killed the keepers being drinking and sleeping.

At the noise and tumult whereof, the king being moved, commanded the gates to be open, to see what it might be, at the which Gadatas and his company rushed in, and killed as many as came in their walk, till they came to the king, whom they found standing with his sword drawn, and manfully set upon him and the other, that with such things as they could get, stood at their defense, and slew the king and all his men.

In this time, Cyrus had sent the horsemen to made a cry in the city, by them that could speak the Syrians tongue, that as many as were taken out of their houses should be dead, and charged them to kill so many as they found abroad. Then came Gobryas and Gadatas thanking God, that they were revenged of the wicked king, and weeping for joy, kissed Cyrus' feet.

When it was day, and they that kept the fortresses understood the city to be taken, and the king slain, they rendered the castles to Cyrus, into the which he put other men, and caused the dead to be buried, and the living to bring their armor forth, and if any did the contrary, to dispatch him without more ado. Which being brought forth accordingly, he bestowed in the forts for munition, and to the sages gave the first fruits of the spoil to be offered to God, and to the rest of the camp, for their travail, he divided house and money accordingly, and if any man thought he were not well served, he might come and show his grief. He commanded the Babylonians to till the land, to pay tribute, and serve them to whom they should be given, and that the Persians and other companions that would there abide with him, should be called lords of the things that they had.

Then minding to order his court a princely state, he thought it good to do it with the counsel of his friends, that he might be less seen without envy, and with more majesty; to the which purpose he devised to come abroad, and show himself to all that would come unto him, and give them audience, which thing being known, infinite people came about him, thrusting and fighting, that his servants could have no rule among them although they did the best they could to keep back the multitude, for every man thrust in afore others, to get to Cyrus. Who seeing any of his friends, would hold forth is hand, and reach them toward him, desiring them to tarry till the multitude were gone. They tarrried, and the people resorted more and more, so that night was come before he had any time for his friends. Wherefore he said unto them. "It is now time to depart, having endured all day without meat."

The next morning Cyrus came betime to the same place, and perceived great confluence of people to be than was before; wherefore having a great guard of Persians soldiers about him, commanded them to keep back all others, till the princes and captains had been with him, to whom being come, he spake in this wise: "Friends and companions, we cannot complain of God, that we have not had our desires in all our enterprises unto this day; but after so many noble victories, if this be our life that we cannot repose ourselves nor enjoy our friends, I bid this felicity farewell with all my heart. Yesterday from morning till night, I did nothing but give audience to the people, and now I see as many or more to trouble us after like sort; whom if I suffer to come unto me, we shall never have done. And one thing makes me smile, that these homely fellows that know not me, nor I them, to presume to be before you that have so long travailled in my service. Whereas I think it meet, that they that would have ado with me, should first have the favor of you. But some man might happily say, 'What meaneth thus sudden alteration? Why did you not so at the beginning?' The answer is ready, that in war the prince must be abroad, he must be doing of this thing and that thing, in pains he may not be inferior to his soldiers, nor in virtues, and many occasions he loseth except he be in sight himself.

"But now the great travail of war being ceased, me think we should seek for some quiet. And because I cannot tell which way to bring it about, and would be glad to do for the best, I am come to know your advice and counsel in the matter."

When Cyrus had spoken, Artabazos (that said he was his kinsman) said this, "Cyrus, when you were young I was desirous of your friendship, and not bold to show it; but after I had been your messenger to Cyaxares, I thought I should have had more leisure and opportunity to have been with you, being for that travail well commended of you, but then came the Hircanians with new business, so that we for your sake, did our best to show them all manner of courtesy; then after our enemy's camp was broken, you had not time to pass the time with me, and I was well content therewith. After came in Gobryas, Gadatas, Cadusius, and the Sacans, and all were honorably entertained and hard for me to have access unto you, than going about the furniture of Persian horsemen, cars, and engines of war, I thought I might have had a time to enjoy with you. When the terrible news came, that all generation of men were assembled against us, though the thing were horrible, yet I thought that God giving you the victory, there should remain no let to our conversation; but now, our enemies overcome, Sardis taken, Croesus prisoner, Babylon won, and all ours. I thought I might have free access unto you; yet I swear that yesterday, and I had not played the man and laid about me with my fists, I should not have gotten to you, nor then another, had not you drawn me with your hand and commanded me to abide; and so I did the whole day without meat or drink. Therefore if we that be chief about you, may have access unto you, so it is, if not, I would counsel all to forsake you, except such as from their childhood have been brought up with you." Cyrus and many others smiled at this talk.

When Chrysantas arose, and thus said, "It hath been very wisely done of you, Cyrus, to show yourself to every man, suffering them to speak unto you, because you have had to do with so many sorts of men, who in camp time be most allured by the presence of the captain; but now that you have got all things as you would, and be in so good state, you may at all times furnish yourself of men, and yourself ought to seek some repose, and not be without an house and family, the greatest comfort in the worked, being shame to us to have our houses, and you to be without."

All the others according to Chrysantas, Cyrus entered the palace, receiving the treasure that was brought from Sardis, and after the counsel of his clergy, sacrificed to Jupiter and the God of household, bending his mind to settle his state. And pondering what a charge he had to govern a city, the chief of the world lately conquered and not well affected toward him, he thought it necessary to have a guard about his person. And considering that princes many times be betrayed by their meat, drink, sleep and bed; he thought it good to provide for the same, and thinking that no man can be faithful that loveth another better than his lord, and that they which have children, wife or woman, be constrained of nature to love the same, he concluded that eunuchs should be most meet to his purpose, being deprived of these matters, and he able to advance them to honors, wherewith they be most won; for being a generation of men most vile, they stand only upon the favor of their prince; and every man thinking himself beeter than they, they bear their hearts to him alone, that accept their sevice.

But it might be thought, that they were weak and effeminate, whereas the truth is not so, for by example of other beasts, as horses, fierce and untractable, being gelded, leave their wildness, and yet be meet for the war; bulls gelded, be not so savage, and yet more meet to till the land; dogs gelded, wait on their masters, not straying abroad, be meet to keep a yard, and not the worse to run. Men likewise, in this case, though they be beraft of voluptuous instinct, yet they be not the less unmeet to serve, in riding, in shoring, in obeying, in diligent doing of their duty, and no men more desirous of honor than they, as appeareth in war, and warlike chases. Their fealty in their lord's perils is so well known, as it needeth no more proof; whose lack of nature is recompensed by use of weapon. Wherefore he appointed all the guard of his person, to be of gelded men.

Yet considering that this was not sufficient, he proposed upon a greater number to rule so great a multitude, and remembering that the Persians at him in their country had but bare livings, for the barrenness of the country, which with continual toil they could not make very truthful, he thought they would be content to lead a better life with him, wherefore he ordained ten thousand of them to ward the palace when he was within, and go about his person when he went abroad. And that nothing might be wanted, he bestowed many other garrisons throughout Babylon, to remain whether he were at home or abroad; and caused the Babylonians to pay them their stipend, whom he entered to keep low, and of all other to make most poor. And this order for the guard of his person, and of the city yet remaineth. Then weighing how he might maintain his empire acheived, and enlarge the same by further conquest, and considering how little the number of his soldiers were in respect of his subjects, he thought good that they with whom, by God's help he had gotten so famous victories, should be still trained in virtue, not leaving their accustomed uses, and living licentiously in idleness, but so in use with goodness, as uncommon did they might do any noble virtue.

Wherefore he called the nobles and chieftains, and said unto them, "My friends and companions, we be greatly bound to the immortal gods, who have granted us to have the things we desired, a country fertile and abundant, houses well apparelled, and slaves at commandment; which things I would not man should think he hold them unjustly, or of another man's. For by ancient law among all men, it hath from the beginning been confirmed, that cities taken, and all things in them, as men and money, be the reward of victory. Therefore let no man think he possess anything unjustly; but if he leaveth anything, that it cometh of humanity. Mine opinion is, O friends, that if we give ourselves to ease and pleasure, after the rate of them that thinks to be none other felicity, and none other misery but to take pain, we shall of necessity set little one by another, and be deprived of all our weal. For it sufficeth not to be good awhile, except a man continueth in the study thereof to the end. And as other arts desposed, be of less price; and strong bodies turned to idleness, fall into diseases; even so prudence, temperance, and fortitude, their exercise being left, be turned into vice. Wherefore me think, that we in no wise should leave the use of virtue to follow vice.

"To begin well, is a great matter, but to bringest to good end, is all. Many a thing is well begun by rashness, but not ended but with prudence and diligence. Wherefore seeing this to be manifest, we ought to apply virtue more than ever we did, knowing that the more goods a man have, the more envy and danger he hath also, specially in a kingdom gotten by force, as ours is. Of the which yet we need not doubt, we having come by it by martial prowess, and not by treachery.

"Wherefore let us endeavor ourselves to that may be our avail, thinking we that be rulers, ought to be better than they that be ruled; whom we will make partakers with us of heat, cold, meat, drink, sleep and labor, but in knowledge and art of war, they shall not meddle with us, but be kept under as tributaries and subjects, we being only worth those arts, whom God have given to use as instruments of felicity. And as we have taken from them their armor, so we may never be without armor, for they that have weapon in hand, have all things that they list.

"Now if a man would say, what are we the better for our victories, if we must still labor and suffer hardness as we did tofore? You must know that those good be the sweeter that be gotten with the more travail; and wise men take labors for sauces to meat. No dish never so dainty can be pleasant, if a man have not a need thereof. And if God would give us the thing that we most desire, and a man obtain that he ould ratherest have, yet should he take no pleasure thereof, except he had a need, for hunger maketh meat good, and thirst, drink pleasant, and labor, rest sweet.

"Wherefore I conclude that we ought still to embrace virtue, that we may taste the sweetness of it, and avoid, that is counted most grief, that is to love the good that we have got. For it is not so grievous, never to have had our desire that after we have had it, to forego it. What reason can we have to be worse than we have been because we have rule? And what a shame is it to be worse than our subjects? Or because we be more happy than we have been? And is happiness wont to engender vices? Or because we have many servants whom we may punish at our pleasure? And how can we punish them, being worse than they? Will we have a guard of strangers, and will not be a guard to ourselves? One thing we must know, that there is no guard so strong as virtue, and he that lacketh it, lacks all other things, which how you ought to practice and use, I need not to rehearse, for as you see the nobles of Persian do, even so I determine that you shall do. And if you see me continually doing my duty, follow me, and I shall see you doing yours, and reward you. Children that shall come of us, must be brought up here, for seeing our example, they shall be made the better. And they, although they would, shall not incline to vice, because they shall neither hear nor see any vitious thing, but be evermore trained in the studies of virtue and honesty.

The Eighth Book of the
School of Cyrus, containing
his civil and princely estate, his
expedition into Syria and
Egypt, and his exhor-
tation before his
death to his
children.

When Cyrus had thus spoken, Chrysantas arose and spake after this sort: "Friends Persians, I have considered many times, that a good prince differeth nothing from a good father, the father always providing that the child should never lack. Cyrus being our prince, hath been always careful for our weal and felicity; but because he of his modesty hath not altogether uttered his conceit, I will express the thing at large, to such as do not well understand the same. Consider with yourselves, what city have ever been taken of the enemies, by them that have not obeyed their prince? What army did ever get the victory by soldiers without obedience? What thing is greater cause of loss of field, than when every man followeth his own way? What good thing in all the world can stand, where men do not obey their betters? What city can be inhabited by law and skill, where every man will have his will? What private house be safe, where servants disobey their lord? What ship arrive at port desired, where mariners will rule the master? We that now be come to wealth, whereby have we attained to the same, but by obedience to our prince? We have been always prompt and ready to do the will of him, both day and night. Things that have been commanded us, we have done them at full. Him we have followed, and idle contentation we have eschewed, and thereby have we finished our enterprises. Then if to obey the prince, be the only way to get Lordship and empire, think there is none other way to save the same, but the self obedience. Before this time we obeyed many, and none obeyed us, now we command and be obeyed of others.

"Therefore as you think meet to command them that be under you, so think it convenient to obey them that be above you; and so much the more, as there is a great difference between you and servants, they obeying for fear, and you for love. Therefore if we will be thought worthy to enjoy this liberty, let us obey our prince; for the city that obeyeth not one prince, but followeth the rude of many, is soon made thrall to one enemy or other. Therefore let us wait at the court, as Cyrus exhorteth us; let us exercise those virtues, that hitherto have holpen us, and now may save us. Let us be prest to serve Cyrus in all his affairs, letting you to know that the profit of the one cannot be divided from the other, having still the same friends, and the same enemies that we have had heretofore."

When this was spoken, many Persians and other the confederates arose and agreed to the same, and accorded that the nobles should be present at the court, and wait till Cyrus dismissed them. The which thing then observed, remaineth yet in Asia, and the kings from time to time followed the order that then was taken, in the which and all other things, it fareth alike. For if the Prince be good, the manners of the country be the better; if he be evil, they be the worse.

After this order taken that the nobles should wait at the court with horse and harness, Cyrus created officers for his costumes and tools, for his works and household, and for every other thing necessary for his state, not omitting keepers for his horse and hounds. Of them that he chose for the ward of his felicity, he did not commit the care to other, but made it his own care, that they might be made the better. For he considered that of them he must choose when any war was, to be made captains, and with them have conference of most weighty affairs; and if he must send any armor in his absence, he must take of them. He considered furthermore that he must use them for governors and presidents of countries, ambassadors of princes, to treat of matters, and to avoid war; wherefore he thought, if these were as they ought to be, his things should go well. If they were otherwise, that all should go to wrack. Wherefore he was diligent in this behalf.

He considered furthermore, that he himself ought to practice virtue; for he knew well enough, that it should be hard for him to entice others to virtue, if he did not embrace the same himself. And to bring all this to pass, he perceived he had need of time, and that the principal care ought to be, for the revenues of his empire, because the charge of the same should be of great importance. And if he did attend only upon these things, he should have no time for other things of the commonwealth, he thought it best both for his own quiet, and for the good order of the thing,that the should apppoint the captains of bands to have the care of the same, the alpheres, the sergeants and masters of the camp, as he did in war. And if he had need of any service, it was enough to speak to one of them. And after this sort he appointed his household matters, so that he needed not but to speak to one man to have many things done; whereby he had more quiet in this empire, than some men have in his private house.

He appointed further what kind of life they should have that should keep him company, whom he would call if they were not at the court; because in his presence, he was sure they would do nothing that should be unseemly; and being absent, he could not be persuaded, but that they were evil occupied, and ordained that they that were present, should have the wages of them that were absent;whereby they resorted very many to Cyrus, lamenting of their injury. He would hear them and give them fair words, but delay their requests; whereby they were the more diligent upon him, and he in in the surer case, by that he did not suddenly chastise them. This way he used to make them well occupied that were present, and to check them that were absent, being the best way to allure them with easy gain that served, and to affray them with great loss that served not, and give none audience to their complaint.

And by this means, he made them good, that else would have been nought, having espies to mark who was away, and ask for them; which thing is yet used of the kings that be in empire, praising them that be present, and blaming them that be absent, himself being example of virtues to his subjects; thinking that as men be made the better by laws written, so by, so by the good customs of a prince, who is a seeing law, they be enhanced that do well, and they corrected that do evil.

Wherefore above all things he bent himself to embrace religion, even in his happy time, and ordained ministers that at the break of day should sing hymns to God, and appoint what days should be made feastful. Which order then taken, remaineth with the kings of Persia; the which manner the other Persians followed, thinking to be thereby the happier, because he that so did, was of all other the most happy prince; and that they in so doing, should be the more dear to him, and he indeed was glad thereof, because he knew that men be more willing to go to the sea, or to do any other enterprise with them that be religious and godly, than with the other. And he considered, that if his men were well affected toward God, they would be better fashioned toward him and themselves.

And one thing he would have known, that he in all his affairs never did any injury to friend nor confederate, but by the way of justice sought to govern and benefit them; whereby the other left unlawful ways, and sought to come up by lawful means. And he thought that he should cause all men to have shamefastness, if he showed himself to be ashamed at any uncomely word or deed; because men esteem more not only a prince, but also others of whom they have nor fear, being endowed with bashfulness. And women they have in most reverence whom they see most maidenlike; and he thought he should cause his men most obedient, if he praised obedience in all things above all other virtues and so he did. And the like in temperance, he provoked his men to be temperate. For when men see the prince void of despite and outrage, the low sort be afraid to use any distemperance.

And this difference he put between a bashful and a temperate man. The bashful see the evil in the presence of others; the temperate flee the same, even in secret, and supposing that either would be the more continent, if they saw him never for any pleasure to be withdrawn from virtue. But evermore embracing honesty he ordained that the worse should obey the better, and that they all should wait at the court with marvelous order and comliness, with civility one to anther, with moderate mirth and pastime.

And for to retain them in warlike pastime, he took them that seemed most meet to go a hunting with him, wherein he thought the best exercise for the war, and truest for the feat of riding; for they must ride in every place, they must match with every beast, they must be quick and learned to manage their horse, they must endure pain and hunger to follow their game, which things the kings still useth. And he himself did exercise all these feats, because he thought no man worthy to rule, except he were better than them that be ruled.

And if he could not go abroad, he would hunt wild deer at home, and used for an ordinary, never to go to meat, but when he had sweat before; nor gave his horse no provend, except they were well chased before. His officers he would have a hunting with him, and them and all others he labored to pass in all honest exercise. And as they exceeded in virtues and goodness, so did he promote them to offices and dignities. Wherefore every man did his best to do well, that he might be so esteemed of Cyrus.

And not only in these things Cyrus thought meet to be better than his subjects, but also in apparel and array of his person; wherefore he wore a Medean robe and comforted his friends to do the same, for by this they should hide such defaults of body as they had, and by their garments seem the goodlier. He would have such shoes, as they might put somewhat under to seem the taller. He would have them paint their faces to seem the fairer, and to rub their skin to seem the better colored. He trained them so, as the did never spit nor snit the nose before company, nor to turn to look at any man, as they that marvelled at nothing; and all this he did, to be in more veneration with his subjects. Whom he minded to make officers and rulers, them he framed to be like himself in all things, and more sage than the other. Whom he made servants, from them he took away the use of arms, and all exercises appertaining to free men, providing so for them, as they lacked neither meat nor drink. When he went on hunting, and had them to chase the deer out of the woods on to the plain, he suffered them to bear meat with them, which the gentlemen might not do. When he made any trip, he used them to drink water as other cattle; and at dinner time, let them have their meat sufficiently, wherefore they as well as the gentlemen, called him father, because he provided for them as for the other.

And by this mean he established the Persian empire, and provided that his person was without all danger. For by taking away the use of arms from the nations won, he made them effeminate and cowards, neither meet to make war. Nor rebel there was none might come about him, except they were very excellent in their feats, whom he he used in the war, to be leaders of men of arms or footmen; or inpeace for the government of the guard of his person. Whom, because he had to do in many matters, he suffered to have often repair unto him, and devising how he might live in most security by them, he entered into many cogitations. Sometimes he thought it good for his safety to take their armor from them; but them he could not see how he could long endure, if they were made unmeet for the war. Therefore the only way was, to make the nobles and chief men more assured to him than to themselves; which thing how he brought to pass, me think it convenient to write.

In all his life afore all other things he used so much humanity as was possible, supposing that as it is hard to love him that hate thee, or to will well to him that will evil to thee, so impossible to be hated of them that loveth thee. Wherefore whilst he was poor and had nothing to give, he used much courtesy of words among them; he was as ready in labors as they be provided for their wants; he rejoiced at their well doing, and lamented at their evil chances. But after he was of ability to do them good, he considered that no benefit was more acceptable to men, than to be in company together at the table.

Wherefore he had the same service for his friends at his table, that he had for himself; and to them that were absent, he would show himself mindful, and send some reward from his own table, declaring that he favored them, although they were from him about their offices, to whom particularly he would send, being in the ward or in another service, and praise them openly at his board, whereby he won their hearts and benevolence. And if he had any other friend that he would set forth, he sent him meat from his table. For even at this day, the people think it a great matter, to see a present sent from the king, and him to whom it goeth, they have in great reverence, and suppose him able to do them good at their needs. And indeed, presents sent from kings' boards, be not only for these causes delectable, but also for their fine making, most pleasant to be eaten, of the which there is no marvel, for as all other sciences be most perfect in cities, so the fare of the king is most delicate. In little towns one man makes a bed, a door, a plow, and a table; yes, and many times the same man buildeth an house and is glad if he can of all these pick out a living. Such a master of many arts, cannot do them all well, but in great cities, because many men have need of every art, one is sufficient for a man's living, and sometime less than one, for one makes women's shoes, and another men's. And sometime one getteth his living by shaping, and another by sewing; wherefore he that with one art alone, must needs do it besst. The like reason is in dressing of meats. For when one makes the bed, covers the table, and playeth the coke, and other things, he cannot do them all well, but where as one is about the boiled meat, another about the roast, one makes the bread, covers the table and playeth the coke, and other things, he cannot do them all well. But whereas one is about the boiled meat, another about the roast, one makes the bread, that appertaineth only to his art, and so forth, of necessity every thing must needs be well done, and therefore the fare of the court exceedeth all others.

Now I will show how Cyrus passed in other things. For as he surmounted all men of revenues and entreat, even so he exceeded all others in giving and in liberality, which thing beginning with him, hath continued with all the kings of Persia. Who hath so rich men as the king of Persia? Who hath so well and rich arrayed men as he? Whose princely gifts be rings, bracelets, and horses trapped with gold? For these no man may have, except they be given of the king. Who hath ever brought to pass by great munificence of gifts, to be preferred in love, to parents, brethren and children? Who so easily could subdue his enemies so far from him, as he? Who after the conquest of so many nations, could get at his dying day, the name of a father, but he, which is the name not of a taker away of others goods, but of a giver to others of his own. Furthermore, they that now be called the king's eyes and his ears, were begun by none other means, but through his liberality and largess. For rewarding them with great honors that advised him of things appertaining to his state, he brought to pass that many did both hear and see things meet for the king to know. Whereof the saying was, that he had many eyes and many ears. He that thinks it better that one man shoud have the office alone to be the king's eye, he thinks not well. For one man cannot see nor mark many things. And if one man had the commission, the other might not meddle. Who being known, men would be ware enough of him; whereas it is expedient for a king, to hear many things of many men, whereby men be afraid to speak anything against him, as though he were present to hear, and to do any treason toward him, being among them to see it. And so not only no man did speak any villany or outrage against him, but also evermore spake most honorably of him.

And nothing made men's hearts to be so knit unto him, as that for little things he would give great gifts. And marvell is none, though he in gifts did excell all others, because he excelled all others in riches. But this is to be marvelled, that he being a king, did pass all others in humanity and courtesy, and nothing grieved him more, than to be overcome in dong well; insomuch as he was used scythed chariots, furnished with men and governors, which did good service in the field; but now they know not their chariotmen, nor who is practiced, nor who ignorant, and so going to the war, before they can abide the brunt of the enemy. Nowadays, they dare make no war without the aid of the Grecians, neither in their civil nor foreign war.

And therefore to end my tale, I dare say, that no nation is of such impiety toward the gods, of such wickedness toward their natural kin, of such unjustice toward all sorts of men, and of such cowardice in the war, as the Persian is. From the which opinion, if perhaps any man do dissent, let him consider their doings as I have, and he will affirm as I do.

Thus endeth the Eighth Book.

Imprinted at London in Paul's
church yard, by
Reginald Wolfe

exercise; and when that Artaxerxes and his family began to set their mind in drinking, they went no more on hunting, but were angry with them that did go. The costume of the children coming to the court, they yet use, but the use of riding or hunting, to be made meet for the war, is dispatched. The children used to hear causes rightly judged, and thereby to learn justice; now he speedeth best, that hath most money to spend. The children did use to learn the power of things hid in the ground, to know the good from the evil; and now they learn the same to do hurt to others. For in no place so many perish of poison, as there.

Now they be more delicate than in Cyrus' days, for then they lived after the temperance of Persia, and now they use the excess of Medea. The one they forsake, the other they embrace, and join more to it. It is not now enough to have soft beds, but also their bed's feet clad with carpets, that the ground should make the less resistance. Of the fine diet of the table, they have diminished nothing of the old, but have added a great deal new. He is now in most price, that can invent a new dish. In winter they do not only cover their heads, bodies and feet, but also their very fingers' ends with thick furred gloves. In summer it is not enough to seek the shadow of trees and hills, but devise other artificial shadows. And he that hath most silver plate is most esteemed; which though a man gets wrongfully, he passes not of it, but increase his desire of unlawful gains.

Every man was wont to be on horseback, not for none other cause, but to prove good horsemen; now they make so soft saddles to their horse, as they use still the thing not for good riding, but for soft sitting; so that no man ought to marvel, though chivalry be decayed in Persia. They were wont that had anything of gift of the king, to have in readiness horsemen and others to serve in the war, and they that warded the palace and had provision, were such as most valiantly might serve their country at all assays. A great number surely, but unprofitable to the war, and noisom to the people; which thing is evident enough for in the country they do more hurt to friends than enemies.

Cyrus put down the use of fight far off with darts, and instituted men at arms with barbed horse, and to see foot to foot; now they use no more the dart, and dare not meet to hand. The footmen bear still the target, pick and sword, but they dare not approach to the nigh fight. Cyrus

The kings and presidents that governed under him, did evermore keep their oath, never failing of their promise made, were they otherwise never so wicked, whereas now for their disordered life, no man have them in credit. Had not this been, many captains and govenors would not have come to have done homage to Cambises, whom he cruelly caused to die. And many barbarian soldiers, in trust to find the son like the father, were one way or other dispatched. And whereas tofore, any man that took any service or charge in hand, or won any province, was greatly honored of Cyrus; now no man is in estimation with the king, but traitors and flatterers. Being like to Leonicus, who leaving his wife, children, and friends for hostages with the king of Egypt, esteemed his oath and promised no more, then served for his commodity.

Wherefore the Asians perceiving this iniquity in the king, became of all others most wicked men. For as the rulers be, even so be the subjects; and from day to day, devised all kind of mischief to get money, punishing not all only the offenders, but also spoiling the innocents; so that now the good men be more afraid of the king, than the evil; wherefore they will no more come at his commandment to serve in war or peace; rather they think it lawful, to rebel from them for their impiety toward God, and cruelty toward man.

And as their minds became infected, so the honest exercise of their bodies they no more regarded. There was a law, that no man should spit or snit the nose, not because they would retain the moisture of the body, but that they would by labor and excercise consign the same. Nowadays this law is no more regarded, and the exercise of the body is utterly abandoned. It was an order to eat once a day, that they might be the more ready to the service of the commonwealth; and now indeed they eat but once a day, but they hold on from morning till night. There was an use that no great pots should be brought to their tables, lest by overmuch drink, they should overload themselves; and now they bring no great ports, but handle the matter so, that instead of bringing in great pots, they are borne out drunken souls.

There was a manner that in their journeys they should bear nothing with them to eat or drink; and now they bear nothing with them to eat or drink, for their journeys be so short that they need not. They were wont to exercise hunting so much as was sufficient for them and their horses'

Next to God, fear the kind of man, which is perpetual. God hath not placed you in obscure or hidden state, but so as your deeds must be manifest to all men, which, if they be just and good, they shall be commendable to all men; if you be evil affected one toward another, you shall be slandered of all men, and no man will trust you when they see, that they, among whom it were convenient that love should be, bear hate and contend one against another.

If I with these words, have showed you sufficiently what you ought to do, I am very glad; if this be not sufficient, learn of examples past, and with the doctrine that is esteemed best, choose the makes for you. You shall find many fathers to have loved ther children, and many brethren loved one another, and you shall find as many that have done the contrary, seeking occasion of discord and novel, and of all these you may choose that makes best for you. And thus my mind you know. As for my body, sons, when it shall be passed out of this life, you shall neither put in gold nor silver, nor any other thing, but immediately in the earth. Nothing can be more precious than to be laid with the earth, which is the mother and nourish of all good things. I have been always benificial, and now I return to that thing that is most beneficial to all mortal men.

Now me think I begin to faint, wherefore if any of you will take me by the hand, or see me whiles I am alive, let him draw near, but when I am once dead, I charge you that no man look upon me. Call the Persians and other confederates unto my funeral, make my feast with joyful exequies, for I shall shortly be in sure place, where I shall feel no pain, being with God or being nothing. Be courteous to them that shall come, as is convenient, to the memorial of him that is a blessed man, and take this for my last lesson: if you be beneficial to your friends, you shall be the more able to overcome your enemies." Having said these words, and taken every man by the hand, he ended his life.

It is evident that Cyrus' empire was most ample, by the confines that we have showed tofore; all the which was governed by his counsel and prudence. For all that were under his jurisdiction, he governed and honored as his children, and they him as their father. But so soon as he was dead, his children fell out, cities and nations rebelled, and everything went to ruin. The occasion whereof I will show, and first concerning matter appertaining unto God.

Therefore, for God's sake, do not lose the occasion of amity that God and nature have given thee, but rather seek to increase it by brotherly amity, which is a charity that cannot be broken; for he that helps his brother, helps himself. To whom is the honors of the brother so dear, as to the brother? Who is more honored of the brother in high estate, than the brother? Who ought so soon to help the brother against the injury of others, as the brother? No man ought to be so obedient to thy brother, as thyself; no man so ready to do his pleasure. For his state, either prosperous or adverse, toucheth no man so much as they. Thou canst look for no such faithful service as of thy brother, neither in peace nor war. What thing is more in hate, than not to be loved of thy brother? What things is more worthy than to prefer thy brother? If Cambises thy elder brother shall honorably entertain his younger brother, no man shall bear you envy. For the which considerations, I beseech you children for God's sake, to esteem one another, if you will do anything that may content me.

Think not, when I am dead, that I shall no more be; because now you cannot see my soul, but of the operation thereof, you know it. The minds of them that have suffered wrong, have you not seen with what fear they suppress murderers, and with what furies they affraye the wicked? Such honors should not be given to the dead, if they thought the soul did perish with the body. Children, I never thought in all my life, that the mind should live so long as it was in the body, and then being separate, it should die, because I see the bodies receive life of the souls.

I think not the soul after death to be a dead thing, although it hath been in a dead body, but as a mind pure and void of contagion, is much more clear than ever it was. Because everything at the death of man do return to his natural couse, but the mind is except, and can neither be seen present nor absent. This is certain, that nothing is more like death than sleep. When as the mind is most free, and doth enjoy the divine contemplation, and forsight of things to come, therefore as the soul separate from the body is immortal, so honor you my soul, and keep well my words. And though it were so, that the soul and body did die together, yet fear the the gods, who is immortal, and liveth everlastingly, and governeth all things with such order, as they see and can do all things, and refrain from wicked act. Whose majesty and beauty cannot be expressed.

friends, I have made lords, and my enemies, slaves. My country that sometime had no rule in Assyria now most famous of all others. I never got thing valiantly, but I have kept it quietly. The time have passed as I have desired; the fear of adverse fortune, have not suffered me to be proud of my felicity, for rejoice too much of my prosperity. Now at the time of my death, I leave you my children alive; my country I leave in happy case, and my friends in good estate; wherefore I may well count myself an happy man.

"How I will declare to whom I leave my kingdom, that there by no business for it when I am gone. Children mine, leif and dear, I love you both alike; but reason and skill requireth, that he that is first born, should have the first place, being more able to govern, in that he hath more counsel and intelligence. I have been taught by my country's use, to give place not only to brethren, but also to our citizens as they were in age, reverencing them in all seemliness, and I have brought you up in knowledge, to honor your superiors, and to be honored of your inferiors; which thing follow, not because I speak them, but because your country command them. You, son Cambises, take mine empire, which with all my power I give you, and trust that God will therein confirm you. You, son Tanoarares, I leave prince of Medea, Armenia, and Caducia; the greater empire and royal name, I leave to your brother, but an happy life with less trouble, I leave to thee. For thou shalt not want that felicity that man can have, but enjoy all the things that may bring happiness to man. To be desirous of glory, to be careful for state, to be enforced to follow thy father's virtues, and to live in continual suspect, things that takes away all delight, be associate with him that hath a kingdom. Cambises, I tell thee this for truth, that this sceptor of gold, is not it, that preserveth a kingdom, but assured friends be the sikerness of a prince. Think not that men be born friends, but be made by benefits; for then every man should be faithful, as natural things cannot swerve from their creation. But friends be gotten, not by force but by benefit. If thou wilt make thy friends for thine assurance, thou ought to begin with not so soon as with thy brethren; and thy countrymen brought up with thee in one place, must be preferred to others that be strangers. They that be born of one seed, and nourished of one mother, brought up in one house, loved of all one parents, and calling one father and mother, how can they no be of more entire friendship than all others?

beloved in every place, that the people contended to present him with most noble gifts. Every city and every private man thought themselves happy, if they might present him. And he rewarded them with things that were rare in their countries.

His father and mother being dead, and he somewhat old, he returned into Persia the seventh year of his empire, wherafter the manner he sacrificed and danced his country dances, and gave rewards after the manner thereof. And sleeping on a time in the palace, him thought, a creature far goodlier than any natural man, appeared unto him, and said, "Prepare thyself, O Cyrus, for thou shall shortly go to God."

Being waked with the vision, he thought his time at hand, and made perfect sacrifices to Jupiter hs country's patron, to the son, and to the other god, with this oration: "Jupiter father, sun, and all you gods, accept these last sacrifices for so manifold benefits received of you, having been by you told what to do, and what not to do, by sacrifices, by stars, by signs and tokens in all mine affairs. Of one thing I most humbly thank you, that in all my victorious and trumphant state, I never exalted myself more than became a mortal man. The which felicity I humbly beseech you to grant my wife, my children, and my friends. And to me grant a present death, convenient to my passed life."

These done and said, he went to his chamber and rested quietly. When time was that he was wont to be bathed, the servants appointed to that office, came, he bade them go their way for he would repose himself. After when time was to eat, and the meat brought, he refused all meat, and took a little drink. Thus continuing the second and third day, he called his children and friends, and said thus unto them:

"Children, and you my entire friends, I perceive evidently by many conjectures, that the end of my life is at hand; which being so, you must speak and do of my death, as of a mortal man most happy; to the which, I have attained from my youth by that I was in my childhood trained in most honest education; and in youth with the practice of virtous things; and in the age of man, in matters meet for a man; and with the increase of time, so increased in strength of body, as I have not found mine age weaker than my youth; nor never enterprised matter, but that I have accomplished. My that he had commanded them. And that they should be example to their inferiors, as he was to them. And these order them made, were from time to time observed, in waiting at the court, in keeping of the forts, and in placing of the noblemen, and in training up their children.

Having spoken and appointed these things, he commanded them to be ready all the year following; for the intended to make an enterprise, and before he so did, he would take a muster of men, horses and cars. Which order the kings of this time follow, and cometh forth with his army, that if any governor have need, he is aided; and if any rebel, he is subdued. And it is occasion that every man is the better kept in his office, the laws be the better obseved, and the rents the better paid, which when the governor cannot bring to pass by himself, he showeth the king, and he takes order in the matter by his power, as they soon be dispatched.

Thus they went forth, and some were called the king's son, some his brother, and some his eyes. To know what was done in every place, being so far separated his provinces one from another, he took this order. Knowing by experience, how far a man might ride every day by fresh horse, he appointed places accordingly, that the fresh man taking letters of the weary, without let might bring the news in most short time, riding day and night without stop. Wherefore it was said them of the people, that his posts went as fast as cranes, which saying although it was false, yet this was true, that it was no small space that they rode. And that thing could not have been so well stayed, if speedy quickness had not been used.

At the end of the year, every president came to Babylon with his men, and Cyrus took the muster, in which was one hundred and forty thousand horses, two thousand cars armed, footmen five hundred and forth thousand with which army he went forth and subdued all the lands betwixt Syria and the Red Sea. Then returning back he won Egypt; and confined his empire from the east, by the Red Sea, from the north, with the Euxine Sea, from the west, with Cypress and Egypt, from the south, with Ethiopia. Of the which confines, some for heat, some for cold, some for water, and some for drought, be inhabitable. But Cyrus in the midst of them led his life, as by months at Babylon in winter, and in the spring, three months at Susa. And the two months of summer, in Bactria, avoiding both extreme cold and heat, lived as it were in a continual spring. And so well honorably, and dwell quietly, where they may give audience to suitors, and at their arrival find their palaces ready."

When he had thus spoken, he appointed many cities and provinces to diverse of his friends, the children of the which did possess the lands and possession that he then gave them. And when he had given this order, he willed them to send evermore to him such things as were the chief commodites of their provinces. He assigned to every man that province, that he best liked; as Megabisus, into Arabia; Artabatas, into Cappadocia; Artacaman, into great Phrygia; Chrysantas, to Ionia and Lidia; Cadusius, into Caria; and Pharnucus in Phrygia by Hellespont and Eolide. To Cilicia, Cyprus and Paphlagonia, he sent no Persian govenors, because they uncalled served him in his wars at Babylon. Only he appointed them to pay a tribute, and live free. The which order then made, still remaineth, the governors of the cities and provinces, the captains of the castles and fortresses, whose names remain in writing with the king. And he admonished them to keep those orders in their offices, as they had seen him keep at home. That they should have horsemen ready of Persians, and their companions; cars and rulers of the same; and that they that had provision, should be attendant at the gate of court, and be prest and ready at the governor's commandment. And that their children should be trained at the court, after the manner of Persia. And that they should wait on the governor ahunting, and other warlike pastime. Protesting to consider and reward him as an increasor and preferrer of the Persian empire, that should have in a readiness, most men of arms, skillful in their feat, most cars meet for the service, and most men trained in knowledge of war. He also advertised them, that they should prefer the nobled men before all others in their assembles. And that their diet should be like his, sufficient for their family, and seemly for their friend. And that they should have garden parks with deer in them, to pass the time, and never go to meat before they had labored, nor give their horse provend without some exercise. Affirming, though he himself were never so good, he could not by any human power, provide for the weal of all, except he were holpen with the favor of them that were good. The which being good ought to favor the good and be companions of their travail. And that they should not think, thathe commanded them these tings as unto slaves, but that he himself would be the first to do anything,

"But if you, Cyrus, being swelled with good success of fortune, shall go about to be Lord of the Persians, as of other nations, drawing all things to the private commodity, or you Persians, being envious of his glory, go about to dissolve his empire, you shall be occasion of much trouble and displeasure, the which to avoid, I think you ought now in this public sacrifice to accord and call the gods to witness of your contentment, that thou, O son Cyrus, shall be always ready with all they power to resist them that shall bring any disturbance to the Persians' laws. And you, O Persians, if any man goeth about to bereave Cyrus his kingdom, or any subject shall rebel from him, shall be ready to aid him and yourselves, according to his commandment I shall be your natural lord and king,so long as God shall lend me life; after my death Cyrus shall be your king, if he be alive. Who when he comes among you, if he will do well, must make your sacrifices even as I do. But when he shall depart, it shall be convenient that you take one of our family, to be your lord and governor, and your minister to God immortal."

These words spoken, they agreed fully together, and after the ceremonies made, called God to witness, and so departed. Cyrus took his leave, and went into Medea, and by the consent of his parents wedded the daughter of Cyaxares, a very fair maid, although some men write he married his mother's sister, who was too old for him. Being returned with his wife to Babylon, he thought good to send governors into every province. And besides them, captains of the castles and fortresses, supposing, that if anyof the governors would go about any novel through their riches, these should be always against them.

Wherefore purposing upon the same thing, he thought it good to call the chief gentlemen and captains, to utter the thing unto them, and signify what way they should take in their provinces; to whom, being assembled, he spake in this wise: "Friends, such garrisons and captains as we left in cities which we won, be still remaining there, to whom we committed none other thing to do, but faithfully to ward the town that they kept; which thing they having accomplished, we will not displace them. Nevertheless, for other considerations, we perceive it meet to send civil governors, that may have authority to command the rest, and to appoint orders appertaining to the state. And to them that I shall sent thither, I think it convenient to assign them house and land, that they may live

Being arrived in Medea, he allodged with Cyaxares, king of the same. And after many salutations and embracements, Cyrus told him, he had provided a palace for him in Babylon, where he might lie as in his own house, and gave him many noble gifts; which being received, Cyaxares sent his daughter a crown of gold, and other chains and bracelets, commanding her to set the crown upon Cyrus' head. Which being done he came and said, "I give the this maid my daughter to your wife. And as your father Cambyses had to wife the daughter of my father Astiages, of whom you are born, so I give you this my daughter; with whom, being a child, you were wont to sport and play, insomuch as she being demanded whose wife she would be, she said, Cyrus' wife. And for her dowry I give you all the realm of Medea, having none heir male to inherit the same."

To whom Cyrus thus answered, that he did accept the parentage, he liked the young lady, and praised the dowry, and every thing contented him, but he would make no contract of matrimony without the consent of his parents. Wherefore giving many tokens unto her, as he thought might please her father, he took his leave and went toward Persia; and being arrived at the confines, he left his army there, and with his friends went to the city with things sufficient to sacrifice, and banquet among the Persians, and presented his father and mother, the ancients and noble men and women with gifts accordingly.

Which fashion the kings use at this day, when they return from a strange country. Wherefore Cambyses calling together the chief of the Persians, and the most ancient and Cyrus with them, he spake unto them in this wise, "I bear my good heart to you, O Persians, and to you my son Cyrus accordingly; for to you, I am a king, and to thee, O son, I am a father. Wherefore it seemeth I ought of congruence to give counsel faithfully to you both. You Persians did honor Cyrus my son, when you chose him to be your captain; he through God's help, hath made you honorable among all men, and most reknowned in Asia. The nobles that have served with him, he hath enriched. The others he hath truely paid, and made the Persians of footmen, valiant horsemen, and increased their dominion; if you in time to come shall continue in this state, all things shall come to pass prosperously.

were pitched and carriages discharged. At one time tents were raised, and sumpters laden. Every thing that was to be done, was done in order and due time. Even as in an house where all things is well bestowed, so in his camp nothing was out of order; provision for things necessary, preparation for their vitails and place, meat for the same, the good appointment of the munition and place for the same, the ready alodging of every man. And as in an house well bestowed, all things is so disposed, as is easy to be had when need requireth, even so much more in a camp ought an order to be had, that things may be done without trouble.

Because the occasions of war be more sudden than others, so the disorder there, be more dangerous than other. Negligent dealing in the war, bringeth much care; and wise government, great avail. Wherefore Cyrus was very circumspect, that his things were done in order. He had his own tent in the midst of the camp, because it was most sure place. Next about him he had his most trusty men, as he was ever wont to have; about whom, the men of arms and the captains of the cars did lodge. The which he placed so, because if any alarm were given, they might have time to arm themselves, which was long adoing; before and behind the which, the archers had their place; then the darters, and all these compassed with the pickmen that they being able to abide a good brunt might hold out till the others were in order. He would have every captain's ensign set upon his pavilion, that as servants in a city knoweth every man's house, specially the great men's, so in his camp every man should understand where he ought to repair, and not need to go about seeking here and there, because every nation and their captain had their place by themselves.

Having thus appointed his things, he thought thus most meet to provide against sudden invasions and tradements, that the doers thereof, might be taken with their own traps. And he esteemed it a feat of war, not only that the battles could march and tarry by it manfully, resisting the enemy on either side, but also to know how to retire and leave the battle in place and time to stay, to torn, to come in succors when time was, to prevent and foresee the drifts of their enemies. And after this sort, he proceeded in journey with great order, that he might be always ready against sudden chances.

them and to their heirs. And they were the most part Medeans and Hircanians. To them that departed, he gave great gifts, that no man had cause to grudge or complain. And besides this, he gave the soldiers that warded his person, the money that he got at Sardis. And further to the colonels and captains he gave great gifts, according to every man's worthiness. And gave moreover to the chief captains, to distribute among the sergeants, alpheres, andother soldiers. At the which largess, some said, he must needs have much money that give so much. Some answered, his nature is rather to give and enrich others, than to keep himself.

At the which words, he taking comfort, assembled his friends, and thus said unto them, "I know that many men desire to be counted richer than they be, thinking thereby to be thought the more liberal and free. In which their opinion, me think, they be deceived. For he that is counted to have much money, and doth not accordingly distribute unto his friends, by and by getteth the name of a covetous man. Another sort there is that desire to keep close their riches; and them I take to be unnatural to their friends, for because it is not known what they have, their friends in their lack do not make their money unto him, but be deceived. I think him the good and plain man, that showeth what he hath, and helpeth as he may. I will show unto you indeed my riches that can be showed, and that that cannot, I will tell it by mouth." And even so he did, with these words:

"Friends, I would you should think thee, to be no more mine than yours. For I do not gather this riches for mine own use alone, but for all them, as shall do their duty, and embrace virtue; and to succor them that shall at any time have need."

Having well settled his state at Babylon, he thought good to go again into Persia; and signified his departure. Which voyage home he made, what train he had, how he harbored, what way he kept in going into his country, we think meet to declare. Wheresoever he camped, his tent was set toward the east, and about it all the guard and pensioners had their lodging; on the right side he placed the bakers, on the left side the cooks. Likewise on the right side, the horses, and on the left, the beasts of carriage. Other things were so bestowed, as every man in every place knew his plate and ground. The carriage was born partly by men, and partly by beasts. Every man came to his appointed place; and at set hours, each man went busily about his office. At one time pavilions

Then Cyrus said, "If any of you will have a wife, make me of your counsel, for I know the art of wooing." Then Gobryas said, "If a man would marry his daughter, with whom must he confer?" "With me," quoth Cyrus, "because I know the art." "What art," quoth Chrysantas. "The art," quoth Cyrus, "to know what woman is meet for every man." Then Chrysantas asked, what woman he thought meet for him. "A little woman," quoth Cyrus, "because you are little. Or else when you would kiss her, you must leap like a spaniel." "It is graciously considered," quoth Chrysantas, "for I am unmeet to leap.

"Further," quoth Cyrus, "you must take one with a flat nose, because you have an hauked nose." Then quoth Chrysantas, "One that have well dined, should lie well with another that is fasting." "Very true," quoth Cyrus. "For a full belly is hooked, an empty, flat." "Well," quoth Chrysantas, "what woman is good for a cold king?" At the which word Cyrus laughed, and so did the other. Chrysantas then said, that he marvelled much at Cyrus' nature, that being cold and still, could be merry and frolick. Cyrus said, for that conceit he should get a name of a pleasant merry fellow. Thus with like mirth and pastime, they passed away the time together.

Then Cyrus took a woman's vesture, and commanded Tigranes to give it his wife, because she had so constantly followed him in the war. To Artabasus he gave a cup of gold; to the Hircanian he gave an horse, and many other gifts, and to Gobryas he said he would give him an husband for his daughter. "You must give her to me," quoth Hystaspas, "that I may have his sentences." "Are you able to find a wife?" quoth Cyrus. "Yes, that I am, I thank God," quoth he. "Where is your substance?" said Cyrus. "Here," quoth he, and pointed to Cyrus. "I am content," quoth Gobryas, and held forth his hand. Cyrus took it, and gave it to Hystaspas, and so they accorded. And Cyrus gave Hystaspas many gifts to send to the young lady, and last of all kissed him.

Then said Aratabasus, "Oh Cyrus, you do not give me such gifts and a kiss, as you have given Chrysantas." "But I will give you," quoth he. "And when?" quoth the other. "Thirty years hence," quoth he. "Therefore you die not in the mean time." And thus ending the feast, he brought them to the gate; and the day following he gave license to to all his friends and companions, to go home to their houses, except such as voluntarily would tarry; to whom he gave house and land, to honorable than him. "Shall I tell you the truth?" quoth Cyrus. "Yes," quoth Hystaspas. "And will not you be angry?" quoth Cyrus. "Rather I would," quoth he, "rejoice to know the truth, and not to have no injury." "Then you shall understand," quoth Cyrus, "that Chrysantas, without any commandment, would do things accordingly as appertained to me. I never troubled to call him to this or that. Further, if there were anything needful to be spoken to our companions, he would advertise me to do it. If for modesty I let anything unspoken, he would express it to them with much prudence. He was always content with the present fortune, the thing that might do me good, he would gladly do it. Of my good fortune no man was so joyful, in sort that of my felicity, I think he was more merry than myself."

Then Hystaspas answered, that he was glad he had demanded the question "And why?" quoth Cyrus. "Because I," quoth he, "will do my diligence to follow the same way to please him." But of one thing he stood in doubt, who he should rejoice at Cyrus' good fortune, either by clapping of his hands, or by laughing, or by other means. "No," quoth Artabanus, "but by dancing after the Persian fashion." Whereat they all laughed.

When the banquet was brought in, Cyrus demanded Gobryas, if he had not now rather give his daughter to marriage to one of his friends, that at his first coming. "Shall I tell the truth?" quoth Gobryas. Yes," quoth Cyrus, "for no need of lie is to be where as question is demanded." "Then," quoth Gobryas, "I had rather give her now, than afore." "Can you tell why?" quoth Cyrus. "I can," quoth he. "Say on," quoth Cyrus. "Because," quoth he, "I saw them here tofore with good heart abide the labors and dangers of war, and now I see them bear with equal mind the favor of fortune; being an harder thing to use well the prosperous state, than the contrary. For pride and contempt is wont to rise of good fortune, and desperation of adverse."

At the which words, Cyrus said to Hystaspas, "Have you heard the sentence of Gobryas?" He answered, "Yes, and if he spake many such sentences, he would rather be a suitor to his daughter, than for a great dowry of gold." "And I can give the many of these sentences," quoth Gobryas, "if you will have my daughter. And because you set not by gold nor silver, you shall give it to Chrysantas, because he is placed above you."

for all men. Because he thought a man to be the most worthy creature; most thankful toward them that showed him pleasures, praising them that deserved it, loving them that were kind, reverencing the Father and Mother, and most mindful of the quick and the dead. So Pheraulas was very joyful to be at liberty among his friends, and the Sacan was glad to be so wealthy a man. He loved Pheraulas well, because he was ever bringing somewhat home, and Pheraulas loved him, because he kept his bond. And thus they two lived.

After the sacrifice, Cyrus called to a banker as his friends that were most careful for his empire and most trusty, as Artabanus the Medean, Tigranes the Armenian, the colonel of the Hircanians, and Gobryas, Gadatas also, who was made master of the pensioners. And when Cyrus had no strangers he sat with him at the table; when he had, he waited, and Cyrus having him in great estimation, and so had the rest of the court. Being come to supper, they were placed accordingly, and the most worthy sat on his right hand, and the next on his left hand, which he did, to signify whom he esteemed best, that they without contention might know one another, and every man see that virtue is the cause of honor. Thus by setting at the table, they had estimation; but not so, but as they exceeded in virtue, so he advanced them in honors. And they that degenerated from virtue, were brought to more base place. And thus he appointed his men.

Having supped, and Gobryas considering everything of his behavior, that being so mighty a prince did not have the company of his friends, but vouchsafed them at his table, sent them presents that were away, he did no more marvel at his great feats in war, but at his gentleness in peace. And therefore when all was done, he said, "Cyrus, I protest before God that I thought you the most worthy warrior alive, but now I think you pass yourself and all others in humanity." "By my trough," quoth Cyrus, "and I had rather show the virtues of humanity, than of chivalry, because chivalry is cause of many men's hurt, and humanity of many men's good." Then Hystaspas demanding, if he would be displeased if he asked him a question. Cyrus answered, rather well contented.

Then he asked him, if he had not been obedient to him, and ready at all his commandments? Cyrus said, he could not blame him. Then he asked him, why he had placed Chrysantas more rendered me double fruit. And after this, coming to Cyrus' service, I have obtained these things that you here see." "Happy you," quoth the Sacan, "as well for other things, as for that you be made rich of a poor one; for I think the getting of goods is very sweet unto you." "Well," quoth Pheraulas, "if you think me the merrier because I am richer than I was, you be deceived, for I ensure you, that I eat and drink with less repast than when I was poor; for now I have much. But I spend much, I care for much, my servants livings, their liveries, alms, provision for my cattle, shepherds for the same, loss when the rot cometh among them. So that I have more care now, that ever I had." "Yes," said the Sacan, "but when you see every thing in good case, you be the gladder, and so enjoy your riches." "Not so," quoth Pheraulas, "for there is no such grief, as to fear to become poor when a man hath been rich. In proof whereof it hath not been seen that any rich man hath been constrained to watch for pleasure of riches, but many that have lost their riches, could not sleep for sorrow." "Nor no man sleep," quoth the Sacan, "when he getteth any thing, for joy." "That is true," quoth the other, "for if it were as sweet a thing to have as to get, the rich should be a great deal more happy than the poor. But he that hath much, must spend much upon his friends, upon strangers, and upon the service of God. Therefore he that hath much delight in money, hath much grief, when he is at any expense." The Sacan answered, he was not of that opinion, but thought him most happy that hath much and spend much." "Then for God's sake," quoth Pheraulas, "make youself happy, and me too. Take all that I have, spend it at your pleasure, use me as you would a stranger, and worse too if you will, for I shall be content with a small portion." "You do but dally with me," quoth the Sacan. Pheraulas swore, he meant good faith. "And that beside this, I will obtain of Cyrus, that you shall not wait at the court, nor be in no garrisons, but be at home, and enjoy your riches. For I will do all for you , and me too. And if I get anything at Cyrus' hand, or by my service in war, you shall have it to make you happy, and me, without care. For if I be discharged of this business, I shall the better serve Cyrus."

So both agreed, the young man thought himself most happy, because he was lord of so much riches, and Pheraulas thought himself more happy, that he was delivered of care, and set at large to do his pleasure. Pheraulas was a man of gentle nature, glad to help his friends, and to do

Armenians, Tigranes; of the Hircanians, the colonel's son; of the Sacans, a privy man outwent them half the race length.

Cyrus asked the young man, if he would give his horse for a kingdom. The young man answered, "For a kingdom I would not forego it, but to a good man, I would gladly give it." Cyrus answered, that he would show him where he should not miss a good man, though he were blindfold. "Show me the place," quoth the Sacan, "that I may hit him with this clod." Cyrus showed him a company of his friends. The young man threw the clod, and hit Pheraulas who was going about Cyrus' business, and did not stay for all the blow. The Sacan opening his eyes, demanded whom he had struck. Cyrus answered, none of them that were present. "Why," quoth he, "is it any of them that be absent?" "Yes," quoth Cyrus, and showed him where he rode among the chariots. "And why doth he not turn?" quoth he. "Belike," quoth Cyrus, "he is not well, with himself." Then the young man went to see, and found it was Pheraulas, his beard being bloody, and with a blow of his nose; when he saw him, he asked him, if he were struck. "As you see," quoth Pheraulas. "Then," quoth he, "I give you this horse." "And why so?" quoth Pheraulas. The Sacan told him all the matter, and said, "I think I have not missed a good man." "It had been better for you," quoth Pheraulas, "to have given him to a richer man; notwithstanding I accept your gift." And prayed God, who suffered him to be hit, that he might prove a good man indeed, that his gift might not be frustrated; and so they changed horses, and rode forth.

The chariot had run also, and to the victors there was given an ox and wine, to make merry after the sacrifice. Cyrus was rewarded with certain cups which he gave to Pheraulas, because he had so well ordered the matter. And the kings of Persia with this manner of riding to the temples at this day. This being ended, they went into the city, and Pheraulas desired the Sacan to supper, and gave him his rewards and others too. And he perceiving goodly appurveyance and rich array, and many servants, said, "Be you of the order of rich men?" "What rich men?" said Pheraulas. "Even of that order that got their living with their hands. My father set me to school, and with his labor found me poorly; being come out of my childhood, and he not able to find me, he made me labor the land as he did, and so I found him to his ending day, laboring a poor little land, but so good as cloak of purple. And he had a crown upon his hat, and so had all his kinsmen; and so have at this day. His hands were bare, his chariotman followed him, not so high as he, either because it was so indeed, or because it was made so. Cyrus seemed the most goodliest and as he passed they honored him, either being so commanded or because they wondered at his goodly and rich array. Before this day, no Persian did ever kneel to Cyrus. The four thousand went afore him, and about him, three hundred scepterbearers on horseback.

Then was brought forth two hundred spare horses for Cyrus, saddle with trappings of gold, then two thousand lancemen, an hundred on a rank, of whom Hystaspas was captain. Then the ten thousand that were first made, whom Chrysantas governed. After them other ten thousand, of whom Dutamas was captain. Then the Medeans, the Armenians, and Hircanians, the Cadusians, and others followed, of which Gadatas had the charge. After their horsemen, followed the chariots, four abreast, of whom Artabatas a Persian was overseer. In his going forth, many men came over the rails to make their suits to Cyrus, who commanded the Pensioners that were about him, and his chariot, to bid them tell their suits to his officers and captains. Of the which calling some of them to him that he would have most honored, commanded to hear the requests; and if they were of any importance, to make relation of him. And they went earnestly about the matter, saving only one Dapherens, and man of proud and haughty nature, thinking to be esteemed the jollier fellow fellow, went very slowly about the matter.

Which when Cyrus perceived, he sent him word not to meddle in the matter, for he would no more trouble him, and to another that was ready in his service, he have an horse, and cause one of his bearers to lead him whither he would; whereby the people gave him great honor.

Being come to the place where they should sacrifice, he offered the bulls to Jupiter, and the horses to the sun, and to the god of the earth and patrons of Syria, such beasts as the sages did apppoint. When the sacrifice was done, he appointed a place of two mile length where he commanded the horsemen to run their horse, divided into three parts, and he himself ran with the Persians, and did best. Of the Medeans, Artabates had the price, of the Syrians, Gadatas, of the seemed most for his honor. After he had given the best robes to the noblest men, he brought forth others of diverse colors, and gave among them, and willed them to clad their men as he had clad them. Then one asked him how he would be decked? To whom Cyrus answered, that he thought himself well arrayed, when he saw them in so good order; and that he apparelled with mean garments, should think himself richly vestured, being beneficial unto them. Then they went and gave the robes to their friends, and Cyrus called Pheraulas, a Persian of the common sort, but diligent, modest, and ready to serve; and that once judged that every man should be rewarded according to his desert, saying unto him, that he would go forth in most comely order, that he would go forth in most comely order that might be pleasant to his friends, and fearful to his enemies.

According together how it might best be done, Cyrus gave the charge thereof to him for the day following; and that he might be the better obeyed, he gave him coats to distribute among the Pensioners and the guard belonging to his person; who said to Pheraulas, that he was become a great man, in that he commanded them in their offices. Who answered, it was nothing so, oak bearers.

And having given the choice of the robes to the principal, he went his way, appointing the order against the morning. The guard they stood on either side the way, that none might come to Cyrus but the noblemen, and there were tipstaves to beat them that were out of order. There were four thousand spearmen, four a rank, and on every side of the court gate two thousand. And all the horsemen were come, and alighted off their horses, with their hands out of their sleeves, as the be wont to do in the king's sight. The Persians stood on the right hand, and the other companions on the left hand, and the chariots likewise on every side. When the court gate was opened, there was brought out four white bulls to be sacrificed to Jupiter and other gods, as the clergy did appoint, which the Persians esteem above all others. After the bulls, were brought horses to be sacrificed to the sun. After this, came forth a chariot of gold to be offered to Jupiter, and another to the sun, then the third cart with purple covers, whom men followed with fire in their hands.

Then came out Cyrus with a Persian hat on his head, and a coat painted with white and red, which none may wear but kings, and a pair of Medean britches down to the knees, and a warlike men, and I get benevolence of all sorts; the fruit of my riches, is my good name and glory, which the greater it is, the better it is, and more easy to bear, and many times makes them light that bears it. And one thing, Croesus, I would you should know, that they that have most money, be not most happy, for then the keepers of town walls should be the happiest men, because they keep all that is in the cities; but he that hath a way to get much money, and spend it well, him I think happy indeed."

And thus Cyrus reasoned effectually with Croesus, understanding furthermore that every man hath regard for his health, and prepares things to increase the same; and to avoid sickness, no man took no keep; he thought good to see for this lack, and called the most skillful physicians unto him, devising with them for medicines, instruments, and other things appertaining to the same. And if they healed any of his friends, he would thank them and reward them. These things he devised for to have the good hearts of his trusty men. And among all other things he propounded plays and warlike pastimes, and rewarded convenient for them, to induce his court to contention and gave of noble feats. Furthermore he ordained that in all matters of controversy, men should choose them judges. They studied on both parts to choose their most friends; he that was overcome, had envy of them that did overcome, and hated them that gave sentence against him. He that did overcome, pretended to have overcome by right and therefore bound to no man. And they that would be most in favor with Cyrus, as it saveth in all cities, have envy out at another, is sort that many had rather receive a loss, than have a benefit that should help his fellow. And this was a cast of Cyrus, that they that were so great about him, should all be occasioned to love him, rather than one another.

Now among the declaration of many of Cyrus' acts, me think it good to show how he came abroad the first time to make his sacrifice, because it is one of the arts that princes use to be in the more reverence. Before he went forth, he took about him all the Persians and other nobles, and gave them Medeans' robes to wear. And this was the first time that the Persians wore them. And when he had distributed them, he told them he would go visit the temples, and desired them to be at the court by break of day, and he ordered as Pheraulas should appoint them. And that they should mark what way might be better done, and tell him at his return. For he would follow that, that wont oft to say, that the office of a pastor and king were like; for a pastor ought to see that his sheep be well kept, and a king that his people well governed: the one and the other, being the felicity of both. Wherefore being of this mind, it is no marvel thought, he labored to pass all others in gentleness.

Of the which he showed an evident proof, when Croesus advertised him, to leave his large giving, that would soon make him poor, whereas he might be made most rich, if he would attend unto it. Cyrus asked him, how much money he thought he might have had, if he had spared after his counsel? Croesus named a great sum. And Cyrus prayed him to send one of his trusty servants with his man Hystaspas, whom he commanded to go to all his friends, and on his behalf to desire them, that they would serve him of so much money as they could spare, because his present necessity required no less. And that they should give the accompt to Croesus' man, with their bills of the same. Thus sending him away with letters of credit, he went and did his message, which thing being fulfilled accordingly, and the letters of accompt given to Croesus' man, he returned to Cyrus, and showed him what riches he had gotten by his journey, besides the money that was brought for him. Wherefore Cyrus said unto Croesus, "Here is one of our treasures, the other may may see and count what money I have if I would use it. Croesus took the count, and found it to be much more than he said it should have been.

The which Cyrus perceiving, said, "You see, Croesus, that I have treasure when I need. Whereas you would have me herd them up at home, and get envy and hatred abroad, and hire strangers to have the keeeping of them. And now I have my friends in good case, which be my treasures in good case, which be my treasures. I have them my keepers of my person and my goods, a great deal more faithful than hired guard men, and one thing I will tell you, that I have that affection that all men have; for I am desirous of money. But whereas I know that money is the cause of much trouble and anguish to them that cannot use it, but hoard it up, tell it, lock it, weigh it, and dieth in desire of it; and albeit they have their houses full of money, yet they can eat no more than they can bear, for they should burst, nor clad them more than need, for they should be choked. I honor God with my money, I desire much, and I distribute much. I help my friends, I enrich my

CANISIUS COLLEGE LIBRARY
PA4495 .C5 1987 c. 1
The School of Cyrus